D1163664

WITHDRAWN

THE
BIRD
TATTOO

a novel

DUNYA MIKHAIL

PEGASUS BOOKS

NEW YORK LONDON

This is a work of fiction, but resemblance to persons now living with us is not coincidental.

THE BIRD TATTOO

Pegasus Books, Ltd.
148 West 37th Street, 13th Floor
New York, NY 10018

Copyright © 2022 by Dunya Mikhail

First Pegasus Books edition December 2022

Interior design by Maria Fernandez

All rights reserved. No part of this book may be reproduced in whole or in part without written permission from the publisher, except by reviewers who may quote brief excerpts in connection with a review in a newspaper, magazine, or electronic publication; nor may any part of this book be reproduced, stored in a retrieval system, or transmitted in any form or by any means electronic, mechanical, photocopying, recording, or other, without written permission from the publisher.

Library of Congress Cataloging-in-Publication Data is available.

ISBN: 978-1-63936-278-3

10 9 8 7 6 5 4 3 2 1

Printed in the United States of America
Distributed by Simon & Schuster
www.pegasusbooks.com

To those who remain captive but whose songs cannot be caged

1

NUMBER 27

Members of the Organization had taken all the captives'
possessions, including their gold wedding rings. But Hel-
en's wedding ring was not a ring. It was a tattoo of a bird. She
was staring down at her finger when someone started shouting
"Twenty-seven! Number twenty-seven!"

He sounded angry, and as Helen belatedly realized that she
was number twenty-seven, she wondered if she was in trouble
because she had just left the queue and run to Amina. She hadn't
believed her eyes when she'd spotted her dearest childhood friend
on the other side of the hall. Amina, too, had opened her mouth
in disbelief.

Their tearful hug hadn't lasted more than a few seconds when
the irate voice announced, "Twenty-seven is sold." The speaker was
pointing at Helen. In his other hand, he carried a cardboard box
filled with all the captives' cell phones.

"Leave her alone!" Amina protested, but her voice was barely audible. All the phones in the box were ringing, their loud tones coming from anxious relatives who kept calling and calling the women captives gathered there, but they got no answers.

The man, who wore a long black shirt that reached his knees and trousers to just above his ankle, pushed Amina so hard she fell to the floor.

Helen bent down to help her up, but the man pulled Helen away and led her to another room. He threw her to the floor and left, closing the door behind him.

Other women sat there on the floor with their heads down. They, too, were labeled with numbers, like those distant planets that have no names.

The one woman who had no number sat at a desk. She handed Helen a paper and said: "This is your marriage certificate. Your husband will come soon."

Helen returned the paper without looking at it and replied: "I'm already married."

"Abu Tahseen purchased you online, and he's on his way here."

If she had not seen it with her own eyes, Helen would never have believed a market for selling women existed. What had surprised her even more was that this market was in a school building. Its name, Flowers of Mosul, was displayed on a banner at the front of the building, which looked just like the elementary school she had once attended with her twin brother, Azad.

But even their principal, the strict Ms. Ilham, would be unable to comprehend the idea of a market for women. For Ms. Ilham, chewing gum had been immoral, even if it was done during breaks.

Azad, who was fond of the Arrow brand of gum, had thought it was no different from the candies that other students ate without any problem, until the day Ms. Ilham summoned him to her office.

Azad had been frightened that Ms. Ilham would hit him on the hand with the sharp side of her ruler, as he had seen her do to students who were late to class. They were supposed to be in their seats before the bell rang so that when their teacher entered, they would all stand up in a show of respect. But to his astonishment, when at the end of her questioning she found out who had given Azad the gum, Ms. Ilham had smiled and said, "Say hello to your uncle Mr. Murad and tell him that gum is prohibited. Now go to your classroom."

———

This room was similar to the principal's office, with its neat table at which now sat the numberless woman busily managing the sale of captives.

"Put on these clothes. The photographer will come soon," she said, handing a plastic bag to another prisoner in the room.

Helen had been surprised by the contrast in the style of clothes imposed by the Organization. In the beginning, they had been forced to wear the niqab, through which only the eyes are visible. Later, they were forced to change into "promo" clothes for pictures and sale exhibitions. The photographer had asked Helen to wipe away her tears in order for him to take the picture.

In other classrooms, members of the Organization were using teachers' desks for paperwork to oversee the selection of boys for military training in the school's front yard. Where on Thursday mornings, teachers and students had once held the Iraqi flag-raising ceremony, the Organization now raised their black flag and recited the pledge to the Islamic State instead of the national anthem.

It had been three months since she'd been taken captive, and Helen had gradually come to understand the laws of this strange market. When a man took her to another classroom for his pleasure and returned her immediately after, it meant that he had taken her for temporary pleasure only, like a customer examining goods in the market. When one of them decided to buy her, he paid the Organization an agreed-upon sum of money, in accordance with a purchase contract with the State's stamp on it. Helen's price started at seventy-five dollars because she was in her thirties. Any buyer had the right to give her to another man in a "rental" contract and then take her back. He could also return her to the market or exchange her for another captive. One of Helen's previous buyers used to temporarily sell her whenever he needed money, then take her back. He finally brought her back to the market, saying, "This one screams in her sleep. Maybe there's a jinn inside her."

About 120 women were crammed into the hall. You could tell which of the women had been raped most frequently by the number of bruises on their bodies. Some tried to hide behind each other, but the guards did not bypass any of them. At night, when the auction was closed, the guards came and took whomever they wanted for pleasure. They pushed the classroom desks aside and raped them in front of each other.

Helen met other captives through the looks exchanged during these ordeals. They spoke with their eyes and communicated through tears.

During a mass rape one afternoon, a captive shouted at the men: "Enough! Would you let someone fuck your mothers and sisters?"

Right away, one of them threw her against the wall, leaving her unconscious. Another woman followed him, screaming incomprehensibly. She spat at him. Helen imitated her and spat at a man nearby. Another captive did the same. Every woman in that room spat on whomever she could in a campaign against the rapists.

Shocked by the collective reaction, the men beat the women with all their might. But eventually the room fell quiet, and the men seemed exhausted from all the beating, and probably felt shame. They left the room one after the other while the captives exchanged looks of encouragement, as if they were patting each other's shoulders, although that would hurt with all the bruises they now bore. Some of the women could not move for several days.

After Arabic and Kurdish, silence was the captives' third language. The youngest among them, Layla, who was ten years old, did not know any Arabic except for the word *tafteesh*, which she learned from the woman who entered the room and pronounced it so that the captives lined up side by side for inspection.

This woman checked the captives' clothes to make sure they didn't conceal any sharp objects. The number of inspections increased daily because suicide attempts among the captives had reached a point that had irritated members of the Organization.

———

Rehana tried to hang herself with a rope she found in the corner of the hall. It had been the school's gym hall, and the rope was a jump rope. A female member of the Organization ran over to Rehana and was able to take the rope from her. She saved her life, then beat her with that same rope.

She was the same inspector who, since the first week of captivity, had passed by the new captives one by one to ask, "Are you married?" and "When was the last time you had your period?"

A captive had replied, "Why this question?" Another screamed, "Why?" And then a third, even louder, "Why?"

The inspector stepped back and yelled at them, "Because our State's law prohibits the sale of pregnant women."

Rehana was supposed to be given for free to Organization soldiers for the sake of domestic service only. This was according to the Organization's code for those aged over fifty, but the broken look with which she came back whenever she was taken and returned showed that the soldiers were breaking their own rules.

"Mama Rehana" was what Layla had called her since the dark night during the second week of captivity when Layla returned to the room, naked and wincing with pain and humiliation. They had thrown her clothes in behind her.

Another captive picked them up, dressed her, and said, "May God take revenge for this girl and for us all." She said it in Kurdish, so the female inspector wouldn't understand.

As a kitchen worker, Rehana had rushed to Layla with a pail of water and stayed up looking after her until morning. Layla opened her eyes to Rehana, who at that moment was wiping her forehead with a wet cloth to bring her fever down.

They exchanged a look of gratitude and sorrow. Rehana spoke Arabic and did not understand Kurdish. Therefore, she depended on Helen to translate between her and Layla—not always, but in the few periods that would pass without any rape. They usually had no desire to speak after rape. They entered the room in a silence that was only interrupted by a greeting from one rapist to another. It sounded odd, like laughter at a funeral.

Thanks to Helen's translation, Rehana knew that Layla had not seen her parents since the day when her mother had braided her hair, and they left home along with the rest of their village, heading toward the mountains. Layla didn't say more because they all knew what happened next, how the men were separated from the women, old from young, and girls from the age of nine and above from the rest of their family members.

One day, Layla had no words, not even for Helen, because Rehana had been found dead. She didn't have any sharp tool, nor a rope. They didn't know how she had died.

"Sadness killed her," said one of the captives. Tears raced down Layla's cheeks. Helen rocked her in her lap as she, too, wept. She held her as long as possible, despite the pain in her back from the beating by Abu Tahseen, who had bought and returned her.

Braiding Layla's hair, Helen remembered the day when Abu Tahseen took her to his home in Aleppo and how she had vomited on him when he was having sex with her. Helen had felt sick all the way to his home. When it happened, shortly after they arrived, he hit her with a stick on her naked back until she passed out. She found herself in the hospital, her hand tied to an IV bottle.

A nurse handed her a pill with a glass of water and asked, "How are you?"

Helen burst into tears and replied, "I'm not from here. I beg you to help me return to my family in Iraq."

The nurse looked right and left and whispered: "How can I help you?"

"Just get me out of here to the street."

"Sorry, I cannot do that. Do you want to call your family, so they can help you?"

"Yes, may God protect you."

"I will bring my phone during my break." The nurse looked at her watch and added, "I'll be back in an hour and a half."

Helen heard the far-off sounds of explosions while she counted the ninety minutes and tried to remember any number for her relatives to give to the nurse. Since his imprisonment, her husband

Elias's phone must have been taken from him, as he hadn't answered any of her calls, and Amina had been taken captive too. Helen didn't know any other numbers.

As if it were a pistol, the nurse slowly pulled out the phone from her pocket while looking at the nearby patients' beds. "I'll leave this with you for five minutes and will be right back," she said to Helen.

"Wait, please. I don't know any numbers. Do you know the code to Iraq from here?"

"Oh, no. Later then, I'll ask around," the nurse said and put the phone back in her pocket.

At that moment, a female doctor entered the room. She picked up and read a clipboard by Helen's bed and said: "You can go home now."

"May I stay one more day?" Helen asked.

"You don't need it," said the doctor. "There are wounded people on their way to the hospital, and we may not have enough beds."

Helen reluctantly got up from the bed. The nurse escorted her to the reception area, where Abu Tahseen waited. As he walked toward her, Helen froze on the spot.

The nurse said to her: "Wait. I'll give you my phone number in case you have any questions."

Abu Tahseen had overheard her. He said: "No, there will be no questions. She will leave from here and return to her country."

"Really?" the nurse asked.

Abu Tahseen turned his back on the nurse and signaled with his hand for Helen to go out with him. Before Helen crossed the threshold to the street, she looked behind her. The nurse was still standing there, watching her.

Abu Tahseen hailed a taxi, then waited for Helen to get into the back seat before he climbed into the front. He might have been afraid that she would vomit on him again. She wondered if he really would take her back home as he had told the nurse. About fifteen minutes later, she heard the driver talking about construction on the road to Mosul, and hope flickered inside her like a lamp in a dark room. She could not suppress the hope that they were indeed on the way to Mosul and not to Abu Tahseen's home in Aleppo.

———

The journey to Mosul took about ten hours. Helen noticed the sign announcing when the highway became the Caliphate Way. At last, the driver stopped at the same school-turned-auction-house where Abu Tahseen had purchased her.

He had taken her back to the same prison. Yet she breathed a sigh of relief to be joining the rest of the captives, if only until she was sold again. Who knows, perhaps a miracle from heaven would allow her to go home. She needed a miracle in order to breathe in the scent of her family again.

"She's sick and not fit for me," Abu Tahseen had said to the guard in the school's front yard.

The guard offered to exchange Helen for another woman, but Abu Tahseen chose to get his money back.

———

The same day Rehana died, Helen was brought outside to be auctioned off again. The schoolyard was packed with customers with extremely long beards, who looked as if they had just emerged from ancient caves.

In the hope of spotting Amina again, Helen searched the faces of the other captives. Had someone bought her dear friend? Helen wondered as she glimpsed a huge person moving toward her. She lowered her head to avoid him.

2

HALF OF A PERSON'S BEAUTY

Helen was worried about the rice, if it was not cooked the right way for Ayash.

She had never been good at cooking. Her mother had once said to her father that Helen should marry a cook, or they would both die of hunger. Her father replied, "Or you rush in and save them with your eggplant dish." Her mother had laughed. He loved to joke about how frequently her mother cooked eggplant and how she had been adding it to every meal.

Helen soaked the white beans in water to make a stew. She had to prepare dinner before Ayash was back from work. Would he come alone today or with his friends? she wondered. Would he come home high, or would he wait until after dinner? How would his mood be? What if he had a bad day at work and disliked the food? Would he just scold her or beat her? Worse yet, he might sell her again.

Two days earlier, she had heard him bargaining with someone on the phone, but it seemed that no deal had been made, and the buyer had not come to take her. Ayash had asked for $400, then lowered her price to $300. He said: "I swear she's worth more. She's sweet, obedient, and smart, but I am in a rush to sell her." He did not mention that she didn't know how to cook rice.

Of all those who had purchased her, Ayash was the best. During the six weeks that she stayed with him, he didn't beat her brutally like the others, who had covered her body with bruises; and when he raped her, Ayash did it alone, not in a group. He even spoke and listened to her sometimes.

When Helen first saw Ayash at the auction, she had been horrified. As she'd lowered her head, she saw feet of different sizes pacing back and forth in front of her. She studied his huge feet and the black trousers that stopped well above his ankles. "My God, don't let this one buy me. Anyone but him," she thought.

The feet came closer, and she was scared. But unlike the others, he didn't open her mouth or check her teeth or smell her. He asked, "How much is this?"

A man standing nearby answered, "Four hundred, but for you, *mawlana*, half price."

Ayash opened his wallet, grabbed two bills, and gave them to the seller. Helen understood it was her turn to leave the school and follow the new buyer. She would follow him in silence because she had learned that objections would do no good. She had learned this lesson the hard way, through beating and humiliation. Every inch of her body and soul had turned blue. Looking back, Helen's heart was pierced by a tearful look from Layla, and she sighed deeply.

It was obvious that this new owner was of a high rank, because they called him *mawlana*, which was what sultans were called in ancient times. She had never heard this word before except for in history programs on TV. A driver in a luxurious black car waited for them outside, confirming her impression.

Ayash sat in the front of the car next to the driver. In the back seat, Helen wore the black niqab they had given her. The two men immediately started talking to each other, and Helen found herself looking through the window at a city she recognized as she would a familiar person who had fallen sick.

The city of Mosul looked pale, silent, and slow as never before. There were no crowds or loud music coming from the shops. Black flags had replaced the neon advertisements. Even the Tigris River, flowing under the bridge, looked completely deserted and oblivious of everything going on above it.

These streets she looked at through the car window were the same ones she used to freely walk, wearing clothes of her choice and sometimes of her own design, inspired by fashion magazines. Once, Helen had imitated the style of a girl wearing her jeans slightly torn. She tore her own pants at the knee. When Helen's mother saw this, she offered to patch them up for her.

From this street in particular, Helen used to buy buttons, fabrics, and threads. Most customers on this street were seamstresses, as well as some shoppers needing to repair shoes or watches or radios. Its shops were small, not exceeding two by three meters each—just a table, a chair, and a lamp. People still called it King Ghazi Street, although the government had officially changed its name to Revolution Street. Helen didn't know who King Ghazi was, but her neighbor Shaima, known as Umm Hameed, had once told her that King Ghazi had always liked to show off. That was why, when he was a sixteen-year-old schoolboy, he had his plane descend to a very low altitude above his school—so his classmates would see him in the plane, which the British called the magic carpet.

The clothing shops looked familiar to Helen, except for the niqabs, which had been put on all the mannequins. Helen and the mannequin were dressed alike, but the mannequin was not for sale.

THE NIQAB IS PURITY and TOGETHER WE TAKE CARE OF THE TREE OF THE CALIPHATE were among the banners now attracting Helen's attention. A few meters away, she saw a handwritten phrase repeated on more than one wall. In a thick font that could be read even from afar, the graffiti read, "I love you, Nadawi." This was the usual nickname for Nada or Nadia. Helen imagined a lover writing on the walls of this city. Did he want to set a contrast to the other, more serious banners, or to vandalize the walls with the huge, sloppy handwriting of that simple phrase? Or was he simply a lover who had lost his mind?

The sudden voice of Ayash interrupted Helen's thoughts. He had lowered the window of the car and was now yelling at a woman walking on the sidewalk: "You, woman! Cover your hair!"

The streets receded and disappeared from Helen's view, as did her former life. The steering wheel was not in her hand to return to that life. Yet she would return as soon as she could, she thought. She would find a hole in the wall through which she could get back to her family.

Again, Ayash interrupted these thoughts as he ordered his driver to stop. He got out of the car and headed into a women's clothing store in the Souq of Prophet Yunus. The shop owner was talking to a female customer but seemed to panic when Ayash moved between them.

Helen did not hear the conversation between the two men, but it was clear the man was fearfully begging Ayash. Ayash did not speak to the customer. She left the piece of clothing she had been bargaining for and hurried from the shop.

Listening to Ayash's conversation with the driver after he returned to the car, Helen understood that he had been giving a warning to the shop owner; the distance between him and the female customer had been less than two meters, and that was a violation for which the punishment was twenty-five lashes. In addition to breaking the law, the shop owner had been flirting with the customer, calling her "my eyes," Ayash said.

"No manners," said the driver.

A few minutes later, they heard a man shouting, "Look at this, Da'usha!" as he pointed at a big mannequin in front of a women's clothes shop.

This time the driver hit the brakes and stopped without any order from Ayash. He probably thought the situation required intervention. Helen guessed the man outside the shop was crazy. No one would dare to use the mocking nickname of the Organization in such a public way unless he'd lost his mind.

When Ayash jumped from the car and approached him, the crazy man laughed and said, "And your excellency is Da'ush?"

Helen covered her eyes with her hands to avoid seeing what happened next as Ayash hit the man. Yet she saw how Ayash knocked him down and climbed over him, choking him and banging his head on the ground.

This time, Ayash did not comment when he returned to the car. The driver put his foot on the gas, and in the side mirror the man appeared, lying on the ground, motionless and bleeding.

Finally, the car entered a residential area. Ayash asked the driver to stop by a small store. Its sign read PICKLES AND OLIVES SALE. Ayash went inside. At first, Helen wondered if he'd stopped to buy something, but this was not the case. An old man came out with Ayash and took down the sign. Ayash got back in the car, murmuring, "They don't know that pickles and anything fermented are not allowed."

On that same residential street, the car parked in front of a two-story henna-colored house. Ayash indicated for Helen to go inside, and he stood beside the car, talking to the driver. The house's front door was ajar, so Helen just went in.

―――

It was furnished and smelled of people who were absent. She felt as if she were about to suffocate despite the fact that she loved the place and its decor, especially the carpet with Persian-style motifs and the turquoise ceramic vase on the round wooden table. The cushions on the sofas were of warm colors that matched the carpet. A large box of toys by the sofa filled Helen with sadness, as she imagined children forced to leave their toys and their home. On the side table was a dried piece of bread. The inhabitants must have left in a hurry and not taken much with them, neither big things like the television in the middle of the wall nor small things like the tiny sandal by the door. She almost saw their fingerprints on the furniture and memories between the walls. She saw in her mind how they'd escaped with only the clothes they were wearing, just as her own people had. They dispersed like billiard balls after a hard hit.

Helen had been by herself when she was taken, but she'd heard from other captives about the caravans of people who fled their homes and headed toward the mountains. Some had made it and others not. Daesh cars had blocked their way, parked in the middle of the road.

In the living room, Helen stared at a framed calligraphy painting on the wall next to the door. She contemplated it but found it hard to read because it was written in an exaggerated, artistic style. She looked closely at it, word by word, and was finally able to read the first word: *half.* Then *person* and then *beauty.* She tried to figure out the rest of the words but could not. The words were drawn as images rather than letters.

She winced when she heard Ayash's footsteps as he entered the house. She looked down while he was pacing the room. He stopped in front of her and said: "My name is Ayash."

Helen did not say anything but glimpsed his curly beard and seemingly neckless head.

"I am Tunisian French."

Helen remained silent.

He walked back toward the TV, then returned and stood before her. "I left my wife and daughter in France," he said in a Tunisian dialect with a French inflection. "I came to answer the call of God," he added, looking toward the window.

Helen remained silent.

"My marriage to you is a jihadi mission in the name of Allah. The State did you a favor because you will become Muslim and thus pure," he added.

Helen wished she could tell him that if he left her, for God's sake, that would be the real favor.

"You are an infidel, and this is not your fault; you were born this way," he said.

Helen looked away.

"You would go to hell if you remained Yazidi."

Helen remained silent.

"Take a bath and come up to my room," he said.

―⁓―

In the bathroom, Helen took her time because she knew that the bath would be followed by prayer and then rape. This was the usual pattern.

In that first building where they'd been kept after they were stolen from their villages, it was in the bathroom that some girls committed suicide. Helen looked at her face in a silver-framed mirror. She was surprised by how normal she looked, despite all the scars she now bore inside. She closed her eyes. They were burning with tears, and she washed her face again. If her heart would allow it, she, too, would commit suicide. But her heart would not let her; she was too attached to her loved ones. If only she could survive this time . . . this difficult time in which she was unable to die or to live.

In the bedroom, she stood by Ayash as he called her to pray with him. *Oh, God, please help me, reunite me with my family, in the name of God and Peacock Malak*, Helen murmured inwardly. She didn't know if she was praying or pleading.

As soon as he finished his prayer, he ordered her to take off her clothes and lie down on the bed. Helen responded mechanically. She did not refuse or resist as she had done in her first days of captivity. No more begging to be left alone. She shrank and curled up because he was staring at her whole body.

He lifted her left hand up and examined the bird tattoo.

"What's this?" he asked.

"Long story," she said.

"I want to hear it," he said.

Helen kept silent, and Ayash repeated his request that she tell him her story. Using his desire to listen to her advantage, Helen thought to put on her clothes.

But before she could do so, he took his off. Helen assumed that he'd changed his mind and didn't want to listen to her. Obviously, he wanted sex. He lifted the bedcover and half covered their bodies and asked again, "What's the tattoo story?"

Helen hesitated, wondering if he really wanted her to tell him. Could she trust him? Who was this Ayash? Was he really one of them? He did not seem to want to rape or beat her. So why did he order her to bathe and take off her clothes? And what did he want if he was not one of them?

In the midst of her bewilderment, Ayash repeated his request, adding: "You can tell me anything. Do not be afraid."

"Are you with Daesh?" she asked.

"Their name is not Daesh. It's the Islamic State in Iraq and Syria. I am a security officer in the Hesba." He explained that Hesba was the religious police. "The State gave me this house and pays the bills for water and electricity. The Islamic State is well organized, and it collects taxes from business owners in accordance with profit. The State provides for our daily needs so that we can work for a cause and not for a living."

Helen resisted asking more questions: What is the cause you are fighting for? Slaughtering people? Kidnapping them and forcing them out of their homes?

After a minute of silence, Ayash touched her. Helen regretted her silence. Perhaps if she had told him her life story, he would have listened to her and not raped her.

"You will enter paradise, you know?" Ayash said.

She remembered what one of them had once told her: that in paradise she would not be a human being but a nymph to delight believers.

"No, I'll not enter paradise. I'll be in hell," she answered. She wanted to say that she would rather be in hell if he and his group were in heaven.

"Why? What sin have you committed?" he asked her.

Helen didn't know what to say.

"You went out with a man secretly?"

"Yes, once I did," she replied.

"You mean you had a relationship with him?"

The question made her afraid, so she quickly answered: "No, he had a relationship with me."

As Ayash was touching her body, Helen froze. She did not let him feel her pain in the bruised parts of her body and was too tired to resist. She'd let him do whatever he wanted since he would anyway.

But perhaps this Ayash was unlike the other beasts who'd enslaved her. Perhaps he was human, and a magic spell had turned him into a Daesh. And then perhaps another power would turn him back into a human being, like in the story of *Beauty and the Beast*. His huge body on her stifled her breath, and she longed to cry.

And in that moment, her parents came to mind. They didn't know where she was. How upset her father would be if he knew what they were doing to her. Her father was tender-hearted, and he always forgave Helen no matter what she did, especially if he saw her tears. Even on that day when she broke the toy camera of cartoon pictures. A relative had brought it for her brother, Azad, and given her a doll, with which she did not know what to do at first.

So she asked her brother: "Do you want to swap?"

He had shaken his head and kept looking through the lens of the plastic camera while turning the side handle to rotate the images inside. There were dozens of images that went around in a loop. Helen asked him to let her see too, but he kept pressing the button, ignoring her request.

She snatched the camera from her brother's hand and ran. He ran after her, and they circled around the house. The camera fell from her hand and broke. Her brother scowled and pushed her. So when their father saw them as they were fighting by the broken camera, he appeared angrier at Azad than at her because Azad was not crying, only she was.

She did not know where Azad was now. Was he looking for her? Did her mother know she'd been kidnapped? Helen imagined her wailing and singing that sad song, the one between singing and sobbing, as she used to do when mourning a missed one, whether a relative or a stranger. It was in their house that the people of their neighborhood used to gather on weekends, and at the end, when darkness prevailed, they would sing. Her mother's voice was always beautiful, whether she sang in joy or in sadness. Their family would sometimes gather in the orchard next to their home, and her father would invite guests to pick fresh figs from the trees.

Her father was well known in the village because he was the only one in the area who knew how to circumcise boys, and he did it so skillfully that some people traveled from other villages to their house, together with their sons. This was how he earned his living, in addition to the gifts that the parents of the boys would bring to their home.

Helen's father never saved anything because he constantly invited people over and provided guests with all that he had to offer. He invited farmers whose crops had failed that season just to give them some money. One time, a farmer came to their house and filled their sitting room with pomegranates because her father refused to take back the money he had given him when he'd needed it.

That was the same day her uncle Murad came over from the city and asked her mother—his sister—to accompany him to see the family of the girl whom he wanted to marry. Uncle Murad suggested that Helen and Azad go with them too. The children always loved going with him to the city of Sinjar.

"I'm coming!" said Helen joyfully. But Azad refused because he'd agreed to go with his friend to the orchard. There was a snake on a tree there, and Azad said they talked and played with that snake.

Her father told her uncle: "You are not going anywhere unless you carry away all you can of these pomegranates. Bring them as a gift to your fiancée's family, Murad."

Helen's mother carried two bags of pomegranates, and Helen did the same. Her father handed two more bags to Murad, and they went on their way.

In the city, after dropping off the pomegranates in his home, Uncle Murad took them to the market. He lifted little Helen up on his shoulders so that she sat high above the crowds of people. She sneezed on his head as she smelled the spices displayed in big open sacks. He stopped in front of a banner that was advertising a new film in the cinema two blocks away from the market. He suggested they go watch it.

Helen was stunned in her seat in front of the big screen, and her uncle exchanged a smile with her mother because Helen was sitting with one leg crossed over the other like a grown-up. When they returned to their home in the village, Helen ran to her father and said: "I was not scared by the film. Only Mama was scared."

"Children have no fears. When you grow up, you'll be scared by those movies like your mother," her father answered.

———

This terrifying film I am watching as a grown-up scares me, Father. It's real. If my life were a film, I would be traumatized by its details. Do you remember, Father, how you once got angry because the teacher slapped me and I cried? You then prevented me from going to school until I convinced you, "It was not a strong slap. I did not feel it, Baba." And you said, "It's unacceptable that someone—whoever it is—touches you or hurts you." If you knew, Father, how many men have hit me in your absence, how many have raped me. Do you remember, once at night, on the roof of our house, how you looked up, and I asked, "What are you looking at?" You pointed up and said to me, "Every one of us has a star there in the sky. Look, that is your star. It's bright like you. I want you always as high as that star. Never put your head down, Helen."

If only I could put my head on your shoulder and cry, Father. Do not let me down from your lap, please.

Tears fell from Helen's eyes as she called out silently to her absent father.

—⁓—

Ayash had just finished with her, and now he surprised her by wiping away her tears.

"Why are you crying? Because I married you?" he asked.

"No, I was remembering my family."

—⁓—

After more than a month in the house, Helen finally dared to turn on the TV. She had resisted because Ayash had warned her not to. He expressed fear that the TV might show her songs and programs featuring infidels. But that evening, a strong desire to watch the news made her take the risk. She wanted to see if the outside world knew about what was going on for her and her people in this part of the world.

They were reciting the Quran when she turned on the TV, and although she was sure that listening to the Quran would not put her in danger, she still kept an eye on the window, fearing that Ayash might return at any moment. After the Quran, a cartoon came on. She turned off the TV, hoping to watch the news another time.

Ten minutes later, she glimpsed Ayash through the window. He was next to the car, talking to the guard. When he entered the house, Helen said to him: "I wanted to ask you if it was okay for me to watch religious programs and cartoons, for example, on TV. I am alone here, and time passes slowly."

"No," he said sternly. "All TVs are to be given to the Organization. But listen, there is a new family on their way here. The Organization gave the second floor of this house to a man from Chechnya known as 'the desert emir.' He signed a contract, according to which he owns a wife and her belongings and children. He is a talented man and a top fashion designer who designs men's clothing inspired by the time of the wise caliphs."

"When will they come?"

"Maybe in two or three days, when the woman gets out of the hospital. She fainted on the way, so he had to take her for a checkup. There they found that she had severe dehydration. Well, she did not ask for water. Anyway, her condition has improved, but she will stay in the hospital for a day or two. She will keep you company when she comes."

Helen was unable to sleep, not only because Ayash snored loudly but because sleep just would not come. From the day she was first abducted, she'd suffered from insomnia. When she closed her eyes, she felt more awake. It was not an awakening in the sense of not sleeping but in the sense of remembering. Helen's loved ones appeared to her whenever she closed her eyes.

But that night, she also thought of the captive woman who would join her in this place.

—⁓—

In the morning, Ayash told her that someone was coming to the house to take the TV to the Organization. Helen stayed in the bedroom while Ayash helped the man carry it into a pickup. When she heard the door slam, she knew Ayash was leaving. Helen left her bed and went into the living room, where there was now an empty space where the TV had been. She knew the front door was locked, but she habitually tried to open it. Every hour she tried and failed. The locked door was just another wall.

Forget the door, she said to herself. Breaking the window glass would be easier than breaking the door. She had lost a lot of weight recently, so perhaps she could pass through the small space between the window's iron bars. She moved closer to the window to inspect it. There might be enough space for her to pass through it and back into her old life. The window was a wall too, though it had more mercy than the door: at least you could see through it.

The person she saw at that moment was the very one she did not want to see. He was the driver who had brought her with Ayash to this place, and he was in charge of guarding her. He stood next to his Chevrolet, in front of the house, talking on his phone. Helen wished that he would suddenly disappear so she could break the glass and flee.

How far she would run! She would never stop. It was a bright day, but who cared? What did bright mornings mean for prisoners? Bright or not, at this moment, what difference would it make?

—⁓—

Helen picked up a pamphlet from the stack on the table. There had been more on this pile yesterday. Ayash must have taken some with him to distribute to the local residents so they would learn that "the employees must say the oath of obedience to the State and promise repentance from previous government tasks. Citizens must hand over televisions and satellite dishes because they broadcast blasphemies and programs from outside the State's area of control. Music other than religious chants is *haraam*." Helen turned the page, reading a sermon from the Faithful Emir about "values that the caliphate seeks to achieve, such as the redistribution of wealth and the fight against corruption" and how "the State will make the caliphate great again."

In the kitchen, Helen opened the cabinets, mainly to find a tool to break the window. Beneath some business cards and bills, Helen spotted a small album, the words *Family Album* written on its cover. Opening it, Helen browsed photographs of the family that had once lived in this house.

Some were in black and white; a jasmine flower appeared in front of the façade of a house. She was not sure if this was the house she was in. She had seen its outside only once, when she'd first entered it. Then there was a picture of an elderly woman with her hand outstretched as if talking to someone who didn't appear in the picture. Another woman, younger, with very short hair and wearing glasses, appeared in several color photos. There she was with two little girls in a park and giant trees in the background. She had such a sweet smile. When someone smiles in a picture, the smile remains forever, despite what happens in reality, which may not always make you smile. Even though he was not with them in any of those other family photos, a man surrounded by various oriental rugs and calligraphic works of art was probably the father.

It seemed that he owned or worked in a shop selling rugs and antiques, which explained the house's beautiful carpets, one of which had miniatures of people surrounded by birds extending colorful wings. Even the clock on the kitchen wall had a classic look with an ornamented frame, although it was frozen at ten past ten. Its two hands looked as if they were pleading for a change while time was out of work.

Helen opened and closed the refrigerator. She was hungry; she had not eaten anything since yesterday morning, but she did not want to eat.

It was as if her senses were out of place, like a ghost with only one desire in this world: to see the real people she knew. If Helen were a ghost, she would also possess their ability to move around unseen. But instead, she found herself in a nightmare from which she could not wake: finding herself with the dead who made her sleep with them in their graves, from which emanated the smell of their corpses. In the nightmare, they wore dark glasses brought from the seventh century, so they saw life through the telescope of that time. They wanted her to see their dead world with them. They denied the existence of a world in which she had her own people, people whom she loved and missed terribly. Helen would trade half her life just to know that they were still alive.

She paced the distance between the kitchen and the living room several times. When she turned, she looked again at the Arabic calligraphy art on the wall. She faced it, determined to read it in full, and this time she succeeded.

So that was the saying, then: "Half of a person's beauty comes from the tongue."

———

This saying's tacit recommendation was not for her. Helen was well aware that she must remain silent and not use her tongue at all in the presence of Ayash's friends. It was not permissible for male strangers to hear her voice. From their point of view, that would be *haraam*. Only in her heart could she say what she wanted.

After the visitors arrived that evening, her voice was locked in her throat and she in her room. In fact, she had three rooms to move around in: kitchen, bathroom, and bedroom.

In the kitchen, she had made food for the men, but she must not take it to them in the living room. She should not be seen by them. Instead, Ayash came and took the tray of food to them. Helen made tea in a large pot that whistled and blew out steam. Its whistle mixed with the religious songs that she heard as Ayash's guests enthusiastically sang praise for the State and its deeds. They didn't have to lock their feelings in their hearts.

The Chechen desert emir was one of the guests in the living room that evening, so when Ayash came to the kitchen to pick up the tea, Helen asked in a low voice about the new family: "Did the Chechen emir bring them with him?"

"No, maybe tomorrow," he said, leaving with the tray of glass teacups.

Helen was eager to meet the woman who would share her prison. This was no regular waiting; it was a yearning for someone like her, for another stifled voice. Even though she had not met her, Helen felt this woman was her close friend. She would make this prison less lonely, or they might even escape together.

Going out into the street wearing the niqab, they would not raise any suspicion. There were police everywhere, but no one would recognize them since all but their eyes would be covered. Not even Ayash would recognize Helen if he passed her in the street.

In any case, he would be busy elsewhere, monitoring and enforcing the State's rules that men left their beards unshaven and women wore the sharia attire. He imposed fines on anyone selling Western clothes, especially T-shirts with foreign words on them. At Friday prayers, if he saw a boy in the street, he would yell at him to get to the mosque. If someone laughed during prayer, Ayash would summon him to disciplinary prison. If he spotted a smoker, he would punish him with twenty-five lashes, plus the number of cigarettes missing from the pack. If he saw a boy wearing trousers that did not fall slightly above his ankle, he would punish the boy's parents, specifically his father, with twenty lashes, and the same number of lashes for the husband whose wife made a mistake in her outfit—for example, if something showed under her niqab. Ayash earned $100 a month for his work, which contributed to reforming society, as he said. The State paid all of his daily expenses, and he did not even need to spend that $100, he explained to Helen.

But she knew that he spent it on drugs. He had taken them in her presence, and he forced her to take some too, almost every night of the past week.

It was obvious that the State did not prevent the use of drugs, but Helen wanted to make sure, so she had asked him: "Only smoking is forbidden, right?"

"Alcohol is also forbidden," he'd replied.

When he said this, he looked at her with such concentration that she guessed he was about to say something important. But she did not expect the words that followed: "Helen, I will release you and go back to my family because our religion says that the one who sets a slave free will be rewarded in heaven."

He rubbed his forehead and asked, "What is your family's phone number? I will sell you to them. I need money to be able to travel. Whoever comes here cannot go back. I know a trusted smuggler, but he is asking for a large sum of money."

"Is it possible to use the Kurdistan telephone directory? I might find someone's number," Helen said.

"I'll see and let you know later," he answered.

"When?"

"I don't know. I told you, later."

⁓

Ayash fell asleep soon after his friends left the house, so exhausted that he neither prayed nor raped her that night. Helen waited impatiently for the next day's arrival with its promise of a companion for her.

Helen didn't know why she kept thinking of the jasmine she had seen in the photo album. In the morning, as Ayash left the house, she rushed to the window to see if the jasmine was actually there. She couldn't see it. More importantly, she did not see the guard either.

It was an opportunity for escape. She could break the window's glass with any tool she found in this house. She would walk fast until she reached the main street, and there she would stop a taxi. She had no money, but when she arrived at her destination, she would ask the driver to wait a little until she retrieved the money from her house or from her neighbor, Umm Hameed.

If they caught her along the way, they'd bring her back to Ayash. If he implemented the State's law, he'd have to stone her to death. Even if he did not want to kill her, he would do it because if he did not, the State would punish him with the same sentence. He himself had told her so.

Perhaps it would be better for Helen to wait for Ayash, so that he could help her escape in an easier but more expensive way. But what if he changed his mind? Or what if the previous night's words were merely said under the influence of drugs? No, she could not wait for him.

Helen rushed into the kitchen, looking for a knife to break through the window.

3

THE LEGO

Wearing the niqab and carrying a large knife, Helen returned to the living room.

There she froze, surprised to see a little girl sitting next to the toybox. The girl, who had her back to Helen, was busily stacking LEGO cubes to make a tall building that rose, tilted, and then collapsed. While Helen watched, the girl started over, building what looked like a house, then pushing the walls to the ground. She was so engaged with building and demolishing that she didn't notice Helen.

Knife still in hand, Helen stood still, afraid any sudden moves would scare away the little girl, like a gentle butterfly that takes off at the slightest movement.

Looking at the industrious child, Helen imagined that she could do the same, demolishing this room. If only she could move the walls just as this girl did. If only the ceiling could be lifted so that

Helen could see the sky above. If the roof was removed, the sky might better hear her prayers. If the walls fell away, she would run into the open air and find her way back to her house.

Not to her house, actually—there was no one there—but rather to the house of her neighbor Umm Hameed, the woman with whom Helen had left her daughter. Helen needed to make sure she was okay.

Her daughter had no name yet. She had been born after Elias disappeared, and she had not been ready to think of a proper name for her. What would Elias have called her if he had been there the day she was born? He would have been very happy to know that Helen had given birth to a girl as he'd wished.

Yassir's name was born with him. Holding him for the first time, Elias had looked at him and said, "Yassir." And because Helen knew of his admiration for the soccer player Yassir Raad, she had not been surprised by the choice. She'd heard it repeatedly from him when he watched games, on tenterhooks. Seeing his favorite player about to score a goal, he would shout, "Yella, Yassir!"

Helen closed tearful eyes and remembered. Umm Hameed must be worried about her, because she had not returned since that terrible day. It could be that her daughter did not even wonder about her absence. She had been a newborn when Helen left her. But she had breastfed her before she had been taken, so perhaps her daughter felt the absence of Helen's breasts?

When Helen stepped back, the little girl noticed her. She screamed in panic and ran up the stairs to the second floor. Helen moved to the window, seeing the reflection of a masked woman with a huge knife. No wonder the child had fled! She glanced at the Chevrolet parked outside.

The driver got out of the car and walked toward the house, so Helen quickly put the knife on the table. After knocking on the door twice, he let himself in and said, "Today Ayash is on a fighting mission, and he will not be back until tomorrow. Do you need anything?"

"No thanks," she answered.

"I'll be here in the area if you need something," he said and went back to the car.

She returned the knife and the niqab to their places and went and stood at the foot of the stairs. She was hoping to hear voices upstairs, to feel less like she was the only one alive in this grave.

But it was not proper for her to go up to them. What if the desert emir was there with them? Those men were not like the people she had known in her life, not even close. Helen and the other girls in her village used to mix with boys without any problem. Even when she moved to the city after her marriage, men did not give her any cause for fear or concern.

She had never met a young man with such a long beard as the Daesh wore. Only certain sheikhs of the temples grew their beards like this, but they were kind and would not hurt anyone. Where had these men come from? And how were they allowed to do all this to her people? Ayash had told her that in the future they would rule the whole world, even China.

So why did he jump out of bed this morning when his phone rang and leave in a hurry? She had mixed feelings about him not returning home today. For months, she'd not had the luxury of being left alone, untouched, and now she'd been given a break in this strange prison where victims rather than criminals were punished.

Yet Helen longed for Ayash to return so that he could keep his promise and set her free.

—⁓—

The water was boiling in the teapot when Helen heard footsteps. She turned off the stove and went to the living room.

A woman came down the stairs, behind her a boy and a girl, the same girl who'd been scared by Helen an hour earlier. The woman nodded to Helen.

Helen said, "Hello. I am Helen, a captive like you."

The woman gave Helen a sad look and said nothing.

Helen stepped back into the kitchen, then returned shortly after and said: "I've made tea. Do you want some?"

The woman nodded, and Helen brought her a cup of tea. Now sitting, the woman looked at her gratefully and said nothing.

Helen pointed to the refrigerator and said: "There's bread and cheese."

The boy looked at Helen as if he wanted to say something, but he turned away and muttered something to his mother.

At that moment, Helen understood that the woman did not speak, because she answered her son with her hands. Helen was impressed by the boy, who understood his mother's signs fluently and translated for Helen.

He said, "My mother says thank you."

Helen smiled at the mute woman's half smile. She had a craving for coffee, so she returned to the kitchen and searched the cabinets, looking for coffee beans. She didn't find any but spotted two magazines squeezed between hand towels.

Her heart trembled when she saw the title of the second magazine, *Nineveh*, the monthly magazine that had employed Elias. This issue in her hand might be its last. Its date of June 2014 on the upper-left corner coincided with the arrival of Daesh in Mosul. They had banned magazines that showed unveiled women, whose fate, they said, was to burn in hell. Her eyes came across an article titled "How to get rid of menstrual pain." Since her imprisonment, she'd been relieved every month when her period came. She did not want to fall pregnant. She kept contraceptive pills in her clothes as a treasure, given to her and others by Rehana. She'd found them with other drugs in a kitchen cabinet. Perhaps she'd swallowed many of them or other pills she'd found and died? Nobody knew.

Helen remembered Layla and the sorrowful look in her eyes when Helen left the market with Ayash. If only Helen had claimed Layla was her daughter, they might have allowed Helen to bring the girl along with her. But now it was too late.

Helen browsed the magazine for an article that might have been written by Elias. The problem was he sometimes published without a byline. She stopped at an article titled "Sun Stroke," which had no byline, and wondered if it was his.

She leaned against the counter and read:

> *It was too hot a spring day when the new war was announced as the "Liberation of Iraq." The temperature had reached 100 degrees Fahrenheit and the dust was heavy, causing the commander of the American forces to hesitate in moving his forces to Baghdad.*
>
> *The sky, however, seemed normal for Iraqis, who were used to being stricken both by the sun and by war; they found nothing strange in the sky that day. No Iraqi could have looked up to the sky and imagined, for example, that foreign soldiers would bring their tanks to these dangerous streets thousands of miles away.*
>
> *When they arrived, the Americans must have suffered headaches from the blazing sun and the confusing reactions of Iraqi citizens. One day they celebrated the arrival of Uncle Sam's distributed sweets, and the next day they cried, "No, no to the American occupation." Some people who had lost*

*their jobs invented a new job for themselves called mujahi-
deen. Their first mission was to kill translators who worked
with the Americans. They branded the translators traitors
and called their mission "resistance." Their second task
was to kidnap people and ask their families for a ransom.
This process they called "collecting donations." A third task
was to terrorize people until they left their homes. They called
that process "providing housing for the faithful."*

*Now their work flourishes, and the Organization has
become a state with a flag, laws, and stamped identity
cards. It's attracting employees from all over the world. Its
new mission is to erase people's memories. New names are
invented for everything. Shakespeare's theater, for example,
became the Sheikh Zubair theater. The gift shop has become
the Gift from God. The court of justice has become the Court
of Destiny.*

The article did seem to bear Elias's ironic style. She held the
magazine close to her chest. Daydreaming, for a moment she forgot
where she was. She didn't notice until she heard the boy's voice.
He asked her, "From this I take?" He had come into the kitchen
to pick up a piece of bread from the table.

Helen opened the fridge and handed him some cheese.

He looked eight or nine years old. He must be younger than ten,
because she'd heard from Ayash that boys aged ten and over would
join training camps and not stay with their mothers.

"What's your name?" asked Helen.

"Zedo."

"And your mother's name?"

"Her name is Ghazal, and my little sister is Joan," he said as he
inserted a piece of cheese inside the bread. "My mother used to

speak before," he added, "but she lost her voice the day they killed my father and two uncles. And they took my older sister too." After saying that, he put the sandwich aside.

Helen regretted opening his wound. She knew exactly what day he was talking about. She closed her eyes and saw the same scene that Zedo was seeing. She witnessed the massacre as if it were in front of her on TV. Men thrown into ditches and shot. Boys without shirts lined up with their hands raised, and Organization members checking them, ordering those who had grown hair under their armpits to join the camps. Others who had no hair yet departed with their mothers to the "guests' place" while they were prepared for sale.

Helen kept her eyes closed, seeing children holding the edges of their grandmothers' dresses and refusing to be separated from them. They would never be separated; they would be buried alive together.

Intuitively, Ghazal rushed over and embraced Helen.

"They took my husband too. I don't know if he's alive or dead," Helen said, tears streaming down her cheeks.

If Elias was alive, she thought, he could not withstand the knowledge of all that had happened to her. When Yassir was born, Elias had been crying for her outside her room.

The midwife later told Helen, "This is the first time I have seen a man show such emotion. How much he loves you!"

Ghazal cried with her, a wordless, rattling sound. When she gestured with her hand, Helen understood she meant to "run away from here."

Helen nodded. They had the necessary clothes, and their men were absent. Ayash and the desert emir had not returned that evening. The captives came to know that when their men were not home and were not relaxing with their friends, taking drugs or reciting prayers, watching clips from pornographic films on their phones or raping captives, this meant they were fighting in battle.

Helen walked to the window and saw the guard leaning against his car, talking on the phone. She thought of a way to get him away from the place even if temporarily.

Putting on the niqab again, she intended to trick the man by asking him to buy them some bread.

But then he surprised her by knocking twice on the door. The guard opened it and said to Helen, "I just received news that Ayash was killed today in the battle, so you have to go back to the guests' place. I have been asked to take you there."

Helen was shocked by the news. "Can I wait here a day or two so I can attend his burial?"

"They did not find his body," he answered. "You should come with me now."

"No, I will not come. I will stay with Ghazal!" Helen cried.

"This is an order you must obey. Otherwise, they will not find your body either."

Helen was about to collapse from screaming. Ghazal hugged her as she cried with her.

"Yella, quickly!" the guard said.

When Helen didn't move, he took out his gun and pointed it at her. Ghazal raised her hand and lowered it, grabbed Helen's hand, and pulled her closer.

Joan cried as she saw the guard approaching Helen with gun in hand. He shoved Ghazal away and seized Helen's arm, pulling her outside. He closed the door behind him with the key and dragged Helen across the yard, at the same time purposefully firing a bullet into the sky. He pushed her into the back seat and closed the door behind her.

Getting in, he drove fast and at the end of the street slammed on the brakes; a child was in the middle of the street. A man ran from a nearby shop and yanked the child away, lifting his hand, thanking the driver.

Helen saw a sign on the front of the shop with the words TAHINI AND DATE SYRUP SALE. She remembered this was the same store which used to sell pickles and olives.

Who would pull her from danger now? Helen cursed the driver who had ruined their escape. And she cursed Ayash, too, for dying when he had dangled the promise of freeing her just the day before.

4

THE BIRD TATTOO

In the back seat of the car, Helen contemplated the bird tattoo on her finger through her tears. She rubbed it gently. It was commonly thought among the people of her village that losing a wedding ring was a bad omen that would lead to the separation of the couple. After their wedding, the rumor had spread throughout her village that this was the reason Helen and Elias avoided traditional rings: the two lovers were afraid to be taken from each other. This had happened to Helen's uncle, who was separated from his wife a month after the loss of his ring. So, they had thought a tattoo was permanent and could never be lost.

But in reality, that had not been why Helen and Elias—at their wedding and to their guests' surprise—revealed bird tattoos on their left ring fingers instead of the usual gold bands. The real reason was that a certain bird had been the cause of their first meeting, and it had become a symbol of their love.

It had been fifteen years since Helen met Elias. She had been twenty years old, on her way from the valley to her home in the village of Halliqi, which sat on the slope of the mountain. She had stopped along the way because she spotted a trapped qabaj bird, its small foot caught by a colorful string attached to the ground near a fig tree. Her family told many tales of how fond hunters were of this beautiful bird and how its beauty was also its curse.

Fortunately, the people of Halliqi, an area this bird frequented, did not hunt nor eat the bird, believing it a bad omen to do so. They held annual celebrations at which they burned empty cages and danced around a fire. They believed this celebration—known as the Day of the Bird—would send comfort to the birds of their region and that those birds would later tap on their windows as a sign that there was news on the way. And since the Halliqians believed that burning empty cages drove away evil, any coming news would most likely be good.

Even the way the Halliqians moved was birdlike. They moved together in groups like flocks. When going to the spring for water, a member of the flock was usually preceded by a volunteer bird. It drank some and waited. If no hunters were detected in the area, it gave a signal to the others that it was safe to approach the water. Like the villagers, the qabaj bird was a simple creature but with dignity. Whenever shot by a hunter, it flew as high as it could until it bled its last drop of blood before falling to the ground like a stone. When wounded, it swayed in a way that resembled a sort of dance. The people of Halliqi called it the "dance of pain," and sometimes they imitated it when sad music was played.

No house in their village was without a flute, drum, or tambur. Even if there was nothing else in the house, there was at least one of those musical instruments, or else how would they play and sing and pass their songs from generation to generation? Most of the villagers didn't know how to read or write—schools were too far away—but almost all of them, young and old, male and female, sang or played music. At sunset, they gathered around the lanterns and sang. When someone died, their singing became sad and was accompanied only by flute.

After singing, their second pleasure was storytelling. Some were real stories of things that had befallen their relatives, and some were imaginary and started with "Once upon a time . . ." Some of their real stories were stranger than the imagined ones.

⁓

Like the other residents of the village, Helen was accustomed to seeing qabaj birds near the fig trees, but this was the first time she had seen a bird caught in a trap. Dropping the pile of firewood she was carrying, she bent down to untie the string.

The bird flapped its wings several times before tapping gently on her hand as if thanking her. As soon as she released its little foot from the string, the bird took several faltering steps. She patted its feathers, and the bird spread its wings and flew into the open air.

Helen startled when she heard someone shouting behind her.

"You there, what are you doing?"

She turned to see a young man running toward her.

"Really? Do you know what you did?" he asked. When Helen didn't answer him, he continued. "For a whole hour I waited for this bird to fall into the trap, and when it finally happened, you simply let it go?"

"I didn't know this was your bird. The poor thing, it was almost dead, and suppose she's a mother and needs to tend to her chicks. Would you separate them?"

Helen wasn't sure why she'd said that, but she didn't expect that her words would have the power on him that they did. First he appeared shocked, and then he looked away at the green-spotted hillside. When he turned his gaze back to her, his eyes were filled with tears.

He walked away and sat on the ground near the fig tree. Lowering his head, he rested his forehead on his hands.

Helen sat down near him, not knowing what to do or say. Then, thinking she should leave him in case he needed to cry alone, she picked up her firewood and went on her way. After about twenty meters, she stopped and turned back.

He had remained in that spot as if he'd replaced the captured bird. She hesitated for a moment and then returned.

When he stood up and wiped away his tears, Helen felt happy, just as she'd felt when the bird rose up in front of her and flew away.

He looked at her and said, "My wife died recently, leaving our little son. She died while she was breastfeeding him. Your words were like salt in the wound."

"Oh, I am sorry. That's terrible," she replied, the firewood again tumbling from her hand.

He picked it up. "Let me carry this for you."

"Thank you, but my house is far away, there on the mountain," she said, pointing into the distance.

"That's fine," he said. "If you can give me some water when we get there, I would be grateful."

"We have the yogurt drink, if you like," she offered.

He nodded, and his eyes glowed with the traces of his tears.

—⁓—

They walked in silence for an hour across rugged mountainous terrain, something Helen was well used to: walking down with her friend Amina for fun, herding sheep, bringing water or firewood back home. But today she was empty-handed and had a spring in her step.

They climbed the rocks—rough but familiar, like wrinkles on the faces of elders. After some five hundred meters, Elias said, panting, "I did not know there were farms on the mountain."

Helen stopped by a tomato tree on the roadside and picked a red one.

"You want it?" she asked.

Elias lowered the firewood, setting it down on a big rock. Taking the tomato from her, he said, "Thank you. Can we rest here a bit?"

She sat on a large flat stone, and he perched next to her, looking at the small shrubs growing among the rocks. Looking at her, he said, "I always see this mountain from a distance and never thought to climb it."

"You came from far away?"

"From Mosul. My name is Elias."

He waited for her to introduce herself as well, but instead she blew a loud whistle.

Seeing his confusion, she explained, "I want to let my family know that a guest is coming." She stood up, and so did he.

At that moment, a large snake curled around the trunk of a small tree in front of them. Pulling Helen away, Elias cried, "Watch out!"

But Helen laughed and said, "Don't worry, I'll carry the snake home with me. It brings good luck."

When she moved toward the snake, Elias said, "No, for God's sake, I'm scared of snakes." A moment later, he seemed to regret this. "Actually, I am not afraid of the snake, but I don't know how to handle it. I've never seen one in the wild."

She smiled and said, "It's okay. You see a lot of them in our region, but they do not hurt anyone."

As they walked away, she said, "We will be there soon."

She put her fingers on her mouth and blew another whistle. In a few moments, a whistle higher and shorter than the first reached their ears.

"That's my father answering me that he welcomes you," she said.

Elias told her that, within this region, he only knew the meadow where he'd gone to catch qabaj birds and sell them in Mosul. It was a much-needed extra income to add to what he earned from writing magazine articles. Sometimes his articles were not published, so he tried to make money from hunting and selling birds. "But I could not have imagined a life there over the mountains," he said to her as he avoided another snake that was lying on a tree trunk.

They sped up as they descended the mountain on the other side. The green valley suddenly opened up before them. They needed to pass through it to reach her home village. The Halliqi tribe had lived there since ancient times. No one knew when they had arrived, just as they didn't know the age of their oldest trees. Many changes had occurred in the world over the centuries, but not in the area around Halliqi.

At least, not until the arrival of Elias at their home that day in the summer of 1999. The Halliqians had no telephones nor internet nor electricity. As for water, they brought it from various springs scattered around the village. Elias knew that life was simple in the villages surrounding his city. Still, he was surprised by such a primitive way of living. Their way of life seemed to him something fantastical and unbelievable in this noisy world at the end of the twentieth century.

The news of the world for them was limited to what a traveler from the city, like Elias, would tell them. They would whistle to the neighbors to come and welcome him and hear the latest news, as if they were listening to the radio. Then they returned to watching their sheep, and handicrafts, and taking care of each other. If a villager spotted a house with no fire coming from its clay oven, they would rush to that house with bread, as a flameless clay oven could only mean there was no flour in that house that evening.

Elias noticed they had no television nor radio and wondered if their good mood was because they did not watch local and international news, or was it due to their relaxed way of life? They did not wake in the morning to alarm clocks but birdsong. They had no specific work schedules and no locks on their doors; they left their doors open all the time to the sun and to visitors. Even the wars that had taken place one after the other in their country had not touched the Halliqi valley.

Any Halliqian hearing such news would hit one palm on the other and turn his head to the right and to the left in regret and disapproval. No police, no sirens, no prisons, no car fumes. Children played outside, and their parents had no fear of them getting lost or meeting strangers. In fact, there were no strangers in the Halliqi village and no secrets. Everyone knew everything about everyone else in that remote spot isolated from the good and evil of the world.

On the wooden slab that served as a table in the corner of the large living room lay a flute—the first thing Elias noticed in Helen's home. As soon as they arrived, he was greeted by Helen's father, who kissed him on both cheeks as if they were close relatives. Helen's mother shook hands with Elias, and he kissed her hand as villagers do for senior women. She pointed for him to sit on the floor on a mattress covered by a colorful quilt. The other mattresses in the room were light brown.

Elias removed his shoes at the door and took a seat. In front of him on the wall was a framed canvas with embroidered figures raising their hands. Above them were stars of different sizes.

At the time, Elias didn't know that Helen was the one who had sewn the thread on the canvas, as she had learned embroidery in art class. She was among the few girls in the village who went to school. The closest school to Halliqi was four hours away. It took three hours on foot to descend from the village to the meadow below and from there another hour by car to reach the village of Sinouni, which had a school.

It had been Murad, Helen's uncle, who suggested registering Helen and Azad at the school, where he was a teacher. In the beginning, Helen's mother had said no because it was too far away, but Murad had convinced her, explaining that they could go three days a week and do their homework in the remaining days. The school allowed this for students who came from outlying villages. He offered to put them up at his home during the days they went to school. He had added: "It's a good chance to spend time with their grandpa and grandma as well."

Helen's love of school had not been for the lessons but rather for the journey. It started in the morning on a donkey, which took her and Azad down the mountain to where Uncle Murad met them with his pickup truck.

Helen rode with Azad in the open back of the car. Buildings quickly receded while they bounced up and down with the road bumps, laughing whenever one of them fell backward or forward. At the end of the day, their grandpa gave them chocolate. Often, Grandmother told him: "I am afraid they will fill up on this and not eat a proper meal." From her grandfather, Helen learned the card game Konkan, while Azad preferred to go out with their uncle.

They did not attend school beyond the elementary years, but Helen continued drawing. Her cloth paintings and colorful embroidery became popular in the area.

Elias was looking at such a painting in the living room when Helen brought him a large pail of water for him to wash his hands and face. He sat on a flat stone in front of the house as she indicated what he should do. He opened his hands, and Helen poured water on them. When he had finished washing, she handed him a white towel.

At that moment, Helen's father whistled loudly several times. "I have just announced a celebration here tonight in your honor so that our neighbors can meet you as well," he told Elias.

"This is so generous of you, but I don't want to trouble you, and also it might be hard to figure out the way back after dark," Elias replied.

"We always meet with our neighbors, especially when a guest visits. Our friends love it. And we expect you to stay with us overnight. We would not expose you to the dangers of the road at night, and it is safest after the sun rises in the morning. The day has eyes, as they say."

"I'm afraid my sister will be worried. I left my son with her, and she expects me to take him back today. Otherwise, I would be more than happy to spend time with you. What if I go and come back in a day or two?" Elias asked.

"In three days' time would be better because it will be the Day of the Bird, and that's an opportunity to join us in our celebration of burning the cages. Did you notice our birds on your way here? They fly low, very close to the ground. They don't like to go too far away from home, but the problem is that every now and then, hunters come from nearby towns and villages with traps which they set," said Helen's father.

Elias glanced quickly at Helen as he lowered his head, and Helen did the same.

Then her mother called from the kitchen: "Helen, come here."

It was the first time Elias heard her name. He did not know why he was so glad to hear it.

Helen returned from the kitchen with a tray and offered him a yogurt drink and fig pies.

Elias loved the pie. "I have never in my life tasted anything better."

Ramziya, Helen's mother, adjusted herself in her seat and said: "A merchant comes over here every month from Sinjar and buys great quantities of these pies from me. He distributes them to the markets."

Shammo, Helen's father, added, "Even in the markets of Baghdad and Mosul!"

"From now on, I'll look for them in the markets of Mosul and remember you," said Elias, looking at Helen, who was sitting next to her father. He stood up to leave.

"Wait a moment," said Shammo. He went quickly to the kitchen.

Elias smiled at Helen, who had also stood up. She looked very like her mother but dressed in a more modern style. She didn't wear the round, white head covering or the traditional loose-fitting robe, tied at the waist with thick, ornamented cotton cloth. Instead, she wore an overall skirt with a cotton shirt. Her coffee-colored hair fell down to her shoulders in ringlets. She was of average height, like her mother, but thinner.

Shammo returned with two large bags filled with small fig pies, a necklace of dried figs, and a large bird-shaped fig pie inside a zipped bag.

"This is far too much to give away," said Elias, but Shammo insisted. "Thank you," said Elias.

"You are welcome," Shammo replied.

"Maybe this is too heavy to carry on foot, Dad," Helen suggested.

He thought about this and replied, "I have a solution," before hurrying out of the room. When he returned minutes later, he pulled a donkey behind him.

"This donkey is an expert on the roads, and he always carries our guests to their destinations and then returns." He patted the donkey's back. "You may ride it, and we'll tie the bags on it. When you reach the bottom of the mountain, just let the donkey go. He knows the way home."

Once on the donkey, Elias waved his hand to them and said goodbye.

"Welcome," replied Shammo.

The Halliqians did not say "goodbye." Only "hello" and "welcome."

5

RED

After Elias got off the donkey and sent it back up the mountain, he stood at the side of the dirt track, waiting for a car to give him a lift to the paved road. He turned back several times to be sure the donkey was headed in the right direction, until it vanished from sight. After a quarter of an hour, he spotted a car coming and raised his hand, waving. The car slowed down and stopped in front of him.

A driver with an impressive mustache and a cigarette in his mouth said: "Hello, where to?"

"If you could take me to the main road, I would be grateful."

"Do get in."

Elias got into the passenger seat, and the driver immediately put his foot down on the accelerator, taking off with a jerk before saying: "I'm headed for Sinouni. Does that work for you?"

"That sounds good. There's a car station there from where I can catch a ride to Mosul."

"Okay. I'll take you to the station, then."

"I hope it's not a burden."

"It's easy. We will be there in less than half an hour."

"Thank you."

"Welcome," said the driver before exhaling an enormous cloud of cigarette smoke.

Elias asked, "Are you from this area?"

"From the village of Hardan. Do you know it?"

"I've heard of it."

"It's like no other place." He took a deep breath and let it out. "Life!"

"Do you know Halliqi?" Elias asked.

"Yes. A beautiful area too, but far away, on the edge of the country. It's not even on the map! It has so many fig trees."

"And qabaj birds," Elias said.

"The qabaj love figs, and so they gather there," the driver said. "It's been said their tweets are so very captivating because the area's delicious figs make them high. Life!" he repeated, now with a sigh.

"I was just up there for the first time. I loved it."

"Its people are out of this world. They welcome you no matter whether you are relative or stranger, and they have yogurt unlike any other. Life!"

"Yes, you're right!"

The driver tossed one cigarette out the window and lit another. "Who do you know over there?"

"A family I have just met. The father's name is Shammo, and his wife is Ramziya."

"Shammo the circumcision man?"

"I am not sure if he does circumcision."

"Yes, who doesn't know him? He's the best."

"Yes, he is."

Elias found a contradiction between the driver's tense expression and his relaxed spirit. He grimaced even more when he smoked. After tossing another cigarette out the car window, he turned on the radio.

"Like rain, your love fell in my heart," the song began, but the driver changed the channel to a news report. Elias wished he'd let him listen to the rest of the song, but he was too shy to make the request.

A stern-sounding news broadcaster said: "According to the latest UNICEF report, the infant mortality rate in Iraq is now the highest in the world. Yet the United Nations Security Council issued a resolution to continue the economic blockade on Iraq, and this is the fortieth time that the council voted on this decision during the past nine years."

A musical break came, and then the reporter returned. "The Iraqi soccer team hopes to take part in the Sydney 2000 Olympics. It is slated to play today with its Jordanian counterpart at the stadium of King Abdullah II in Amman." The reader concluded his news report, saying: "This summer the world will witness the final lunar eclipse of the twentieth century, and the phenomenon will last for three hours over Europe, India, and the Middle East. Iraq and Syria are the only two Arab countries that will witness a full eclipse, and the clearest view of the eclipse will be on the Nineveh Plain."

"Oh, the eclipse. We must be ready," the driver said, slamming on the brakes as a single sheep crossed the road.

Elias bounced in his seat, then said: "Is he lost or fleeing from the herd?"

He did not expect a response, but the driver answered him, laughing: "Or just chilling on his own."

Silence fell between them, and Elias busied himself observing the vast fallow plains at the side of the road.

"I have to get some gas," said the driver, turning into a station.

Elias got out of the vehicle and went into the station shop. He returned carrying two cans of Coca-Cola and two small bags of salted nuts to share with the driver.

"I like pistachios," the driver said.

Elias was about to say "Life!" but instead he smiled.

At the car station, Elias thanked the driver and purchased a fare on a small bus which could carry eighteen passengers. The bus driver stood by the door, calling out: "Yella, two passengers to go!"

Elias climbed on and was followed by a woman carrying a large plastic bag. The driver waited for the woman to reach her seat, as she was walking very slowly. Strands of her gray hair appeared from under a blue scarf, and on her hunched back she wore a long-sleeved jacket despite the hot weather. Three minutes into the journey, she called out to the driver: "Where's the soldiers' center?"

"There's no such place, auntie," the driver replied. "Where do you want to go?"

"I don't know. My Hajji gave you his life. His will is to return the bag to the center."

"Which bag?" the driver asked.

"This is it. Everything's inside it: his khaki uniform, helmet, belt, and boots. He wore them all his life. Now they are useless."

"Why do you say useless, auntie?" asked the driver, switching lanes and passing a slower vehicle. "What about the struggle, patriotism, and sacrifice?"

"Don't worry, son, they're all in the bag," the woman said. "Just take me there."

When they reached the last stop, the woman asked: "Are we there?"

Next to Elias, a passenger said to the driver: "Poor thing, take her back to her home, and the fare's on me."

———

Elias rang the doorbell of his older sister Sana's house. As soon as she opened the door, he handed her a bag of figs.

"Where did you get this?" she asked.

"From Halliqi village."

"I've not heard of it."

"Me neither. I didn't know it existed. But it's very special."

"I wonder what took you there, brother."

"The qabaj bird. I will go again in three days and will need to leave Yahya with you, if that's okay."

"Yes, of course. You must have a big hunting mission ahead."

"No, I will not hunt birds anymore."

She looked closer into his eyes. "You are strange today. What will you do there, then?"

"I will celebrate the Day of the Bird with the people there and perhaps write an article for the magazine about this special ritual," replied Elias.

At that moment, the air-conditioning started up, making a noise, blowing hot air at first, then cool. Sana said: "Thank God, the electricity came back. The heat was killing us."

In the corner of the room, eight-month-old Yahya was playing with his cousin Rula, who was three years older than him. She was facing him with a straw fan, and he took it from her and put it in his mouth. She said, "Ew."

Elias knelt on the floor by them. He told Rula, "Close your eyes." When she did, he put the fig necklace around her neck. "Guess what this is," he asked.

Eyes still closed, she touched it and said, "What is it, Uncle?"

When she opened her eyes, Elias said, "You can eat this necklace."

"All of it or just one?" she asked.

Her mother, Sana, came closer to her and said, "One fig at a time, sweetheart." And she whispered to Elias, "I bet you this necklace will soon disappear."

⁓

Sana had moved from Sinjar district to Mosul in 1995 when her husband, Karim, got a job in the registrar's office at the university. A year later, Elias and his wife had joined them; his in-laws were also in Mosul, so moving to the area was easy for him, as he worked from home as a freelancer. Elias's eyes filled with tears whenever he remembered how his wife died as she was breastfeeding Yahya.

She had complained of pain in her heart but was certain it would go away in a minute or two. Instead, she died, with a newborn crying in her lap as if he understood what was happening.

Now Yahya was in his arms as Elias walked to their house, which was two blocks from Sana's. Once there, he put Yahya in his small bed and lay down on his own. Elias's mind soon took him back to the Halliqi valley. He found himself smiling at the thought of lovely Helen.

At dawn, Yahya woke him up, and Elias rushed to prepare milk for his son. The strange thing was, at the moment he'd opened his eyes to Yahya's crying, Elias had thought of Helen too. Even as he fed his son, he never stopped thinking about her. He found himself eager to walk with Helen, even if a snake accompanied them. Later, he would go to the market to buy a gift for her family. He thought of buying sweets, so Helen could taste them. He changed his mind because an edible gift would disappear. He wanted to give them a permanent gift but didn't yet know what it would be.

—⁓—

Carrying Yahya on his shoulders, Elias spent half a day at the Saray market, looking for the gift. It was a hot summer day, but the lavishly decorated high roofs of the market protected the shoppers from the sun's heat. They passed through the market halls on his right and left until Elias stopped for a rest at the Hadba cafeteria, known for its natural pomegranate juice mixed with ground walnuts.

The waiter passed by the front table, clicking a glass *istikan* of tea with a little teaspoon. Yahya laughed at it, and the waiter watched and came toward them, continuing to click on the *istikan*, making faces and clowning around for Yahya, who kept laughing. Elias ordered tea for himself and pomegranate juice for Yahya.

"All ready, my eyes," the waiter cooed at the baby.

The voice of Nazem Al-Ghazali blasted from the radio, singing "She of Black Eyes," and before the end of the song, Elias stood up and took Yahya in his arms. He paid his bill and left in a hurry. He had finally realized what he wanted to buy.

He left the Saray market, heading to Al-Hammam alley, which led to Jabbar's shop for new and used devices. As Elias expected, the voice of Nazem Al-Ghazali was also blaring loudly from the shop. The owner of the store was known for his love of Al-Ghazali songs; indeed he played nothing else.

On the right-hand side of the shop was an old radio that looked like an ornate box, a meter long. Next to it were other large Philips and Marconi radios that all looked as if they were more for decoration than for daily use. On the left were smaller, more commonly used devices. Elias selected a red radio bearing the local Harp brand and went to pay for it.

Another customer holding a similar one, but in white, asked the shop owner: "How much is this radio of noise?"

The seller replied: "Seventy thousand dinars. The noise comes only when you first turn it on, and then it disappears. The foreign radio is twice the price."

When it was Elias's turn, he said to the seller with a smile, "Radio of noise and batteries, please."

―――

Elias did not fall asleep that night until two in the morning, perhaps because he had drunk a lot of tea while writing a new article just after midnight. He wrote: "When the sun shines on the village of Halliqi, it appears new and fresh, as if it shines there before anywhere else in the world. At sunset, shade gathers under the trees and between the houses, and soft breezes blow, so no fans are needed. It's a magical area, despite its ruggedness, with its natural variety of hills, valleys, rocks, and those springs that flow underground like feelings kept secret. To discover its beauty is to experience a euphoria as if you had just found an ancient secret that would make a real difference in your life. Life has hardly changed in this village over the past centuries. If we were to add the village to the map, we would draw it in the northwestern corner of Mount Sinjar, near the border of Syria, in a range of mountains overlooking the valley."

He stopped there, deciding to complete the article after his much-anticipated trip the next day.

―――

What Elias could not have predicted was that Yahya would wake up with measles the next morning. He was a quiet child and did not cry without reason, but that day he wept because his entire body was covered in rashes and red spots. When his temperature spiked, Elias ran with him to the clinic.

The doctor recommended a medication that would bring his fever down and said that Yahya would need at least a week of care to recover.

Day after day, Elias was relieved to see Yahya's condition improving. Elias started playing with him and joking, "Your measles only came now, sweetheart?"

When the child slept, Elias's mind went to Helen: Was she thinking of him as he did of her? Had she felt sad when he did not show up? He couldn't understand how this could happen to him when he had only spent a few hours with her.

Elias didn't leave the house during the week, and on the eighth day, Sana arrived at his door. "I've been wondering why you haven't brought Yahya over. Rula is asking about him too."

"He was sick with the measles. It's contagious," he replied, leading her into the kitchen, where he was preparing food, the baby nearby in his high chair. "He's fine now. The doctor will see him on Monday to make sure he's fully recovered. If all goes well, I'll bring him by your place on Tuesday early morning, so that I make my trip to the village before the sun's heat gets too strong."

In his high chair, Yahya's face was stained with soup.

Sana approached him and said: "Nothing wrong with him, just like a rose."

"If you saw him a week ago, he was like a red rose from the fever," said Elias.

That evening, Elias put his son to bed and sat next to him, thinking about the mountain village that took visitors a hundred years back in time. He was too late for the Day of the Bird, so was it still appropriate to visit? More importantly for him, would Helen be happy about his visit, or was he just another visitor to her?

He went to the kitchen, where he kept a beautiful qabaj bird in a cage. Over her eyes was a black line, like kohl eyeliner. Her feathers were striped with brown, and her voice made the place especially atmospheric. She'd bring a good price if Elias sold her like the other birds he'd sold. But he'd kept her as a companion for the last year. He wondered if Helen and her family would forgive him if they knew he was keeping a bird in a cage.

<hr>

Tuesday, August 10, 1999, was no different from the rest of the hot summer days, but still the sun filled Elias with energy and happiness like never before. He walked west toward the mountains, carrying the red radio in his knapsack.

He stopped by the spring in the Halliqi valley, scooping up its water to drink from his hand. The spring was his sign: from there, the path started up to the village, which seemed small from such a distance, as if the road to it were endless. The village houses appeared to be delicately painted on the mountain, and one would not know at first glance that they were built from the rocks of the mountain itself. All of them looked similar, with a square shape, flat roofs, small windows, and doors of raw, unpainted wood. The clusters of houses were separated by a variety of trees bearing figs, almonds, oaks, mulberries, and nuts, and the hills on the approach were spotted with sheep and cattle.

After two hours of walking, Elias sat on a rock, contemplating whether he might be lost. He thought it had taken longer than the last time he'd walked this way with Helen. He looked around, and not far away he saw a flock of sheep.

He walked toward them and asked their shepherdess: "Do you know the way to Helen's house?"

"Helen is a girl my age?" she asked with a knowing smile. She had a mole on her cheek and long, braided hair.

"Yes," he answered, at once bashful.

The girl pointed and said: "See that hill over there? Behind it there is a stone-paved walkway for mules, and then there are fig orchards. Cross them until you reach the sumac grove. Beyond it is Helen's house."

"Thank you."

"Welcome."

As he followed the shepherdess's directions, Elias felt as if he was in a wonderful dream. It seemed the birds were calling Helen's name over and over. He recalled her heart-shaped face—her pure heart was reflected on her face! She seemed to him brave and confident, even if she was a bit strange; she whistled and was unafraid of snakes. While perhaps unusual-looking by general standards, she was attractive. The contrast between her light hazel eyes and wheat-colored skin added to her allure. But beyond all that, there was something especially alive and unique about her, though he did not know how to describe it.

6

WHEN THE WHALE
SWALLOWED THE MOON

E lias did not knock on the door, for it was wide open, and there was no movement inside. As he stood at the door for a few minutes, he heard a long whistle. When he turned toward the sound, he saw Helen's mother, Ramziya, the palm of her left hand on her mouth.

She walked toward him in her ample white robe, which was tied at the waist with a yellow cotton belt, and a white turban. Ramziya greeted him warmly, and before he could reply he heard a whistle from far away, then another one with a different tone, consisting of two syllables, not one.

"That's my neighbor," she said. "I invited her for tea, and she told me that she would finish what she was doing and come later."

"That's sweet," he said. "But I thought I heard two whistles."

"Yes, because my neighbor is far away, my closer neighbor passed the message on to the other neighbor, then returned the answer to me."

Elias smiled. Their whistling seemed to him in harmony with the whistles of the qabaj birds, as if one were the original sound and the other its echo.

He said: "Sorry that I am two weeks late. My son got sick. Otherwise, I would not have missed the opportunity to celebrate the Day of the Bird with you."

"Don't worry. Today is also a special day. Whenever a guest arrives, it becomes a celebration. How is your son now?"

"Fine, thank you. He had measles, but now he's okay."

"Thank God," Ramziya said as she extended her hand. "Come in, please. Shammo is in the sumac grove, and he will be home soon."

"Is it okay if I go join him?" he asked.

"Why not? The grove is nearby. Let's walk there."

"I almost got lost, but a shepherdess showed me the way to your house through the sumac grove," Elias said as they walked.

"There is no other sumac grove in the village. It was a fig grove before, but from neglect it turned into sumac."

"I didn't know that figs could turn into sumac," said Elias.

"Sumac thrives in the dry desert soil," she explained, "so we have a saying that figs have gone and sumac has come, describing the bad son of a good father."

"Aha. Sumac is problematic, then, but it's also tasty, especially with onions."

Helen's mother laughed. "Yes, true. We season a lot of our food with it. Even Umm Khairy sometimes comes to take of this plant. She says it is an anti-inflammatory. She is smart, *masha'llah*. No disease passes before her without a solution."

"Is she a doctor?" he asked.

"Umm Khairy is the village doctor, even though she did not study at school. She inherited her knowledge from her father, so she knows how to cure diseases using herbs. Measles, for example, she would treat with olive leaf. Even when she can't cure a disease, she provides boiled herbs to numb the pain until you can get to the Sinjar clinic."

When they entered the grove, Shammo was bent over a small bush, with Azad next to him.

Ramziya called out, "Come, Azad, greet our guest."

After greetings and hugs, Shammo rubbed a green oval leaf with a pointed tip and said to Elias, "Smell this."

Elias smelled it and said, "It's like lemon. Let me help you today with the gardening," he added. "I'll be happy to learn more."

"Not now. We have to prepare for dinner and then tea with the neighbors." Shammo turned to Ramziya and asked, "You asked the neighbors to come, didn't you, Ramziya?"

Ramziya nodded and said, "Let me go home ahead of you to cook the bulgur."

Azad also asked permission to leave, saying, "I will be with Dakhil until dinnertime."

"If you want to help me with the garden work, we can come back tomorrow before the lunar eclipse," Shammo said to Elias.

"Oh right, tomorrow, August 11, total eclipse," Elias said. "The best view of it will be from right here on the mountain."

"God willing, it will be all right. We will do what we can to save the moon from the whale," Shammo said. In a straw basket, he began gathering small red fruits from clusters of flowers just above the soil. He paused to explain. "Let's take some fresh sumac seeds with us. We will sprinkle them with water and salt and cover them with a piece of cloth that stays over the fruits without touching them. We leave them for a day or two. When they have dried, we put them in a sieve and rub them until the husks separate from the seeds. After we get rid of the seeds, we leave the husks in the shade for a short while until they turn the beautiful red color you know. Maybe you can take some with you to Mosul."

"I love red sumac. By the way, I also have a red gift for you," Elias said, raising the bag in his hand.

"I wonder what it is. But wait, let's go home first for all to see," Shammo said, smiling.

The two men left the orchard. Just five bushes away from the house, they encountered Azad again. He was patting a snake, together with another young man.

Shammo watched for a moment, then said to Elias, "Azad and Dakhil befriended this snake early in their childhood. They pass by it every day on the way home, and it's as if it knows them and waits for them. It comes down to that branch for them whenever they pass by.

"Helen told me the snakes here are peaceful," Elias said, hoping to hear something about her, but Shammo only said, "Yes, they are."

—⁓—

Ramziya was grilling eggplants over charcoal when they entered the house. When Azad arrived fifteen minutes later, he headed directly to the coal pot. He grabbed the eggplant from its funnel and began removing its grilled skin.

Ramziya poured oil into a large flat pot to fry the grilled, peeled eggplants. Shammo whistled, and Elias hoped it was to call Helen.

His wish was granted. Helen entered a few minutes later, carrying a water jug. She greeted him and went to the kitchen, then returned with layers of thin, dry bread. She sprinkled water on it, and it became soft. She put it in a handmade straw basket and added it to the rest of the food that was laid out on a mat on the floor.

Shammo went into the kitchen and brought back the pot of bulgur. He asked, "Ramziya, did we forget anything?"

His wife brought the powdered sumac.

"Perfect. Yella, Elias, help yourself," Shammo said.

They sat around the dinner mat and waited for Elias to start the meal, as was their custom when eating with guests. Elias served himself some salad, and everyone did the same. Helen sprinkled sumac over her salad, and Elias imitated her.

Shammo told Elias, "You should try the eggplant," and Elias took some. Here they wrapped eggplant in a thin bread. He did as they did.

After they were done, Elias said, "I brought this gift, I hope you like it." Before them he placed the red Harp radio and added, "This may entertain you because it tells you the news of the world."

They seemed all excited, so Elias was happy, especially when Helen and Azad returned to the room to see the radio.

"There is no radio in the village except at Aliko's home," Ramziya said. "He is so protective of it that he allows no one to touch it, and he calls it the magic box."

Elias pressed the power button and turned the wheel to set the channel. A broadcaster's voice mingled with some noise. He turned the wheel left and right until the voice became clearer. He spoke in French. Azad said, "It also has a foreign station."

Elias turned the wheel and stopped it at a song by Demis Roussos titled "Far Away." Azad jumped up and performed some dance moves, and they all laughed.

"This is a wonderful gift," Helen said.

Shammo agreed, saying, "Thank you, Elias, for this magic box."

"Glad you like it," Elias replied. He felt good that he'd bought the radio, despite his low income that month.

At sunset, Azad and Helen each lit a lantern, which they placed in front of the house as a signal they were ready to receive guests. Shammo carried out a large teapot and placed it over burning charcoal. Next to it was a big tray of small tea *istikans* and a bowl of sugar cubes.

Neighbors soon began flocking to the yard shaded by mulberry trees, bringing with them their musical instruments. In front of each house in the village, there were such areas for hanging out with visitors. They laid their instruments under a mulberry tree and went to help themselves to some tea and chatted with each other. Most of the men wore similar attire: wide trousers, a jacket of the same color and fabric, with a large cloth belt in a different color. Some of them wore white head coverings. Young women didn't cover their hair. Only older women wore the traditional turban.

Shammo walked around with Elias, introducing him to the visitors.

A young man with a mustache and a light beard approached and said, "Hello."

Shammo introduced him to Elias. "This is Abdullah, my nephew. He lives in Sinjar."

Elias told Abdullah that he was originally from Sinjar as well, and they spoke for some time. The two men seemed almost the same height, about six feet, and both had wheat-color complexions. Both wore white shirts and modern trousers, except that Abdullah's were gray flannel and Elias had on blue jeans. Perhaps if Elias lost a few kilos, he would be the same size as Abdullah.

"This is my childhood village," Abdullah said, "so I visit it from time to time."

"When did you move to Sinjar?" Elias asked.

"More than twenty years ago. My father moved to Sinjar to work with his brother, growing vegetables. His dream was to own a garden, but he died before achieving it, and I myself have worked to achieve the same dream."

Elias wanted to ask him whether his dream had come true or not, but Abdullah excused himself when another man called his name. Looking for Helen, Elias saw that she was standing across the yard next to a girl who looked familiar. It took Elias a few moments to recognize her. She was the shepherdess who had shown him the way to this place.

He walked over to them, and Helen introduced them. "Amina is my friend. Elias is our guest."

He shook Amina's hand, excited that Helen had uttered his name.

"Thank you for showing me the way here when I was lost," he said to Amina.

"Actually, there are three girls named Helen in this village," Amina said, "but I guessed you were asking about my best friend's home."

The three of them smiled. Elias wondered if Helen had told her friend about him. Did she feel something special toward him? Could she know how happy he felt around her?

Visitors began taking seats on the ground in two curving rows, an adult row behind a children's one.

"Time to sit down, right?" Elias asked them.

"Yes," Helen replied. "Someone will tell a story, and then the audience will have the right to ask questions at the end."

Elias nodded and moved to the side, allowing Helen and Amina to join the crowd. He saw Shammo waving for him to sit next to him, so Elias did. Abdullah sat cross-legged in front of the two rows of people, as it was his turn that evening to tell a story.

When all eyes had turned to him, Abdullah began to speak: "Once upon a time, there was an emperor named Genghis Khan, who was expanding his empire by bloodshed, genocide, and the invasion of cities. When he was on his deathbed, he asked his grandson Hulagu to complete the conquests of Asia that he had begun. Hulagu implemented his grandfather's will as far as he could. At that time, Baghdad was the capital of the Abbasid nation and the meeting place of scholars from all over. Its popularity reached the ears of those near and far, including Hulagu, so he decided to invade it. He headed there with his army and surrounded the city. After he destroyed its walls and killed thousands of its residents, he abolished its landmarks of civilization and architecture. First, he targeted the library, known as the House of Wisdom. He threw all the books into the Tigris River until the water ran black with ink. When he saw that the people of the city were so greatly upset, Hulagu asked them to bring the best scholar in Baghdad to him. None of the scholars agreed to meet with the unjust ruler, except for one, a scholar whose beard had not yet grown. The young man agreed to meet Hulagu on one condition: that he could bring with him a camel, a goat, and a rooster. On the day of the meeting, Hulagu looked at this young man from top to bottom and said, 'So they could find no older scholar than you to send to me?' The young man replied, 'If you want a bigger one, I have a camel, and if you want a bearded one, I have a goat. If you want someone loud, there is a rooster waiting outside.'

"As he realized that he was in front of an extraordinary person, Hulagu rubbed his chin and said, 'Do you know why I came here?' The young man answered, 'It is our actions and our sins that brought you to us. We did not appreciate God's grace, so we went too far in making problems instead of solving them.'

"'So you people are trying to get me out of here?' Hulagu asked.

"'If our differences don't divide us, you will not be able to stay here,' the young man replied."

Abdullah stopped, and a girl raised her hand with a question. Abdullah nodded to her.

"Why did Hulagu target the library first?" she asked.

"Because he knew that the library was the pride of the Baghdadi people at that time," Abdullah replied. "They used to say that the whole world opens in your hands the moment you open a book."

"I don't have a book to open," the girl said.

A little boy raised his hand and asked, "How would I see the world through a book?"

"Everything in the universe is written in letters," Abdullah answered, "and the letters make words and meanings that can take you anywhere in the world—all while you are sitting and reading."

Elias raised his hand, and Abdullah looked at him, awaiting his question. Elias said, "I have an idea. I know that schools are far away from here. How about if I volunteer to teach reading and writing to whoever is willing?"

Without raising their hands, the villagers started whispering and talking, too excited to follow the rules.

From his spot in the middle of the yard, Abdullah said to the crowd, "I ask you to keep quiet for a moment because I want to say something to our guest."

When they stopped talking, Abdullah resumed, "On behalf of the Halliqi tribe, I thank you, Elias, for your initiative. The people who know how to read and write here are fewer than the fingers on one hand, and they, although few, can help you in this great task." He turned to his fellow villagers. "What do you think, my brothers and sisters?"

Shammo joked, "Abdullah is the best person to deliver a sermon among us."

Abdullah laughed. "I am ready to help Elias with what little I know."

Elias looked at Helen, smiling, and she understood him. She said, "I will volunteer."

"Azad also knows how to read and write," Ramziya said.

Azad responded, saying, "I don't mind helping."

Shammo said, "Hey, Elias, our homes are open to you, as you know, but I am afraid we will cost you a lot of time. You live hours away from our village."

"I love this village," Elias said, "and I would be happy to come, let's say, once a week. If I teach one letter per week, everyone will learn to read and write within months."

Abdullah got up, saying, "Let's celebrate, then. Time for some music."

Several adults and children scrambled to pick up their instruments. A group of children climbed the branches of the trees to watch. Some of the adults went to drink more tea, while others sat, ready to play. One man started strumming his tambur, and the others joined in like a trained band.

Elias could not resist looking at Helen as she played the flute. She looked even more beautiful when she was playing. She wore a light purple dress that fell to her feet. Her long, embroidered sleeves had wide ends, pointed like fins.

A villager started humming the opening notes of a song, another answered him with a matching section, and then they all joined in, singing as a group. The volume rose, and the rhythm became faster. Azad played his tambur, followed by rapid strokes on the drum by another young man. So began the fast debka tune.

Shammo stood up to open the dance, and Ramziya joined him. Others held hands, raising their bodies up and down to the ground, forming a large circle. Shammo left the circle and approached

Elias, inviting him to dance with him in the middle of the circle as a special greeting for his guest.

They both danced barefoot, raising one hand and lowering the other, like the dance of two friendly birds.

To end, the musicians played a quiet melody that melted Elias's heart, and he started humming along with the rest. Four girls danced to this tune. They stood swaying gently, and the wide folds of their dresses swayed with them. They moved to the right and to the left, raising their hands over their heads and opening them to the horizon like tree branches. They walked after each other with their right hands waving toward the audience, then one of them went forward and made several turns. The music intensified, then she paused, bending her head a little bit, lowering her body to the ground like a wounded bird. The three other dancers stretched their hands toward her and raised her up, and the four of them walked together lightly, returning to their places as the music slowed with the dance's end.

It was past midnight when the neighbors put their instruments on their backs and left. Elias was shy about sleeping with the family in their house.

Shammo, as if reading his thoughts, said, "You are most welcome, Elias. You know what? We forgot to show our guests the radio. Perhaps next time we can turn it on and surprise them. Come with me. I'll show you your bed."

Elias followed Shammo up to the roof of the house. There were two low beds, not more than two feet high. A third bed was higher, and above it was a rope with a folded linen cloth attached by clips. It looked like a white tent. Elias guessed it was the bed of Shammo and Ramziya. Along the bed cover on the other side were stacks of dried figs.

Shammo folded and pulled up the cover with the figs inside and placed it all on top of a large rectangular stone on the side. He leveled the bed with his hand and said to Elias, "This is your bed."

Lying down, Elias craved those figs. He would not have minded if Shammo had left the figs with him on the bed. After a moment, he abandoned the wish, smiling. He thought that if this wish came true, he would be fatter in the morning. He'd been trying to lose a little weight, but he had a weakness for eating at night, especially pistachios. He looked up at the glittering stars, thinking that he would at least lose some weight walking to the village every week to give his lessons. He saw hope shining like an additional star in the sky. When he imagined Helen going to sleep, he dropped his eyelids to cover her.

He awoke to the hot morning sun. No one else was on the roof, so he went downstairs. The windows of the house were all open, but nobody was there. He looked out the window and saw Ramziya baking in the clay oven and some children sleeping under the trees. Inside the living room, the radio had been placed next to the flute on a slab meant to be a table.

He picked it up and browsed the channels until the voice of Fairuz came singing, "You see how big is the sea/that is how much I love you." Shortly before the end of the song, Helen entered the room with a small basket of eggs. She paused to listen to Fairuz, and an exchange of smiling looks with Elias filled his heart with warmth.

"Did you sleep well? she asked.

"Very well, and you?" What he wished to ask her was, "How did you sleep in my eyes last night?"

"I couldn't sleep," she replied.

"Why?"

"I don't know."

Azad came in and said to Helen, "I'm not sure we can go to the spring today. We barely have time to grind the pomegranate and oak husks before getting ready for the eclipse."

"Let's have breakfast first," Helen said.

"What if I go to the spring and bring you water so that you can finish your other chores?" Elias suggested.

"We go to the spring for the sake of washing bed linen, not just to bring water," Helen replied.

When Elias did not answer, Helen added, "We go with the neighborhood boys and girls because we all wash them together, and we have fun doing this. You may come with us this time if you like."

"I am happy to," Elias said.

"So Elias can go in my place today," said Azad, looking at his sister, "and I will grind the husks, but we have to hurry a little."

"Let me tell the neighbors that we will join them soon," Helen said.

Helen went out and whistled twice. A fragmented whistle came as a response. Azad brought the teapot from over the burning coals, and Helen emerged from the kitchen with yogurt, boiled eggs, and warm bread.

After a quick breakfast, Helen left and returned with the donkey Elias already knew.

"Let's go?" Helen asked him.

"I am ready, but don't we need to bring the linen?" Elias asked.

"No, it's not our turn today," said Helen. "Every time we clean the linen of one home, we wash each other's too, so we don't get tired."

Elias and Helen walked with the donkey to a house where a group of young men and women had also gathered with their donkeys. Elias recognized some of them from yesterday's gathering.

After they exchanged greetings, they distributed the linen on the backs of the donkeys. After there was some on the back of Helen's donkey, they started the journey down to the valley, talking and joking along the way.

Elias said to Helen: "I see that girls and boys here mix and go out together, unlike in the city."

"We all know each other here," she said.

"How many people live in the village?"

"Maybe five hundred."

"The majority are big families, aren't they?"

"That's right. We are one of the smaller families in the village. I heard from my mother that Azad and I came into the world as a miracle. She and my father were old and without children, and then the unexpected happened and they had twins. Azad says he's older than me, although only by a quarter of an hour."

"You both are the sweetest miracle."

Helen smiled.

———※———

At the spring, they laid down the blankets. On each one, they poured water and sprinkled powdered soap. Then they all stood on a sheet, holding each other's hands and beating the surfaces with their feet, like a group dance. When the cover was clean, the young men placed it on a large piece of wood to dry out.

Helen stood next to Elias, so of course she held his hand. They jumped over the linen with the group, and his heart almost jumped from his stomach to the cover in front of them. They repeated it with every sheet. Elias wished they would slow down and take their time so that he could keep his hand in hers even longer. *But there will never be enough time*, he thought.

"It is never enough," she said.

He looked closer at her. Had she heard his heart say such a thing?

"We have to hurry before the whale swallows the moon," she added.

Helen and the other girls picked small rocks from the ground and rubbed the heels of their feet with them by the spring. Meanwhile, the men, including Elias, folded the clean linens for the donkeys to carry.

When Helen arrived home with Elias, her family was waiting for them, planning to eat early together before joining the others. The villagers would climb as one up the mountain they called the Dog Tooth. Surrounded by lower mountains and hills, it rose up high from among them.

Shammo carried a lantern. Ramziya handed Helen, Azad, and Elias plates and big spoons, and they all headed toward the mountaintop. They were among about four hundred people, all carrying lanterns, pots, trays, plates, and large spoons; they were all ready to save the moon, especially since they were in a spot high enough to hope that the noise they made would reach the whale's ears so it got scared and fled, leaving the moon to proceed in peace. The Halliqi villagers would not forsake the helpless moon suffering inside the whale's mouth. If that happened, the moon would turn red with blood, and disasters and wars would befall the country.

Elias had first learned about the whale swallowing the moon in September 1980. He had been six years old. He heard his mother talking to her neighbor through a cloud of cigarette smoke: "Did you hear about the prediction of Hajji Abu Al-Timman? He wrote in the newspaper that there will be a lunar eclipse over Iraq. A large whale will swallow the moon, and as a result, darkness will prevail and a great disaster will befall us. His prediction came true; otherwise, who would think about the war with Iran?"

"I also heard, and this is just between us," said the neighbor in a low voice, "that it was actually the government that invented the character of Hajji Abu Al-Timman so that people would blame the war and everything on the poor whale. Well, if Hajji Abu Al-Timman is a real character and not a fake, I think he must be crazy to recommend people go up to the roofs of their homes and bang on pots and trays—all to scare away the whale!"

That war had continued. With the passage of days and an increasing number of dead and wounded in the city, people again started talking about the whale that had brought woes to the country. And so they went up on their roofs to bang pans as hard as they could, their eyes bulging as they looked up toward the sky and chanted, "You who are high beyond where stairs would reach, our moon is in trouble. We ask you for help."

Two days before the war finally ended, Elias's father was killed on the battlefield. They brought him home wrapped in the Iraqi flag, and a black banner with white letters that read: MARTYR FOR THE NATION'S HONOR. It was one of thousands of similar banners hung on the façades of homes during eight years of war.

Two and a half years later, Elias went with his mother and sister again to the roof of their house like the other people in their area. They took ladles and pots with them because the whale was again proceeding to swallow the moon.

Elias, then seventeen years old, was unnerved to see the moon gradually disappearing in the sky, especially since there were already threats from America to wage war on Iraq. And then Desert Storm brought armies from around the world because Iraq swallowed Kuwait—like that whale—and the Americans were trying to scare Iraq to get Kuwait out of its mouth.

But instead of ladles and pots, they used bombs and missiles. Elias recalled electricity being cut off in the city and ambulances rushing to transport the wounded to hospitals. Sirens preceding aerial bombardments.

Whenever Elias's mother heard an explosion near their house, she'd say, "Damn the whale. How much trouble it has brought!" When the war ended, people said, "Finally, the whale left the moon alone." They exchanged congratulations, their cries of joy mingling with the sound of the bullets they shot into the air. People returned to daily life and had almost forgotten about the custom of banging on pots, were it not for the war that broke out at the end of 1998, this time named the Desert Fox.

And so they remembered the whale again. There was no eclipse that time, though they prayed the prayers of the eclipse and made offerings in order to ward away evil from their country. Elias's mother did not witness the Desert Fox because she had died a year earlier. Her doctor had recommended that she stop smoking, but she didn't listen. She said, "If I quit smoking, I would still die on the same written day, albeit in good health."

⁓

Elias's feelings about the eclipse today were different. His mind was not preoccupied with the moon so much as with a village girl whose smile was warm like a round loaf from the oven. Despite warnings from some clergymen that darkness during the last eclipse of the twentieth century might mark the end of the world, Elias was unconcerned. He was not nervous about the end of the world. On the contrary, he felt his world had just begun, there above the Dog's Tooth.

The horizon appeared to be split in two: one darker than the other. Within minutes, darkness prevailed, and the noise rose to frighten the stubborn whale away from the moon.

Elias's heart was also beating because at that moment Helen turned toward him from behind Azad, who stood between them. Elias exchanged a look with her, then gazed up at the moon, then at her again. The lights of the villagers' lanterns surrounded them on all sides, like a necklace sparkling in the dark. Elias thought he had heard the distant whistling of the qabaj birds, as if they, too, from afar, were contributing to the moon's rescue.

7

A IS FOR AMOUR

The eclipse only lasted two minutes here in Mosul," Sana said to Elias, "but they made a big deal about it. Anyway, tell me, how was your trip?"

Elias replied, smiling, "Listen, there is a girl I intend to marry."

"Is that so? What wonderful news. Where is she from?"

"From the Halliqi tribe. She lives up in the mountains."

"Go and ask for her hand. Go tomorrow."

"I'll go on Friday, the twentieth of this month. I have agreed to go up to her village every Friday."

"Brother, you are complicated."

"I'm not so sure. Anyway, can you do your complicated brother a favor and take care of Yahya every Friday?"

"Yahya is not a problem. But marry that girl so that she can become a mother to him. Wait, I remembered something. This Friday I have an appointment in the evening."

"Then I will go the Friday after."

"No, go to your girl, but be back before six P.M."

"Okay."

Elias left the village after the lunar eclipse, but Helen thought about him all evening, and then again at night when she closed her eyes, she saw his oval face. His eyes shone when he smiled, as well as when he was sad. Either way, smiling or sad, Elias's looks gave Helen an extraordinary warmth that penetrated her heart, prizing it open like a pistachio.

She stayed up late, thinking about how their hands had touched while cleaning the covers near the spring and how they'd looked at the moon together and tried to save it. In the end, the moon had reappeared, beautiful and safe.

She woke up at dawn and found herself in love with him. She felt that two wings had grown out of her soul, so she flew to him. Her body looked for that spirit and longed to be one with him. She felt the need to tell everyone that she loved him, but she definitely would not tell her family. In fact, she only wanted to tell Amina. Outside the house's front door, Helen whistled, signaling to Amina that she would accompany her today in herding the sheep.

Her friend answered with a whistle of approval.

That morning, a slight wind caused the grass to sway a little. The sheep walking beside the friends slowed to eat the grass, then rushed ahead of them.

Helen asked Amina, "How come you didn't come to the Dog's Tooth on the day of the eclipse? I looked for you and did not see you."

"Do not laugh at me," Amina replied. "I fell into a deep sleep next to the tree while I was tending my sheep. I was startled when I heard the sound of banging on pots and pans. At first, I thought it was the sound of the bells around my sheep's necks. I was terrified, thinking they'd run away while I was asleep. How I rejoiced to find them all near me, not a single one missing. They never run away from me—even when my father slays one of them in front of the rest. They may become sad, but they never run away. Every time that happens, I close my eyes so I don't see their blood when it flows."

"Animals' love for us is true love," Helen said.

"These sheep understand me more than my family do. Nobody understands me but you and my sheep," Amina said.

"I love you, my friend."

"You seem in a really good mood today, Helen."

"I'm happy, and I love everyone, including your sheep, more than ever before."

When Amina laughed, Helen said, "I want to tell you a secret."

Amina waited, and Helen finally blurted out, "I love Elias."

"Your guest? He was looking at you fondly when you were playing the flute."

"After he left the first time, I couldn't wait to see him again."

"Be careful. Don't let anyone notice."

"It's not really in my control, but I'll try to hide my love for him."

"Will he teach reading and writing, as he promised?"

"He starts on Friday. You're coming, aren't you?"

"No, I'm busy during the day."

"Nothing will happen if you leave the sheep for one day. Come on Friday, please, for me."

"Okay, I'll come when I hear the whistle."

———

Trying to conceal her feelings for Elias, Helen was determined to avoid looking at him, for fear that her eyes would give her away. But just a minute later, she had forgotten her decision and exchanged smiling looks with him. He was enthusiastic about his lessons and had brought with him paper, pens, and a box of chalk. Sitting with the three volunteers under the shade of the berry tree, he prepared his lesson before the students' arrival.

"What do you think?" he asked. "Should we teach one or two letters a day?"

Abdullah said, "Give them two letters and see how things go."

"Okay," said Elias. "Let's distribute these papers and pens for them to practice with. I suggest that we divide students into groups so that each of us works with a small group. And if you are ready, we can start."

Azad gave a loud whistle to start the lesson, and students flocked to the courtyard in front of Helen's house. Just as she was looking around to see if Amina was among them, her friend came from behind her and put her hands over Helen's eyes.

"I know it's you from the smell of sheep on your hands," Helen said.

Amina pulled away her hands, pressing them to her waist in protest, and Helen winked at her. Amina took her place on the ground with the rest of the students. They ranged from ages six to seventy, with grandparents in the back behind their grandchildren.

Elias welcomed them. "You look wonderful with the mulberries surrounding you!" He seemed to be looking through the crowd for Helen. "Today we will learn two letters. The first is called alif. It's written like number one. Like this," he said, holding a piece of chalk.

He paused for a moment and said, "Oh, I forgot to bring a board to write on, but that's okay." He wrote the letter on the tree trunk beside him. The volunteers rushed to distribute papers and pens so those in attendance could copy the letter, but some of them preferred to draw the letter on the ground in front of them with a stick.

Elias continued: "The second letter is called ba. We write it like a dish of rice with a dot below. If we put A plus B, the result is AB—father—like this."

The students repeated after Elias, "Alif ba father."

"Now I give you a question and you write the answer," Elias said. He wrote: "b + a + b + a ="

The volunteers exchanged smiles as they heard one of the grandmothers reminding her grandson to put a dot under the dish of rice.

Elias divided the class into groups to complete the exercises with the help of the volunteers.

"I have to ask permission to leave early today," Abdullah said.

"Wait for me, I will go down with you," said Elias. "I also have to leave. Azad and Helen may complete the exercises."

Elias stepped closer to Azad and said, "I am sorry, but I have to pick up my son before six. Please say hello to your parents for me, and I will see you next Friday." While looking at Helen, he waved goodbye and left with Abdullah.

They silently descended from the heights of the village until Elias broke the silence. "The air is so pure here. There's no pollution."

"I spend time up here whenever I can," said Abdullah, "but today I have an appointment with a friend, a merchant in Sinjar."

Several more moments of silence followed until Elias said, "You told me, Abdullah, that you had been dreaming since your childhood of having a garden. I wanted to ask you, did your dream come true?"

"I was thirteen when I left school to work in my uncle's garden. What fascinated me the most there was the beehive. One day, my uncle allowed me to take care of that hive, and it became my own secret world. I used to watch how the bees worked. They were a very organized and productive society. If you look at them from afar, you may think they are moving about randomly, but as soon as you look closer, you discover their purpose. Brother, even the sound they make is like a symphony led by the queen, who flies high. But sometimes I have had to kill some queens."

"Why?" Elias asked.

"For the kingdom's safety," Abdullah explained. "Sometimes the hives become weak, so I merge them to strengthen them, but if there is more than one queen, one of them will fly away and take with her her own army of bees. And that is a greater loss. Just as it is not permissible to have more than one wife in a house, so it is not permissible for there to be more than one queen in the hive. My Yazidi group knows how much I hate polygamy."

"I would think it's quite hard to please two women," Elias said. "Unfortunately, these days it has become more common and fashionable among our people. But tell me, are you still keeping bees?"

"Of course," Abdullah replied, "let me tell you. One day I saw an orchard on our street for sale. I asked my uncle to come with me to negotiate for it. I had saved nearly a thousand dinars, but the owner asked for nine thousand dinars, equal to the price of two houses in Sinjar. My family met to discuss the issue. Of course, I expected them to tell me that purchasing this orchard was impossible, but I was surprised by my mother's initiative. She gave me a small box of gold, which was her dowry and the gifts from my late father to her over the years. She told me to sell it and add it to my money. My sister-in-law did the same and gave me all her gold. When I bought the orchard, it had ten beehives. After three years, there were over a hundred. Whenever I watch the queens and their movements, I remember the women in my life and their generosity to me. From the income I made from the orchard, I was able to marry and raise my children. Honey has enabled me to earn a living, but more importantly, it has earned me friends."

"Did you fall in love, or was it an arranged marriage?" Elias asked.

"Neither one nor the other," said Abdullah. "Sari was a girl my age who lived on the same street, and we used to go together to the river where young men and women of our village would meet to wash dishes and their feet, especially during the summer. Sari and I were good friends and talked about anything and everything that was on our minds. Even at village parties, we danced together. My mother thought we were in love, so she spoke to Sari's mother, asking for Sari to become my wife, and Sari agreed. When my mother found out that I was unhappy at what she had done, she was very surprised. 'I've seen the two of you happy together, and I wanted to make it official,' she said. Sari heard that I did not intend to marry her, and was of course hurt. She is very sensitive. She would not talk to me afterward and would leave the river if she saw me there. I regretted losing our friendship. It meant so much to me. And I missed being around her. I told my mother that she had actually done well when she'd asked for Sari's hand. But this time, Sari rejected my request and said she would never accept me as a husband. One day I waited for her at the river. When she arrived with her dishes to wash, I said to her, 'I have a few words to say. Please listen to me.' She finally looked at me, and I said, 'You will always be my closest friend, and I hope you will marry the best person in the world, but I also hope that we will remain friends forever.' She smiled and said, 'Are you coming to the weekend party?' I said, 'Yes, I will.' But as the days passed, our river meetings became more beautiful because our hearts met on their own. When I asked my mother to go and ask for Sari's hand again, she said, 'No, I will not do this. The girl has already refused.' I finally convinced her that Sari had agreed and that she had to speak to Sari's mother. Now we have two boys and two girls. Thank God we are a happy family." Abdullah paused and took a breath. "I've talked a lot, I'm sorry."

"Not at all. Tell me how honey earned you friends."

"As you know, our region is close to Syria, so one day I thought for the first time in my life of taking a trip to Syria, both for business and pleasure, as they say. I took along jars of my honey to sell, and with the earnings I would visit new places. By chance, a merchant I met there liked my honey and offered to help me export honey to Syria on a regular basis. My business flourished and my travels multiplied, and I got to know more wonderful merchants and friends."

"Like the man you will meet today?"

"Yes, Saleh is a dear friend of mine, and I introduced him to my uncle's family, so he buys figs from them and distributes them in stores. My uncle's family has a stone basin in which they pound figs using oak wood until the figs are smooth like dough. They make fig pies in shapes of animals and birds, in addition to necklaces of dried figs."

"I tasted some. They were delicious. Your uncle Shammo told me about that merchant."

"Today he wants to meet with me about a very special matter."

"I hope it's good."

"Let me tell you, but please keep this between us, because it is still just talk."

Elias nodded.

"My friend Saleh wants to marry my cousin Helen," Abdullah said, "and he wants me to go with him to ask for her hand."

Elias took a moment to recover before asking, "When?"

"I don't know yet. When I meet him today, we will agree on a suitable date."

"And what does Helen think about this?"

"She doesn't know yet. Today I told her father, so he will tell her mother, who will ask Helen. I expect everything to go well, because my friend lacks nothing. He would be a good catch for any girl."

"He is lucky, too, because Helen is very kind-hearted."

"Of course, my cousin is one of the best."

———

With heavy feet, Elias arrived at his sister's house. Right away, Sana asked, "What's up? Have you asked for her hand?"

"Someone asked for it before me."

"Has she agreed?"

"I don't know."

"I mean, did you tell her anything?"

"No."

She kept quiet for a moment and then said, "Don't worry. If she's your destiny, no other will take her from you."

———

That week felt like the longest in Elias's life. He was eager to see Helen but also anxious to hear whether she had already agreed to marry the fig merchant.

His worries took sleep from his eyes. Sometimes reading helped, so on Thursday night he picked up a magazine and turned the pages while lying in bed. He didn't usually care about astrology, but he was desperate to receive any kind of message, even if it was from stars millions of miles away. So he browsed the horoscopes page.

His sign spoke of money and support and challenges. He envisioned various challenging possibilities, including an unnerving scenario that after he finished that week's lesson, Shammo would invite him to stay overnight to attend Helen's wedding.

His throat was dry, so he got up and went to the kitchen. After he poured a cup of water for himself, he went to look closer at his bird in the cage. He wondered if she was unhappy.

"I vow to set you free if Helen becomes my wife," he said.

But Elias could not wait for his wish to come true to fulfill his vow, so at dawn he went again to the kitchen. As usual, he put out food and water for the bird. As soon as the bird finished her morning meal, Elias opened the door of the cage, and with a gesture, invited her to leave.

Elias waited a minute, but the bird did not leave her cage. Elias took her out himself. *Life outside may be riskier than in the cage*, he thought, *but it's worth living.* He kept her a minute in his palm, then opened his front door and encouraged the bird to explore the morning light and go on her way. The bird took two steps in his hand. She remained in the same spot, as if afraid of the big world in front of her.

Elias took the bird back and decided not to release her there but instead in another environment in which she would be more comfortable, near some fig trees.

He felt relieved by his decision. But for some reason, he felt sure his vow had been accepted and his wish was about to be granted.

8

THE LAST SONG

Walking up to the mountain village on the morning of his second Friday lesson, Elias fantasized that he'd find Helen by the fig tree where they'd first met. That day, she'd reminded him of his wound and made him cry. He needed to cry again. Love made him want to cry.

The strange thing was that she was there just as he'd wished. She sat with her back against the tree as if she had been waiting for him.

Too excited to greet her, Elias sat down next to her without saying a word. He noticed the letter *F* and the word *fig* had been written in chalk on the tree trunk. He asked, "Whose handwriting is this?"

"I don't know," she said, "but you will find letters and words written everywhere. On trees, on rocks, and on the ground."

"Really? How can that be?"

"The group were so enthusiastic that Azad and I continued with them for two more letters, and it seems everyone has been writing letters and words with chalk and sticks just about wherever they could. Even during the evening gathering, they recited them with the music they were playing," she said. Then with a smile: "They are eagerly awaiting your second lesson. What letters are you bringing us today?"

Elias pulled a piece of chalk out of his pocket and said: "Let me show you."

He wrote on the tree trunk: "L + O + V + E = LOVE. Example: I love you."

"Read this," he said.

"But I don't love you," she replied.

"I only gave an example," he said.

Helen laughed and read aloud: "I love you." She repeated it: "I love you. I love you, Elias."

He wrote her name on the tree trunk and drew a heart around it. Helen took the chalk from his hand and drew a cupid's arrow breaking through the heart.

"You remember the qabaj bird I was going to catch, which you set free?" When she looked at him and did not answer, he continued: "Now I wish to burn all cages except one."

"Which one?"

"The golden cage, so that we may enter it."

"I would not enter a cage, even if it was gold," said Helen. "My soul is that of a bird."

"I'm a bird like you, and your name even means bird's nest. So let's get married in the nest, not in the cage," Elias said.

"How?"

"You mean how to get married? Or how birds do it?" He laughed.

"I mean that my family may not accept it."

"Then we elope."

"Like the story of Khansey and Rasho?" she asked.

"I don't know that story. Tell me."

Helen hesitated a little. Elias looked at her with a smile and leaned toward her, waiting, so Helen recounted the tale: "Rasho was an orphan living alone in Karsi village in Sinjar. He was a singer and a brilliant flautist. The villagers used to see him barefoot in alleyways, and they would stop to listen to his music, enchanted by his powerful voice. Some would bring him food so he wouldn't die from hunger. One day, a rich pomegranate merchant passed by him and admired his singing, so he sat chatting with him and ended up taking him home. He took care of him as if he was a member of his family. Rasho helped the merchant's family grow pomegranates, and his situation improved. He had a house now and new clothes. The merchant had a daughter named Khansey, and as the days passed, she and Rasho fell in love. He sang about her black eyes and her captivating smile, and she listened to him, her passion aroused. Their love matured silently and heavily like ripe pomegranates. One day Rasho was delayed in the orchard and didn't have time to eat lunch. Khansey brought him a meal she had prepared herself, and while he ate, the couple sat on the ground exchanging looks of love. Rasho told her, 'We must bury our love inside us because if your father knows, he will be very angry, and he has the right to hope for your marriage to someone who deserves you more than me, although with less love for you because no one could love you as I do.' Khansey replied, 'I will not marry anyone but you, so let's elope.'"

Helen adopted the voices of the characters, so it was easy to tell who said what.

Rasho: 'I ate from your father's bread and would not do anything that brings shame upon him.'

Khansey: 'Don't be a coward. Get up and kidnap me.'

Rasho: 'No, I will not.'

Khansey: 'You see that big rock? If I reach it and you do not kidnap me, I will be nothing but a sister to you.'

Rasho: 'So be it. I will not betray the trust.'

"Khansey went about ten meters and then turned, saying: 'This is the last step.'"

Rasho: 'Stop, you're crazy!'

"He followed her and said: 'If we elope, where would we go?'"

Khansey: 'I don't know and don't care.'

Rasho: 'Let's go to the house of Khalaf Khan Ali. He's the chief of the Haskan tribe in Sinjar.'

"When they got there, Khalaf gave them tea and date pie and asked them: 'Where are you from, and where are you going?'"

Rasho: 'We will not eat or drink unless you give us your word that we are safe here.'

"'You have it,' Khalaf said.

"'I am Rasho, a poor man, and this is Khansey, a daughter of the well-known Qerani tribe. We eloped and seek your help and that of God so that we may be married.'

"Khalaf said to his men around him: 'Get ready to go to Khansey's parents so that we may first reassure them that Khansey is with us and safe.'

"As it has always been in our region, problems dissolve when the chiefs of tribes intervene to solve them. So when Khalaf returned from Khansey's family, he said to his men: 'Bring the drum and mizmar. Today is the wedding of Khansey and Rasho.'

"But the happiness of the two lovers did not last. A plague spread, and many people in the area died. Days after their wedding, the disease reached Khalaf's home. His wife and seven children as well as many of his relatives died. When Rasho started to feel unwell, he said to Khansey, 'I am going for a little walk.' After a few steps, he fell down and knew that his end was fast approaching. He crawled to a large rock and propped himself up against it. Khansey rushed to his side and rested his head on her arm. She listened to him as he sang his last song. They call it the song of Khansey and Rasho."

"How does the song go?" Elias asked Helen.

"I don't know."

He looked to the sky, as if trying to remember. "I know it. Wait a minute."

On this trip, Elias had brought with him a small chalkboard to use in teaching the alphabet. He took out the board and began writing on it. He laid it on the ground and seemed completely immersed in writing.

Helen stood up and strolled over to a rectangular rock, leaning against it. Looking into the far hills, which were spotted yellow and green, she saw a boy gathering objects that had fallen from the back of his donkey. After some time, Elias came toward her, so she got up off the rock and went to him.

He said to her: "Listen, I will read to you the lyrics of Rasho's song."

This morning
I woke up in love with you
I heard a bird singing to you
And a bird's love is all in song

This morning
I will climb the mountain
The stars over there are more beautiful
because they glow in your eyes

This morning
I will follow the birdsong
wherever it goes
because it takes me to you

"How do you know the song when you don't know the story?" Helen asked.

Elias laughed and did not answer.

"You made up that song just now, didn't you?" she asked.

"Rasho's song is more beautiful for sure," said Elias. "This one was written quickly."

"So you write songs?"

"Sometimes I write songs, and sometimes I write ads for magazines."

"Ads about what?"

"About anything. Like the deterrent Tarzan, used against insects and mice, or about the energy drink that gives strength and inspiration."

They laughed together, but when he looked at her, she looked away. Then she looked back at him.

"Go to that rock and tell me to kidnap you," he said.

"No, I wouldn't say that, even if you jumped down from the mountain," she replied.

They laughed again. He placed his hand on the tree trunk behind her and moved closer. He was about to kiss her.

A whistle came from afar, and Elias stepped back.

Helen looked at where the sound was coming from and found it was from the boy with the donkey. "His whistle is an invitation to take us home," she explained to Elias.

"What if you go with him on the donkey and I follow you?" he suggested.

"No, I like walking," she replied.

The boy came down to them and said to Elias: "Hello, teacher, do we have a lesson today?"

"Yes, as soon as we arrive."

"I can take you both on my donkey."

"Thank you, my dear," Elias said, "but we will walk and collect some firewood along the way. See you soon."

After the boy and donkey departed, Helen said: "We could not have ridden that donkey with its huge load."

"Especially since I am heavy and fat," Elias said, putting his hand on his stomach.

"Not really," she said.

"This week, in particular, I messed up and ate too many fried potatoes. When I am worried, I crave salty food."

"Why were you worried?"

"First tell me: Why did you say your family would not accept me as your husband?"

Helen hesitated to speak, and Elias stopped walking.

When they resumed walking a moment later, she said, "Because they gave someone else the word, and breaking one's word is a source of shame in our area."

"Who is that person?"

"A fig merchant who has been doing business with us for a long time."

"What do you think of him?"

"Saleh is a good person."

"So will you marry him?"

"I don't know."

Elias kept silent. Without speaking, they climbed the hill.

Then she asked, "Are you upset?"

"No, why would I be? You are free to marry whoever you want."

"No, I'm not free."

"How?"

"In our village, a girl cannot refuse a good marriage offer unless she has a good reason."

"I love you, and you love me. Is that not a good reason?"

"Love alone is not enough for our people."

"Can I convince them and ask for your hand formally?"

She smiled in approval.

He looked deep into her eyes. The color of honey was not an adequate description. Her eyes held oceans of honey within and filled his world with a warm glow.

"Let me see the hand that I will ask for." He took her hand to his lips and printed upon it a gentle kiss.

The distance to Helen's house was much shorter than before, Elias felt. He hardly noticed the journey. He was astonished at how time's passing seemed to vary depending on how engaged he was in what he was doing.

"I would like to live with you for a very long time. I don't want to die young," he told Helen.

She wondered why he said that.

—⁂—

Some students were already sitting in the gathering place in front of the house, awaiting their lesson. When Helen arrived with Elias, she said, "I'll tell the rest of the students that the lesson is about to start."

"Yes, sweetheart bird, give your whistle," Elias whispered.

The space filled up with students until there were no places left, and Elias started the lesson. He took the chalkboard out of the bag to write on it and realized his song for Helen was still written there. He had not brought an eraser, so he pulled a berry leaf from the tree and quickly erased the romantic lyrics. He wrote the letter L and said: "Let's write a big word with few letters. Love."

The students imitated him, carefully writing the word. Some wrote it on paper and some on the ground in front of them.

From the back, Abdullah commented, "I wish this word was a little longer so that we could take more time when writing it."

Elias laughed, and they all laughed. He passed out exercises for the volunteers to work through with their groups.

At the lesson's end, Elias managed to take Helen aside and whisper to her that he wanted to talk to her father. She told him that at this time of day, Shammo could be found in the sumac grove.

———

Elias found him cutting bushes. As usual, Shammo wore a long-sleeved shirt and trousers that were loose around the thighs, tapering at the heels, and tied at the waist with a braided rope.

Elias greeted him, and then said, "I have a special request, and I hope that you will grant it."

"You are special, so your wish is our command," Shammo replied.

"Very briefly, I wish to ask for the hand of your daughter, Helen."

Taken by surprise, Shammo became silent and pensive. Finally, he said, "I will consult my family and give you our answer next time."

Elias thanked him and got ready to leave, but Shammo said: "Please don't leave without having lunch."

"Okay."

"I hear the villagers are happy with your lessons," Shammo said as they walked home.

"It's my pleasure."

"I want to tell you something, and I hope you understand me."

"All ready."

"Another man spoke to me about Helen, and I wished him well. It's not that I favor him, but as we say, blessing is given to the one who asks first."

———

Helen noticed that Elias seemed downcast during lunch. He barely ate the rice and stew. She was afraid her father had rejected his request. Immediately after tea, Elias asked for permission to leave.

"Wouldn't it be better to stay until morning?" asked Shammo.

"I am grateful to you, but I know the path well now, so there is no problem even in the dark," Elias replied.

9

ROLLER COASTER

In their bed on the roof beneath the linen curtain, Shammo spoke with Ramziya: "Today Elias expressed his desire to marry Helen. We agreed to Saleh, but we should tell Helen, just in case."

"Don't worry, I'll talk to her. Saleh is perfect, and he suits her the best," Ramziya said.

"Elias is a nice person too," said Shammo.

"But he was previously married, has a son, and no steady income," Ramziya said.

The next day in the living room, Ramziya seized the opportunity to be alone with her daughter, who was sewing an orange shirt she'd designed. Ramziya said: "You are not going to marry Elias, right?"

"Why not?" Helen asked.

"Think carefully, daughter. Marriage is not for one or two days. It is for your whole life. Saleh would provide you with a comfortable life. He is rich and owns a house and shops. Elias is educated, true, but does not have a job, so how will he provide for a family?"

"Oh, Mama, aren't you the one who always says that God helps whenever there are good intentions?"

"Saleh's intentions are good too."

"Why do you hate Elias?"

"I don't hate him. On the contrary, he is a kind person, and I hope that he finds a good wife—just not you."

"Crazy." This was how Amina described Helen when she learned of Helen's intention to reject a rich merchant and instead marry Elias, who had nothing. The two friends were on their way back from the valley, their arms full of firewood for their families.

"What does love have to do with marriage?" said Amina. "Love whoever you love, and marry the right one," Amina said.

"Who is the more crazy between us, Amina?"

"Well, my mother says men are all alike. Anyway, why do you like Elias more than Saleh?"

"I don't know exactly. But the whole world is different when I am with Elias. Even songs have a deeper meaning, as if they were written just for me."

"Your love is fire," Amina sang as she extended the vowel in the word *fire*, imitating the great singer Abdul Halim Hafez.

That evening, when Helen returned home, her mother told her that they had invited Saleh and Abdullah for dinner in two days. "You should get ready," said Ramziya. "This is an opportunity for minds and hearts to come closer."

Helen didn't say anything. She hurried up to the roof, even though it was not time yet for sleep. Still, Helen lay in her bed till morning. Elias was in her dreams when she slept, and when she woke up his smile was the first thing she thought of. She was not ready to exchange that smile for all the fortunes of the world. Why must she meet this other man? And what would she say to him? That she loved Elias? Helen was annoyed, not only because of Saleh's visit but also because she had a stomachache. She felt dizzy.

In the morning, she drank some tea but didn't eat breakfast. She was nauseous all day, and this lack of appetite caught her mother's attention.

Ramziya said: "Come with me, my daughter. Let's go to Umm Khairy."

Umm Khairy was a single woman in her midfifties who lived with her son, Khairy, and her mother and aunt, both of whom were widows. The boy Khairy had been an orphan when, aged thirty, Umm Khairy adopted him. The villagers said that Umm Khairy was not born to get married and that she was too smart to do so.

When Ramziya and Helen arrived at her home, Umm Khairy escorted them through a corridor into a large bedroom that had been converted into a clinic. On one side of the room was a narrow bed and a chair. Another side had Umm Khairy's desk, on which were flasks and small tools. On the wall over the desk was a picture of a stick with a snake wound around it and two wings on top. The other two walls were lined with shelves bearing herbs in glass containers. Helen sat on the bed and Ramziya on the chair.

After she examined Helen, Umm Khairy said: "This is a virus. There's no cure, other than drinking lots of liquid. But I will give you a relaxing herb because the stomachache may be due to stress."

The next day, Helen lay in the corner of the living room for most of the day.

When her father passed by her late in the afternoon, he stopped and took a seat beside her, putting his hand on her forehead. Then, in the kitchen, he squeezed two pomegranates and brought her the juice to drink.

She sipped some so that he would not be disappointed. Shammo had asked Abdullah to postpone the date with Saleh until Helen felt better.

On Friday, Helen was absent from Elias's class. Not only because she was still weak, but she was reluctant for her father to see her with Elias now that he knew she loved him. It was normal to mingle with any man in the village without embarrassment, but not once they were engaged in a love affair.

Elias presented the villagers with new letters, but he appeared distracted. When he finished the lesson and the class was departing, he stood by Abdullah and said: "It is not like Helen to miss a lesson."

"She is sick," Abdullah replied.

"Why? What's wrong?"

"Just not feeling well."

Elias reluctantly said: "Abdullah, I need your help with a delicate problem."

"Whatever I can do, I will not hesitate."

"Can we talk in private?"

"Are you leaving the village now or staying?"

"Leaving."

"Let's go down together and talk on the way."

———

As Elias was bewildered at how to start, Abdullah took the initiative. "How are things with you, Elias?"

"Okay. But I want to ask your opinion about something because you seem understanding and a romantic as well."

Abdullah laughed. "How do you know that I'm a romantic?"

"From your response to the word *love* in the lesson. I liked your comment."

"Well, I may not look like a romantic, but it's true that inside I am. And you?"

"I don't know if I am a romantic, but I am in love."

"Good thing."

"Well, there is a problem."

"What is it? Don't tell me it is unrequited love."

"No."

"Thank God. I hate love from one side."

"What if a third party is involved?"

"What do you mean?"

"Suppose two people are in love and agreed to marry, then another person comes to separate them because he also wants to marry the girl."

"Aha? This is not permissible, especially if the girl does not want him."

"Thank you. What if that third person is your friend?"

"Who are you talking about?"

"Saleh, the merchant who wants to marry Helen."

Abdullah was silent for a while and then said: "Saleh does not know there is another person involved in this."

"I love Helen, and she loves me, and she does not want to marry your friend. Can you help us?" When Abdullah did not immediately respond, Elias added: "Of course, your friend is richer than me and more privileged, but I am sure my love and respect for Helen are greater than his."

"Money is not everything, Elias. That's it. Leave it to me. I'll talk to my uncle."

Elias didn't comment but was grateful to Abdullah.

"Every problem has a solution," said Abdullah. "But if love is a problem, it is better to remain unresolved."

"Didn't I say you're a romantic?"

The following day, Abdullah met with Shammo and Ramziya in the sumac garden.

"Previously I came with my friend Saleh, asking for your consent for him to marry Helen, and now I'm asking you *not* to agree to it," Abdullah said.

"Oh, God who can change everything, how come?" Ramziya asked.

"It is because I love my friend Saleh, and I don't want him to pursue a lost cause," Abdullah said.

"You mean marrying Helen is a lost cause?" Ramziya asked.

"Helen has the right to choose her life partner because . . . because it's her life, isn't it?" Abdullah said.

Shammo shook his head gravely. "I swear this is the first time I have seen my dear Helen wilted like this. The poor girl is not eating or drinking. But I am also embarrassed at the shame of breaking our word to Saleh."

"Breaking one's word is better than breaking a person's heart," Abdullah said.

"Here we go. Give us your beautiful sermons, Abdullah," Shammo said.

"Leave the news of the broken word to me," Abdullah said. "I'll talk with Saleh. He's open-minded and understanding."

"Yes, I have no doubt he's a good person," Ramziya said.

"May God protect him for his people," Shammo said to Abdullah. Then he turned to his wife. "Go tell Helen so that she becomes healthy and happy again."

—⁓—

It was before noon on September 7th when Helen hurried from her home, eager to tell Amina that her family had accepted Elias as her husband.

There was something like a telepathic connection between the two friends. The moment Helen thought of Amina, she heard her whistle of invitation to accompany her to the almond trees on the upper slopes of the mountain. It was the time of the year when the villagers usually harvested almonds from the trees—"before the bear eats them," as Shammo would say. Helen replied with a short whistle, informing her friend that she would join her immediately. She walked toward the small hill where they often met before ascending the mountain.

Amina was already there, so when Helen arrived, they started their journey right away.

"They say love makes the mind fly away, and so it does to viruses," Amina said.

"Very funny, silly. You should prepare yourself to be seated next to me at the wedding as the bridesmaid," Helen said.

"When is the wedding?"

"I don't know exactly. Elias does not yet know that my parents have agreed. I'll tell him after the lesson."

"Yes, don't tell him before."

"Why not?"

"So that he doesn't go so crazy with joy that he can't teach us."

They laughed.

"He is a good teacher. Look." Amina wrote her name on the ground with a small branch.

After the Friday class of September 10th, Helen waited for Elias to be alone before approaching him. He was by the berry tree, his bag on his back and his hand in a cage. He lifted the cage up to his chest and said to Helen, "Maybe this cage would be good to burn on the Day of the Bird?"

It took Helen a moment, looking at the empty cage, before she answered, "Yes, it would."

Elias handed her the cage and said, "Today on my way here I stopped by the fig tree and released my bird."

"You had a bird?" Helen asked.

"Yes, I used to take care of her," Elias said. "I thought she was happy, but I learned from you that happiness without freedom is incomplete. She was hesitant about flying at first, but just a few minutes after hearing the voices of her qabaj friends, she joined them."

Helen smiled and said, "Thank you for setting her free."

"Well, I was relieved to do it," Elias said. "I'm hoping that a bird will tap on my window with good news."

"I hear a bird now telling me that you could talk to my parents about wedding matters," Helen said.

She did not expect Elias's strange reaction. He put his fingers to his mouth and whistled loudly.

"Who is this for?" she asked.

"I don't really know. For the birds and the mountains and for everyone! To tell them I am happy!"

"You just blew the fire whistle."

"It is fire," he said, and pointed, "in my heart."

Seconds later, Shammo ran from the sumac grove, frightened by the fire signal. A few minutes later, a neighbor boy, Dakhil, arrived too, panting with a large pot of water in his hand.

"Sorry," said Helen. "The whistle was an accident."

Elias covered his face, terribly embarrassed. Dakhil left and Helen withdrew, leaving Elias with her father.

Shammo breathed a sigh of relief at the news that there was no fire. He gave a warm hello to Elias, and the younger man felt relieved too.

"Come in, Elias," Shammo said, pointing to his door.

Inside, Elias took his usual place, sitting on the mattress.

"You must be hungry after the trip and teaching," said Shammo. "How about some yogurt while we wait for dinner?"

"I never say no to yogurt."

"With figs?"

"And I wouldn't say no to figs."

"What do you say no to?"

"No to colonization," Elias answered lightheartedly.

Shammo went into the kitchen, laughing, and returned with a bowl of yogurt and a basket of figs. The two men sat beside each other amicably as they ate.

A few minutes later, Ramziya burst into the room, panting. "I ran behind the house to see if there was a fire because someone had whistled the fire alert. Thanks to God, no fire. How are you, Elias?"

"Fine, thank you. And you?"

"Okay," she said, and went into the kitchen.

Elias looked up at Helen's painting on the wall, then at Shammo. "I wonder if you have had a chance to discuss and consider my request to marry Helen."

"We are happy to grant our approval. As for the details, it is better to discuss them with Ramziya."

Elias stood up, hugged Shammo, and kissed him.

When Ramziya returned with a tea tray, Shammo said to her, "I told Elias that we give him our blessing to marry our daughter." Ramziya sat down next to her husband.

"Helen will always be in my eyes," Elias said, looking at Ramziya.

"May God protect your eyes," Ramziya replied.

"By the way, I applied to work for the *Nineveh* magazine," Elias said. "There is an employee who will retire next month, and I will take his position."

"Congratulations," Ramziya said. "That is good news."

"I have money for the wedding. Shall we throw the party in two weeks?"

"No, Elias," she answered. "We need more time to prepare. As you know, here in the village we do everything with our own hands, and now it's not even the wool season. We also need to go to the city to buy wedding supplies. I'd say we need two months at least."

"So does that mean we can set the date for the last Thursday of November, for example?" Shammo asked.

"Yes, that sounds reasonable," said Ramziya.

The thought excited Elias, and he said, "How about you all come down to the city of Mosul with me? Then I can take you to the market, and on our way, we can pass by my sister's house, and you could meet her."

Ramziya gave Shammo an inquisitive gaze, and her husband said to her, "It's a good idea. You and Helen may go down with Elias, but don't forget to buy me and Azad some Arrow chewing gum."

Elias smiled. "I'll bring the gum with me when I come back next Friday. And then after the lesson, we'll go down together? Of course, you may stay in my home or my sister's. Deal?"

Ramziya nodded, and Shammo said, "Deal . . . so long as there's gum."

They laughed.

—·—

Yahya was in the high chair when the doorbell rang. Sana ran to open it for the guests she had been eagerly awaiting. She welcomed Helen and Ramziya, exchanging kisses with them before inviting them into the sitting room. She'd already made tea with cardamom, leaving it on a low flame, and had prepared baklava and cake.

Elias took Yahya in his arms. He brought his son and introduced him to Ramziya first. She kissed his head and handed the baby to Helen. As he sat in her lap, she smiled down at him.

The little boy has his father's brilliant eyes, she thought. She had a mixed feeling of joy and anxiety as she suddenly had a new son placed in her lap. For some reason, she had never given him much thought. To have a son without pregnancy or childbirth was a confusing experience.

"Where is Rula, Sana?" asked Elias.

"She went with Karim to her cousin's birthday party, but they'll be back soon."

Sana brought in the tea tray. Elias carried the baklava box with one hand and the cake with the other. He offered both to Ramziya. And when he offered them to Helen, she let Yahya take a piece of cake first.

Elias said, "He will not let you drink your tea comfortably."

"It's not a problem," Helen replied.

Elias left the sweets on the table in front of the two guests and took a seat. Sana tried to take Yahya from Helen, but the boy refused.

"This is the first time I've ever seen Yahya stay in someone's lap," Sana said.

Elias smiled and said, "Of course, the sweets are right in front of him." And he said to himself, *The sweet woman is behind him.*

When they finished drinking their tea, Elias asked his sister, "Are you coming with us to the market or waiting here for Karim and Rula?"

Sana thought a little and said, "It might be easier if you and Helen buy the wedding rings on your own. What do you think, Ramziya?"

Ramziya hesitated, so Sana added, "Let's take our time, and in the evening when the weather is more pleasant, we can go out and shop together."

"As you like," Ramziya replied.

—⁓—

When he and Helen reached the end of the street, Elias pointed. "My house is there in Sarchakhana. The house is more than two hundred years old, I think. A historic house, as its owner says.

More importantly, it is close to the Ancient Bridge. After we cross that, there's a forest, and beyond that is the amusement park. Have you ever been to an amusement park?"

"Yes, once when I was little, I went with my uncle Murad."

"Let's go. What do you think?"

"Won't we be late getting back home?"

"No, no. Let's do it."

When they arrived at the park's entrance, he said, "First, we should ride the roller coaster."

"Right away?"

"Yes, then all the rest is easy by comparison."

The ride's sharp turns pushed their bodies close to each other, and when their cart went up to the highest point, Helen closed her eyes and screamed. The cart fell very quickly, then slowed down until it settled on the track.

Afterward, they strolled a little and found themselves in front of an outdoor cafeteria.

"Are you thirsty? Let's get a drink," Elias suggested.

In the cafeteria, the waiter listed the drinks available. Helen chose orange juice. Elias asked for Erbil yogurt drink.

"You sure like yogurt," Helen said.

"If one of our countrymen landed on Mars, guess what he would do there?"

She paused, making a show of thinking very hard. "What would he do?"

"He would open a restaurant selling kebab and Erbil yogurt drink."

"Funny. Do you know how to cook?" she asked.

"No, I only know how to eat."

"Well, you should know I'm no good at cooking—I find rice especially difficult to manage."

"Oh no, I like rice."

"So you eat rice and potatoes but say dieting does not help?"

"I take your point. Let's go ride the Ferris wheel. It's the best thing if the cart stops there at the top."

Helen looked up at the Ferris wheel and feigned a shudder.

"Oh, baby," he said. "I know you were really scared on the roller coaster."

"Like you weren't. You were clutching the bar so hard your knuckles were white."

Elias shook his head. "But seriously, who was more afraid?"

"You."

"Here, let's see who is stronger," he said, putting his elbow on the table.

She tried with all her strength to win. Their hands tangled, slightly bending to the right and to the left. In the end, Helen defeated him, or perhaps he let her win.

"You're strong. Do you play a sport?" he asked.

"No, but I go up and down the mountain every day, you know. And you?"

"I play soccer sometimes."

After leaving the park, they stopped at the Everything for A Dinar store. Elias bought a transparent bag with balloons that had words written on them for different celebratory occasions. He told Helen: "Let's distribute these to the students in the next lesson and ask them to read them as an exam. What do you think?"

"It's a sweet idea," she replied.

Elias picked up a red balloon from inside the bag and blew it at Helen's face as she laughed. The words *I love you*, written on that balloon, grew bigger as he blew into it.

In front of the store, a woman had spread out her wares on the sidewalk. One particular item attracted their attention: a ring engraved with a bird similar to the qabaj.

Elias picked it up and gave it to Helen to try on. It was big on her. Elias tried it, and it was small on him. He put it back on the display cloth and asked the saleswoman: "Do you have any other sizes of this ring, auntie?"

"No, but I have these other shapes. All beautiful, take a look," she replied.

"We want this bird ring in particular," Elias said.

"What a shame," said Helen, "not in our sizes."

They were two steps away when the woman called after them. "Come, come. If you like this bird's shape so much, I can do it for you both as tattoos." She pointed to the tattoo parlor on the opposite side of the street. "There's my place: the kit and everything."

After a moment of consideration, Elias asked Helen, "What do you think?"

"A tattoo had not occurred to me, but if you like it, I like it too," Helen replied.

The woman stood up, gathered her stuff, and motioned for them to follow.

Her place was tiny, barely the size of a chicken house in the village. The only furniture was a chair and a desk, but a good type of original wood desk with drawers. On the desk sat a huge book; also needles of various sizes, strings, tubes, and small square bottles with colored inks.

"Where do you want the tattoo?" asked the woman after she lowered the abaya down over her shoulders and lifted her long sleeves. A huge silver charm necklace with seven eyes was now revealed on her chest. Its turquoise color matched her earrings, which were shaped like crescent moons. Her eyes were noticeably wide in a thin face tanned from the sun. Despite the wrinkles on her face, the way she carried herself suggested a much younger woman.

Elias looked at Helen, and she said, "Like that ring, right?"

"You mean on the ring finger?" Elias raised his left hand slightly and looked at his ring finger. "Why not?"

"Most of my customers get tattoos on their arms," the woman said, "but I can do it for you both on the ring finger as you want."

When she finished inking the bird on their two fingers, they smiled, pleased with the depiction. The woman's needle was so fast and fine that there was little pain. And what pain there was, they did not mind, so happy they were about what was to come.

"Is there anything else I can do for you?" the woman asked.

"No, thanks, auntie," Helen said.

"I ask really because I have something else to offer you." She picked up the big book from the table. "I will tell your fortune from this dictionary, and whatever you choose to pay me will be a blessing from God."

Without waiting for their answer, she closed her eyes while muttering incomprehensible words, and stroked the book with her thin hands. She opened it very slowly, then fell silent for a while. She said, "I see a roller coaster."

Elias raised his eyebrows at Helen as the woman resumed: "I see a person whose life is ascending and descending like a roller coaster, then settling in a faraway place. That person will be lost but will find a door of hope, and then all they must do is find the right key. It's not easy to find the key, nor is it difficult. There is an arduous journey, but there are also people who will help. At every station, a person will be waiting to help." The woman was about to say something else but refrained, finally closing the book and putting it back on the table.

As they crossed the street, leaving behind the woman's tiny tattoo parlor, Elias said to Helen, "It's so strange, as if she saw us together on the roller coaster, right?"

"She did a good job drawing our tattoos, but her fortune-telling made me uncomfortable," Helen said, looking at the tattoo on her finger.

"Who cares about the talk of fortune-tellers?" Elias said, and after a pause, "I wonder what key she was talking about."

"I thought you didn't care about what fortune-tellers say," Helen said, smiling.

10

THE WORLD AS FLAT

The village students, old and young alike, practiced writing letters, words, and sentences on paper, rocks, and tree trunks. As for those they wrote in the dirt, the rain wiped them away, so they became part of the clay memory.

At the end of the last lesson, on November 19, 1999, Elias said, "Congratulations. I am very happy to say that you have learned all the letters in the alphabet. Today, you graduate."

"Should we have a party?" an adult student asked. He wore white from head to toe: his head cap, dishdasha robe, and linen shoes.

"Let's celebrate this evening," Elias replied.

"Should we bring our musical instruments?" asked a villager whose hair was arranged in four long braids coming down from under a white cap.

"Of course," Elias replied, "and I have news I think you will be happy to hear. Helen and I plan to marry, and our wedding will take place here on Thursday, and you are all invited."

The students whistled their congratulations.

They passed on the wedding news from one person to another, and Helen's parents distributed sour-sweet candies to the village houses in place of invitation cards to confirm the date. Neighbors and relatives began preparations for the celebration. They brought extra water from the spring. They gathered more wood than usual, setting up the gathering area and decorating it with lanterns. They ground coarse wheat with wooden hammers to soften it as they sang the songs of the wheat, wishing the new couple's blessings to multiply like those bouncing grains under the hammer. They cooked feast meals, with bulgur on top. And to the party, they carried trays of food that the bride's family would return to them, with gifts inside the dishes, for one never returns a dish empty.

Following tradition, Elias and a group of young men stood on a hill. The others wrapped a colored handkerchief around his head, and he became the Pasha. In order for him to play the role, he had to accuse one of the attendees of having done something bad while the accused tried to defend himself. If the group decided that the accused was guilty, he lost a sum of money. This would be spent at the party, or the groom could donate it to whomever he wanted. But if the group decided the accused was innocent, the vindicated man pulled the handkerchief from the groom's head and took it to the girls from the bride's group, where he would get a gift.

One by one, Elias looked at the smiling village men surrounding him, and in the end, he charged one, saying: "Your crime is huge. You missed the lesson last Friday."

The young man took a moment and then answered, "I was busy planning an important meeting with the Pasha."

The guys put their heads together. One declared he was innocent, but three others protested strongly. One young man declared, "We are the opposition."

Elias laughed while the guy swiftly pulled the handkerchief off his head and departed amid the hustle and bustle.

With the sound of drum and mizmar, the debka circle formed, and the trills of women's voices sounded in the mountains. The celebration continued until the early hours of the morning, when the bride and groom left on two rented horses. They would return the horses to two young men waiting at the bottom of the mountain. On the unpaved road, there would be a car and chauffeur waiting for them.

When the young couple on horseback reached the plain at the bottom of the mountain, Elias glimpsed their very own fig tree, where they had first met. He stopped his horse, and Helen did the same. He jumped down and grabbed her hand to help her down from the horse. He remained holding her hand while their eyes met.

Elias moved the wedding veil from her face, and he heard the echo of a drum, or perhaps his heartbeat. He noticed her eyelids closing, and he bent so their lips met for the first time. When they opened their eyes, they saw something as warm as that kiss. Her horse had rested its head on the neck of the other horse. Elias and Helen exchanged a smile.

He pulled her hand, saying: "It is not right to interrupt their hug. Come. Let's sit by our tree until the two lovers remember we are here."

They sat down, and Helen rested her head against her husband's chest. They looked almost like their horses.

"The party was sweet, wasn't it?" Helen asked.

"The party is over, and my heart is still beating the drum and the mizmar," he replied.

"Recite me a poem," she asked.

Elias looked up, then at her, and began:

"O sea, my heart is a ship, sailed to you
I have prevented my love from sailing, yet it did to you
and never came back, my heart that went to you
don't ask me what was it that went to you
as if went to me when it went to you."

"Wow." Helen was about to ask him to repeat it but noticed the horses had moved a little farther away, so she jumped to her feet, in fear that the two animals would run away and leave them in the dark.

Elias quickly grabbed the lead of Helen's horse, and she got on the beast's back. When she was settled, he, too, got into the saddle of his horse. Facing her, he said, "These are our limousines."

———

To Helen, the city seemed a flat world. There was no going down to the valley or up to the mountains. Still, she was fascinated by many things, the first of which was electricity, which lit the whole room equally. Not accustomed to it, Helen did not complain about the continuous blackouts, unlike the rest of Mosul's residents.

She liked to watch TV and felt that wherever she moved in the room, the presenter continued to look in her direction. Each morning, she opened all the windows as she used to in the village, even though she didn't see any fig trees or qabaj birds. There was, however, a bitter orange tree in the small garden in front of the house and a swing that she liked to sit on with Yahya in the evenings when Elias went to work.

Impressed by the changes that Helen made in the house, Elias called them artistic touches. She had embroidered a rectangular canvas and hung it on the wall, and another small square one which she put on the table. There was a low stone bench along the wall on one side of the living room, which Helen transformed by covering it with a quilt embroidered in warm colors. Elias loved it so much that this became his favorite place to drink coffee. She adored the Turkish coffee with cardamom that Elias made. She now took a bag of coffee beans with her to the village on their usual Friday visits.

Each member of the new family yearned for those weekly visits even though the journey now took longer because they had to stop on the road from time to time so that Yahya or Elias—carrying him—could rest a little. Sometimes Elias insisted that he needed to carry Helen on his back—despite her refusal. He would take her hands from behind his back and raise her up in the air, laughing while Yahya jumped around with joy.

After three years of regular visits, Yahya had become greatly attached to the Halliqi, especially Amina's sheep. He often cried when it was time to leave the village.

Sometimes Amina accompanied them when they went back to the city and would spend a day or two with Helen.

Once, on the way back, Yahya, who had just turned four, asked Amina, "Can the sheep please come home with us?"

"I wish," Amina replied.

On the third Friday of March 2003, Yahya was waiting for his family to take him, as usual, to the highland farm fields so he could run between the cattle and chickens or go with Azad to pet the snake. But life in the country had become tense. America had just invaded Iraq, and its people were nervously awaiting whatever might happen next. The sounds of sirens in Mosul also made many residents unwilling to leave their houses. But that evening, Helen was feeling sick and dizzy, and they had to go to a nearby clinic. The doctor told them that Helen was pregnant.

"Your belly will be so big that I will no longer be able to carry you on my back," Elias commented on the way home.

In response, Helen pinched him and said, "Your belly is big too."

"It's only a gesture of solidarity with you," he replied, laughing.

———

Three months passed without a visit to the mountaintop village. It was the longest Helen had ever gone without visiting her people, and she especially missed Amina. She remembered how once, when they were little girls, Amina had been upset because Helen went to her uncle's house in the city and stayed for a week without telling her ahead of time.

At the time, Helen had said, "So what? What's wrong?"

Amina answered her, "Nothing's wrong. I just felt lonely without you."

She hoped that Amina again felt lonely without her. She was thinking this while standing in her front yard, holding a hose to water the garden, when Amina arrived with Azad.

Helen could not resist spraying them with water, just as they used to do every year on the Water Spray Day at the beginning of July. That was when villagers sprayed each other with water to give blessings. Also, when someone left the area for a distant destination, they'd sprinkle water behind them as a means of warding off danger.

Helen threw aside the hose and ran to them. Holding them close, she said, "Come on in."

Azad sat in the swing next to Yahya and said, "I prefer to sit outside here."

Amina followed Helen into the living room, carrying a paper bag.

Helen made tea and heated up some klecha date pies. She placed some on a tray for Azad and Yahya as well and put it on a small table by the swing. She went back and joined her friend in the living room. Amina took a sip of tea and said, "I was packing my stuff and found this bag. Take a look."

Helen opened the bag and found it contained drawings she'd made as a girl. She was surprised, for Amina had never told her she'd kept her drawings.

"There is sunshine in all my drawings," Helen said, looking through them with a smile. "You kept them all these years, Amina?"

"I was hoping they'd be worth a fortune when you became a famous artist."

Helen smiled and said: "So now you are returning them because you realize they are of no value?"

"I brought them only to show you for fun. I'm not giving them back."

"But why did you say you were packing your stuff?"

"Because I will move to Hardan village. I came to invite you to my wedding party on December 4th. The night before it will be the henna party."

"Congratulations. Who is the lucky groom?"

"His name is Cutto."

"Cutto?"

"He's truly cut from a tree. In fact, he was named after his Turkish great-grandfather. In his time, a hundred years ago, their clan was annihilated by the Ottomans. Any Yazidis who were not killed tried to flee Turkey. Cutto the great-grandfather was wrapped in white cloth as a baby and left atop a pile of fallen leaves under a tree. He was found by Khunaf, a woman fleeing Turkey with the rest of the Yazidis. When she found Cutto, Khunaf was not married, yet she raised him as her own. Khunaf remained single, but since she had a son, she was considered a married woman, even though she was a virgin. The people who heard his story called the boy Cut Off Tree—Cutto—and that became his name. His grandson was also raised by his mother, Nassima, single-handedly. His father died before he was born, and his name became Cutto of Nassima. Even on his identity card, his name is Cutto Nassima, because they thought this was his full name."

"How did you meet?"

"In the winter, he came to buy wool from my father. In the spring, he came and asked for my hand. He said on Khidr Elias Day that he had dreamed that he drank water from my hands, so he decided that I was his saint preemptor."

"Nice. Do you love him?"

"At first, I did not love him or hate him, but I grew to love him after the engagement." Amina smiled and added, "He told me he wished he was one of my sheep because I take such good care of them."

"Take care of him too, Amina. From what you say, I can tell he's nice."

"Yes, he is. He agreed that I could take my sheep with me. At first, he said, leave your sheep and I'll buy you other ones, but I refused. I want my own sheep."

"Other sheep are not the same as yours, although they all look alike," Helen said and stood up to pour more tea.

Amina nodded, so Helen refilled both their cups. Amina took a piece of klecha from the dish in front of her and said, "Tell me. How is marriage for you, Helen?"

"I am pregnant, four months."

"Is that true? It doesn't show on you."

Helen lifted her shirt to show Amina her belly.

"Perhaps you will not be able to get up the mountain to our wedding," Amina said. "If that's the case, I will completely understand."

"My due date is the end of October, and I would not miss your wedding, even if I give birth on the path up the mountains."

At that moment, they heard gunshots.

"They say random bullets hit passersby at night," Helen said.

"We don't hear any gunfire in the village, but we have heard from visitors that a war has started again," said Amina.

Helen went to the door and called Azad and Yahya to come inside.

"When will Elias be home?" Azad asked as he entered with Yahya.

"He works the evening shift. He doesn't come until midnight," Helen replied.

They stayed up until one A.M. waiting for Elias.

When he arrived, he told them he was late because tigers had escaped from their cages in the zoo, causing chaos and traffic accidents. "Cars were slowing down and driving out of their lanes. They could not believe their eyes when they saw the giant cats on the roads. Rumors were that the tigers had killed pedestrians on the bridge. Some said the tigers had been taken down by all the gunshots they were hearing," Elias said.

———

The next morning, the sounds of gunfire had subsided, so they decided to take a walk in the market before Azad and Amina left. In a small gift shop, Helen paused in front of a handmade tablecloth. With a natural motif, it was similar to the colorful, stitched fabric pieces she made. She approached the old man running the shop and said, "How much is this piece, uncle?"

"Ten dollars. It's handmade," the man said.

"I know how to make these. If you need more of them, I can bring them to you," Helen said.

The man thought a moment and said, "Bring me a sample to see."

"Okay. I'll be back tomorrow," Helen replied.

Helen had drawn a bird on a square cloth and embroidered its wings with colored thread. When she brought it to the shop owner, he asked, "Is this a handkerchief?"

"I thought it was a cover for a small table, but it could be used as a handkerchief," she replied.

"Okay. Make it a little smaller so we can display it as a handkerchief. If you bring me ten, and if I sell them, I will give you half the profit. What do you think?"

Helen was happy with the offer. As soon as she got back home, she started drawing tree leaves, animals, and birds on square fabrics.

That evening, she showed them to Elias, and her husband whistled. "Oops! I am afraid that was another emergency-call whistle."

Helen laughed and said: "It was."

"Really?"

"No, just kidding."

"Anyway, here no one understands the language of whistling," said Elias.

"So do you really like these handkerchiefs?"

"They are wonderful, especially this one." Elias picked up a bird cloth. "I'm not showing a bias for this beloved bird, but really, this handkerchief is the most beautiful."

"They will be displayed in a gift shop, and I get a profit from each piece sold."

"I guarantee you at least one will be sold," Elias said. "I'm buying this."

Two months later, the store owner asked Helen for more of the bird handkerchiefs. They were his best-selling handkerchief.

"Did I not tell you?" Elias said.

―⁓―

On a cloudy evening in November, Helen's thoughts were swaying with the garden swing. Her due date had passed by more than a week. She remembered her mother's words that when the fruit ripens, it falls down, and so do newborns: they come when it's time.

That moment, a child's colorful ball cut through her thoughts as it flew over the wall between her garden and the neighbor's. It settled in the branches of the citrus tree.

With her big belly, Helen tried to raise herself and shake the tree branch to release the ball. As she tried to do so, a boy and his mother appeared at the gate. The mother asked Helen for permission to enter and retrieve the ball.

After introducing herself as Shaima, the boy's mother said to Helen, "Be careful. Don't hurt yourself."

Helen halted her tree-shaking efforts, turned, and said, "I thought I could bring it down."

"If you don't mind, my son is quite the agile monkey, and he can get it."

Helen laughed and nodded her approval to the boy.

"When is your due date?" Shaima asked as her son climbed the tree.

"It already passed."

When the boy jumped down with the ball in his hand, Helen smiled at him and said: "Ah. You got it quickly. What's your name?"

"Hameed."

"What grade are you in, Hameed?"

"Second."

"Masha'llah."

———

The following day, Elias was in the yard, walking back and forth and wiping away his tears. Helen was inside with the midwife. She'd been screaming in pain for two hours.

For a moment, he thought he heard a newborn crying. He took a few steps toward the inner door and then returned, thinking the child's voice was probably his imagination. No, it was real!

The midwife emerged from the house and said to Elias, "Congratulations. Mother and son are both fine." This woman, who had delivered most of the neighborhood's children, motioned a stunned Elias into his own house.

He rushed to Helen's side and kissed her forehead.

She did not move and appeared to be asleep. But she heard him when he uttered, "Yassir."

———

After a few hours, Sana came with Rula and Yahya to see Yassir. She brought a pot of dolma with her. Elias retrieved a tray from the kitchen, turned the pot over on it, and put it on the table.

They heard heavy knocking on the door. When Elias opened it, an American inspection team consisting of fifteen soldiers burst into the house's three rooms.

One of them, looking at the big tray where steam was still rising from the stuffed vine leaves, told Elias they were searching for terrorists.

Elias invited the soldiers to taste the dolma, and they each took one. They thanked him and left. Elias closed the door behind them, saying, "They liked the dolma."

"Was there enough?" Sana asked him.

"It would be enough for them all, but they only tasted it," he replied.

Then came another emotional moment. One by one, Sana gave them goodbye hugs. She was about to leave for Sulaymaniyah. Her husband's work had moved to the university there.

―――

There were more and more tanks on the city streets, and the townspeople became increasingly anxious and confused. Within that general anxiety, Helen felt a private anxiety, like a baby kangaroo within a bigger one. This was the worry of a young mother over her newborn: Helen could not be sure she was doing the right thing for Yassir when he cried.

Elias reassured her that nothing was wrong with the baby as long as he was neither hungry nor dirty. He quieted down when his mother carried him.

"See? He only wants attention," said her husband.

―――

Helen was not supposed to leave the house until forty days after the birth, as the postpartum period required. But she did not want to miss Amina's wedding, so Elias carried the baby, and

Helen grabbed Yahya's hand, and they all headed up to the village.

As soon as Helen entered her parents' home, her mother greeted her, trilling with joy, blessing the new baby by putting the seven-eyes pin on his white cotton garment, saying: "What? He cries a lot? Nothing wrong, just gas."

Shammo said, "Let me circumcise him."

On this visit, Elias would remain in her parents' home, and Helen would go to the home of Amina's parents. The henna party was for women only. They put henna on their palms and feet, singing and dancing around a tray of candles and sweets to celebrate the bride's last night at her parents' home. Married women gave Amina advice, some of it funny: "Love is blind, but remember that it opens its eyes well after marriage." "Do not run to your parents at the first fight." When it was Helen's turn, she said: "Treat your husband as you treat your best friend."

—⁓—

A week after Helen returned from the village, her neighbor Shaima, Hameed's mother, knocked on the front door. She had brought a baby towel as a gift for the newborn.

After that visit, which the neighbor initiated to bless Yassir's birth, a friendship developed between the two women. They frequently visited and left their doors unlocked so that any member of the two families could enter the other's house at any time.

Whenever Helen went to the market, she left Yahya and Yassir with Shaima. When Hameed returned from school hungry and his mother was not done with the cooking yet, he would eat at Helen's home. Shaima was six years older than Helen but looked much older when she put the abaya on her head.

On some holidays, Hameed liked to sleep in the same room as Yahya and Yassir. But on November 11, 2005, he had to sleep with them. His mother and father had gone out and did not return home. That evening was the joint birthday party of Yahya and Yassir. Both had been born that month, a week apart.

Helen had made two cakes, putting seven candles on Yahya's cake and two on Yassir's. After they had blown out the candles, Helen put before them a large, wrapped gift and said, "This is a gift for you both to share and enjoy with Hameed."

They rushed to tear off the wrapping paper, finding a miniature soccer table designed for two people to play on. They could move the side handles of plastic soccer players and try to make them push the ball to the opposite goal. Like his father, Yahya loved soccer, so he was very happy with the gift and started playing with Hameed.

Elias and Yassir stood there watching. Elias said, "Yassir and I will have our turn next."

—◦—

The following evening, Shaima returned. She was panting and out of breath when she arrived at Helen's house.

"Where were you?" Helen asked, getting her a glass of water.

"We stayed at my brother's house and did not sleep all night. You don't know what happened?"

"What happened, Shaima?"

"A gang kidnapped my nephew and demanded twenty thousand dollars for his release."

"Oh my God. This is terrible."

"They sent his picture. Behind him were masked men holding swords. His mother fainted when she saw it, and my poor brother tried to sell his restaurant to pay the ransom. I contributed as much as I could, and some of our relatives stood with us as best they could. My brother asked the gang to lower the price, but they threatened to return the boy to him in a garbage bag. My brother quickly borrowed the required amount and paid them. Most important, thank God, they returned the boy. He is traumatized and silent and does not even want to tell us what they did to him."

Helen disappeared into the bedroom. After she came back, she tucked $500 into Shaima's hand and said, "I saved this from the handkerchief sales, and I wish I could give more than this to help your brother pay off his loans."

"Thank you, Helen. I will pay it back as soon as possible."

"Don't worry."

"Tell me. How are your parents doing?"

"Last night my father came to me in my dream, and he was worried about me."

"Why was he worried?"

"My front tooth was broken."

"Oh. They say we must recount our bad dreams in the bathroom so that their effect passes away."

11

BLANK SCREEN

On their roof during the next lunar eclipse, Yassir said to his father, "The moon is not there. Did the whale really swallow it?"

Yahya was also curious. "How could a whale swallow the moon when it swims in the water and the moon swims in the sky?" he asked.

Elias had been waiting for weeks after hearing news of the full eclipse, during which the moon was expected to turn red. He gave Yahya the same answer that he'd heard from his mother when he was a little boy: "The poor moon was thirsty, and when it turned to the river to drink, the whale saw it and jumped after it."

A light drizzle did not prevent Helen, Elias, and the two boys from banging trays on the rooftop, as did many of their neighbors that mid-April day in 2014. But they did not see the red moon that evening, nor did anyone in Mosul. Still, they did their best to fight the invisible whale, just as Don Quixote had battled against his windmills.

Helen didn't know why that night under the moon came to mind two months later. She specifically remembered the words of an American priest she had seen on television earlier that day. The man had said that because the eclipse coincided with religious occasions in the region, the bloody moon portended horrific events in the Middle East.

Perhaps she remembered this because she was frustrated at not being able to go up to the village and attend Azad's wedding party on June 5th. For the last few years, Ramziya had been mentioning to Azad names of girls she knew, hoping he would consider one of them a potential wife. He didn't take any of it seriously until he turned thirty-five, which was considered late for marriage in the village. His bride was ten years younger than him. She belonged to a big tribe, and her relatives planned a huge party.

But it was not Helen's pregnancy that prevented her from attending the event. A curfew had been imposed on Mosul. A radio broadcast announced that an armed group now controlled the city's western side. The curfew was a security measure so that the police could regain control of the situation.

Standing near Helen when she heard this on the radio, Yassir, now in fifth grade, said, "This means no exam and no school today, thanks be to God."

The curfew was supposed to end in three days' time, but the armed group was gaining territory. Some people returned to their jobs, while others continued to shelter in their homes, unsure whether or not the curfew had ended. The streets were almost empty of pedestrians, while long lines of cars appeared at gas stations.

Helen went next door to Shaima's house to try to relax.

Answering her knock, Shaima motioned her inside. "Come in, Helen. The world is upside down."

"Oh my God, what is happening?"

"I've heard that a big gang called Daesh is occupying Mosul. They're raising black flags and killing whoever stands in their way. Oh, when will our problems end?" Shaima said and asked Helen to sit with her at the kitchen table.

"Where did they come from?" Helen asked, squeezing her hands together.

"I don't know where they are from, but they've taken control of the airport, government departments, the banks, and oil fields. They have patrols between the regions. Even Abu Hameed, who has never closed his shop before five P.M., came home early today. He told me all shop owners closed and left because gang members were roaming the markets and taking money from people and merchants by force. They somehow know how much each of them earns."

"How could they possibly know that?"

"They seized ration card files and found out the details of each family's livelihood."

"So their plan is well thought out."

"Certainly."

Looking deflated, Shaima fell silent for a moment. Then she pointed to the street and said, "Have you seen Umm Qasim? She's happy and distributing baklava. She says Daesh are the best people because they've provided water and electricity."

Just then, Hameed rushed in. Spots of oil and soot covered the teenager's clothes. He greeted Helen and disappeared down the hallway.

Shaima poured tea into the *istikans*. After the first sip of tea, she told Helen, "Hameed has started working with his father in car repairs. He's eighteen, no longer young, and it is better for him to learn a trade since he does not like to study."

She lowered her voice a little and added, "But Hameed hates working with his father and invents all kinds of pretexts to be absent from the store. So the atmosphere here is tense, and they are always fighting."

———

One night, Helen stayed up with Elias to watch the film *Titanic*. They cried together at the scene of people drowning. That scene came to Helen's mind the next day after she walked with Elias on the Ancient Bridge over the Tigris River.

There was a capsized boat in the river. Elias commented, "Our ship will not sink, not because our captain is more skilled but because our river is without water or salt."

They were on their way to the gift shop so that Helen could make her usual delivery of handkerchiefs. From there, Elias would continue to the Nineveh offices. Helen was wearing Shaima's abaya. She had heard the gang harmed women whose heads were uncovered.

When she had first put it on, Elias had joked with Helen, singing the beginning of a song: "How beautiful is your abaya." But he kidded less and less these days. He seemed bewildered and worried like never before.

On the street, she held her husband's arm and said, "Try not to be too late today."

He stopped walking for a moment, and so she did the same. He gave her the deep look she knew well. Finally, Elias said, "I think before going to work I should get you and the family up to your parents in Halliqi."

"No. No need for that."

"The situation here does not look good."

"I'll get home quickly," Helen reassured him. "You go to work, and I will pack a bag and wait for you."

"Don't forget to include some Arrow gum for your father and Azad."

———

When Helen returned home, she called Amina. Ten years earlier, mobile phones had become available in some villages of Sinjar. Ever since, the two friends had spoken almost every day. The phones had not yet entered Halliqi village, but Helen heard the local news from Amina.

"Why are you still there?" Amina asked immediately.

Helen did not answer, and Amina added, "Our town is filled with people fleeing Mosul. They say a terrorist organization has captured the city."

"Yes, it's a huge mess, and there are barely enough vans to get people out," Helen said. "The students' final exams were even canceled. We hear this group of thugs plan to change the textbooks and cancel art classes. Elias did go to work today, but he is applying for a long vacation. If we can find a taxi, we will leave tomorrow. And then we will have to climb the mountain on the donkey. My belly is so big this time; it's difficult for me to walk any long distance. I am eager to see my parents. We will stay with them until the situation calms down. I hope to see you there, Amina."

"I'm there every weekend," Amina said.

"Bring Ahlam with you, so I can see her as well."

"When is your due date?" Amina asked.

"Five more weeks. Elias does not want to stop until we have a girl."

That night, Elias did not return from work.

Helen could not sleep. She didn't know how many times she had called him. No answer. There was no answer in the morning and no answer that evening.

She went next door to Shaima's. "I will bring the two boys to you and go to the magazine's office. Elias did not return home yesterday."

"Calm down, Helen. Let's ask around first."

"I'm scared," Helen said, crying.

Abu Hameed was eating his breakfast. Shaima's husband stopped eating when he heard Helen crying. He stood up, looked out the living room window, then turned to Helen. "I will go and ask about Elias. The roads are not safe, but I know how to get there."

Three hours passed. Helen had no alternative but to wait. She studied the geometric figures on the tiles in Shaima's kitchen. It was the first time she'd noticed the small square motifs overlapping on the ground like labyrinths. Inside the squares were drawings of wildflowers. On the table were artificial flowers.

Helen had never seen artificial flowers. In her village, all flowers were natural.

Shaima brought her a plate of pastry and said, "Eat something. Do not forget that you are two. You must feed your second at least."

But Helen was unable to swallow anything, especially since she was feeling pain in her stomach. It was a pain not unlike that which Helen had felt when her mother told her she would become the wife of Saleh, the fig merchant.

Finally, Abu Hameed returned.

Helen looked at him with tearful eyes, waiting for him to say something. It was as if she were in front of a doctor examining an X-ray to diagnose her disease.

"I could not enter the Nineveh building," he said. "It was surrounded by guards carrying guns. But I visited a friend of mine in the area who has extensive connections. He promised me to ask about Elias and call me as soon as he finds out—"

The landline rang before Abu Hameed completed his sentence, so he grabbed it and raised it to his ear.

A moment later, he lowered the headset while looking at Helen.

Her blood froze in her veins. From his look, she expected bad news. "Tell me what happened, please."

"They took the magazine staff as prisoners of war," he said.

As a wave of grief washed over Helen, Shaima said, "They might release him. They may ask for a ransom and let him go."

Back at home, Yahya searched the kitchen cabinets for something to eat. He picked up a piece of biscuit, and with the other hand grabbed the bird-shaped dough, asking: "Is this for eating or just display?"

Elias had kept that dough all these years since the day Shammo had given it to him. Helen had found it in his kitchen cabinet a week after their marriage. Elias said it had been made in an artistic way and was too beautiful to eat.

"It's for eating, but I'm afraid it's expired," Helen replied.

Yassir took a ball from his pocket and threw it against the wall to bounce back, but Yahya jumped and grabbed it.

At the same time, the new human being within Helen was demanding her attention by hitting the wall of her stomach. Helen wanted to stop the boys playing ball inside, especially because she was feeling nauseous, but she had already forbidden them from playing on the street because of the growing risk of kidnap, so she let them play in the sitting room.

She went to her bedroom. The clamor they made was, after all, better than when they were completely silent. Or when they nagged and asked her when their father would come home.

A hard question. She too wanted to know the answer. Three weeks had passed since Elias's disappearance, and she was out of her mind with worry. She closed her eyes during the day instead of at night, and when she urgently needed to go to a nearby shop to buy something, she felt as if she was walking in her sleep.

Today, she was even more frustrated because the TV screen was blank: there was no sound or picture. She'd been following the news since that terrible day when Elias went to work and did not return. She missed no opportunity to listen to the broadcast, with vain hopes of hearing something about the prisoners.

She went to Shaima's house and found her TV screen blank too.

"I knew they would stop broadcasting," said Shaima. "They announced in the mosque that television programs are forbidden." She was breastfeeding Mustafa, to whom she had given birth four months ago. Her husband was busy breaking up the wood cabinet for firewood to cook. Gas was no longer available, and breaking the wood up was easier than standing in an endless queue for one tank of gas that would be sold for an unimaginably high price.

Helen returned home, feeling that her life had become a blank screen. She looked at her phone, as she'd been doing compulsively, hoping that Elias would somehow manage a call to reassure her that he was alive, or that someone would call her to ask for a sum of money in exchange for his release. She would somehow manage to get whatever they asked. At that moment, the phone rang, and she immediately answered.

"Hello."

"Hello."

"Azad?"

"How are you, sister?"

"Fine," she said, suppressing a sob.

"Is there any news of Elias? We heard what happened."

"There is no new news except that they turned the magazine building into a prison."

"I will come down now to bring you and the boys here."

"No, Azad. The roads are too dangerous."

"I am here in Hardan, I am calling you from Amina's phone. Here she is. Talk to her."

"Hello, Amina."

"You are in our thoughts, Helen."

Helen burst into tears, and Amina cried with her.

"Tell Azad not to come to Mosul."

"He's already left," Amina said.

———

Shortly after midnight, Azad arrived to a tearful embrace from Helen. When she'd calmed down a little, she said, "Thank God the gang did not intercept you on the way."

"A strange gang," Azad said. "I heard one of them calling through the loudspeaker in the car garage that everyone who works in the government sector should sign the repentance card and swear on the Quran not to belong to any political group. Anyway, I paid triple the fare for a driver who had links in the patrol control points. He will take us back to the village. He also has fake identity cards just in case."

"The strangest thing about this gang," Helen said, "is that they don't hide their crimes. On the contrary, they seem proud of them and demonstrate them in terrifying videos."

After a terrible pause, she said, "Two days ago, I watched a YouTube video of masked men beheading people they called traitors. Fountains of blood poured from the dead. I glimpsed someone who looked like Elias, but it was not him. I saw him very briefly and closed my eyes. Why would they kill Elias? No, it wasn't him. Surely not."

These last words came out from Helen's mouth in a jerky voice.

Azad sat, rubbing his forehead. He lowered his hands and said, "Early in the morning when Yahya and Yassir wake up, we will all go to the village. Okay?"

"I can't. My body is too heavy, and I have agreed with the midwife on our street that she will help me give birth. She even postponed leaving the city because of me. But I want you to take my two boys with you."

Hameed was sleeping with Yahya and Yassir. When he woke up in the morning, Helen introduced him to Azad, saying: "Hameed is the son of my neighbor, and he is like my son."

"Do you want to come with us to the village?" Azad asked him.

"Yes, come with us, please. You will like the village," Yahya told Hameed.

Hameed refused, saying, "I have to go to work." He asked to be excused to leave.

The doorbell rang. Azad looked through the living room window and said, "The driver is here. We also have to leave now."

Helen hugged each of them and said, "Let Amina know when you arrive. She will tell me."

Azad nodded and said, "See you soon."

——*w*——

A week after they left, Helen was wiping sweat from her brow between knocks on the midwife's door. The pain in her lower back was intense, and she could barely stand.

This was the third time she had come. The previous two times, contractions had come, but the baby did not. If the baby did not come this time, Helen would have to find another midwife. Her midwife was Christian, and all Christians had to leave Mosul a few days later.

The gang had now declared itself the State, with the power to impose its will. Among their new laws was the takeover of Christian homes. They inscribed the letter N in red marker on the homes of those they called "Nazareth." This was a warning for them to get out or be killed, even if their people had lived in these houses for hundreds of years.

"Sorry for the inconvenience," Helen said when the door opened, "but this time the pain is too strong to bear."

The midwife rushed to grab her bag and accompanied Helen back to her home, which stood about thirty meters from the midwife's house.

Helen walked slowly, stopping now and then and moaning in pain. Finally, she was inside and in her bed. The contractions were sharp and close in time. After two hours of pain, Helen pushed the fetus forward, but it slipped back again. The midwife urged her to push harder, and this time the baby's head came out. The midwife asked her to stop pushing and to breathe calmly. While Helen trembled with the effort, the midwife grabbed the newborn's body. She wiped traces of blood off the baby with a cloth and waited a little longer. She had brought Yassir into the world with Helen eleven years ago, and now she wrapped this baby girl in a white cloth. She settled her in Helen's lap and went out saying, "Now I can leave. We have no life with these monsters. Just like this newborn baby, we'll leave with nothing."

"Wait. Let me pay you," Helen said, struggling to move.

"No, my dear. God willing, when Elias returns safely and sees his beautiful daughter, he will pay me." The midwife abruptly left Helen and the baby girl with no name and no father.

—⁓—

They slept throughout the day and stayed up at night in the dark. The baby girl cried, so Helen brought her to her breasts to feed her.

Helen searched for Elias in the baby's features. She found him in two dimples in her cheeks.

Ten days later, when the umbilical stump dried off, Helen took her daughter to Shaima. Helen asked her neighbor to take care of her until she returned. She intended to go to the magazine office and ask about Elias.

"You cannot go," Shaima said. "Less than two weeks have passed since the birth of your child."

"I can't handle it anymore, Shaima. I waited all this time throughout my pregnancy."

"Then put on my abaya and cover your head well so they don't bother you."

The baby was sleeping when Shaima took her. Helen kissed her tiny hand and gave Shaima a tearful, grateful look. Helen adjusted the black abaya, went outside, and headed toward the bridge.

In the middle of the road, she saw armed men in a pickup truck wearing black headbands. She turned her face in the other direction and walked as fast as she could. She avoided looking at the scenes of devastation, but they passed before her one after another. Even when she lowered her head, she saw scorched tires thrown into the street. Raising her head, Helen saw on the walls the banners of the "Islamic State on the path of the caliphate." The hotel at the corner of the street looked deserted, with big holes in its facade and debris scattered in front of it. The hair salon where Helen used to go was closed, and the bridal makeup ad had been removed from outside. Using lipstick could lead to thirty lashes.

Hairdressing had become a dangerous profession, for both men and women. One of Shaima's relatives, who was a barber, was punished with fifty lashes, after which he was hospitalized. His cousin had asked him to shave his hair and beard on his wedding day. As he did so, the barber's hand was trembling because he knew it was a risk, but at the same time he wanted his relative, the groom, to rejoice, and he hoped that his action would pass unnoticed, that perhaps they would not come to watch him on that hot afternoon. Three days after the wedding, they arrested him and closed his salon.

Helen walked streets that were empty except for a few others who kept looking behind them fearfully. In the past, these streets had been so crowded that people would not apologize if they bumped into each other. Gone were the scents of tea, spices, and perfume. The sellers who displayed their items on the sidewalks, street vendors, and café-goers—all disappeared.

Close by the magazine building, Helen smelled gunpowder. At the gate was a boy who looked about Yahya's age. But even though he was carrying a gun, she felt she could talk to him. "My son, may I ask you a favor?"

"Go ahead," he replied.

"My husband works for this magazine, and he has not been home for more than a month. I came to ask about him."

"What is his name?"

"Elias."

"I don't know him."

"I heard he was taken prisoner here."

"No prisoners here."

Just then, a car pulled up in front of the building and a bearded man got out. Looking at Helen, he said to the boy, "Who is this?"

"She came to ask about her husband because he was an employee here," answered the boy.

"So your husband must be a government agent," the man said.

Helen lowered her head and took a step as if to leave, but the man grabbed her hand and pulled her along the sidewalk and into the building. From there, he forced her into a room where there was a man with an exceptionally long beard. The man who had brought her had a shorter beard. He said, "This is the wife of an agent."

"Do you have an identity card?" the long-bearded man asked Helen.

"No, not with me."

"If you are Christian, you should have left Mosul by now. Why are you here?"

Helen didn't answer, so the man resumed, "You must be a spy. Do you want to confess by will or by force?"

"Confess what?"

"Who sent you to us?" he asked.

"No one."

"Where are you from?"

"I live here in Mosul."

"But your accent is not of Mosul. Where are you originally from?"

"From Sinjar."

"Yazidi?"

Helen did not answer, so the man shouted at her: "Yazidi—yes or no?"

"Yes."

When she uttered the word, the short-bearded man left, soon returning with two other men. They spoke a language Helen did not understand. Nor did she understand why they were looking at her as if they had found a strange creature who had just landed from another planet.

12

IN THE CASTLE

On the 2014 calendar next to the fridge in Amina's kitchen, the second day of August was circled. This was a special day for the Yazidis. After forty days of fasting, it was their Eid, and one of this holiday's traditions was that a married woman leaves her husband and goes to sleep overnight at her parents' home. This was what Amina did that day.

Like any other year, they would gather around delicious food and stay up all night. Why worry when they could sleep afterward for as long as they pleased? When they woke to the morning sun, they would open the windows to let the light enter their homes. The shepherds would go with their sheep to the fields, and the farmers displayed watermelons on the side of the roads, ready with large knives in case any customer wanted to ensure the chosen watermelon's inside was red, not white.

Life was supposed to flow like the river. And it did for three hours, after which it deviated from that course forever.

The people of Sinjar heard loud explosions, unlike any known in previous wars. They rubbed their eyes, confused, somewhere between awakening and sleep. The explosions were so loud they even reached the isolated village of Halliqi.

———

Ramziya thought it was the sound of thunder in the sky. But she soon realized her mistake, as she had never heard thunder in the summer. She had no idea what was happening at the foot of the mountain. She had learned of Elias's disappearance and, like everyone else, wanted to know if he had returned home yet. On this particular holiday, Helen's parents were especially worried about her: she had not come and did not respond to Amina's continuous calls.

Azad decided to leave his pregnant wife with her parents and go down the mountain with Yahya and Yassir on that third morning of August 2014 to Amina's home in Hardan village. She'd call Helen from there or go to her in Mosul if they couldn't get hold of her.

At the last moment, Shammo quickly put on his sandals and told Ramziya he was going with them.

"You've never in your life been to Mosul. Wait, I'll go with you," Ramziya said, and she, too, went to change her clothes.

Right then, a neighbor entered their home. Shammo rushed upstairs and said to Ramziya, "You have a guest, and I don't think you should come with us at this time. We will find Helen and be back."

———

Once they arrived at Amina's house, she tried phoning Helen again. Then again and again with no answer. Amina suggested they stay overnight at her house and try calling Helen again the next morning. Her husband, Cutto, welcomed them over dinner.

When they had finished, he said, "I heard the news. I hope it is all rumor." They all looked at him, and he said, "Daesh have arrived in the Sinjar district, and some people have fled to the mountains."

Azad nodded. "Yes, many people were heading up the mountain as we were coming down."

"I also noticed many buses in the street. Is that normal here?" Shammo asked.

"No, not normal," Cutto answered.

Cutto's mother, Nassima, put the teapot on the stove and said, "My son, why is all your news bad these days?"

"If they sell good news, I'll be the first to buy it," Cutto replied.

When Yassir whispered to his brother that they should return to Mosul, Azad overheard him. He told the boys, "When morning comes, we'll go."

—⁓—

Two hours after midnight, they awoke to sounds like a large hammer in destruction mode.

Amina jumped back in fright when she pulled open the front window's curtain. Many cars were parked in front of the house, and there were masked people carrying black flags.

"Daesh are here!" shouted Amina.

"What does Daesh mean?" Shammo asked.

Outside, loudspeakers called on the villagers to surrender their weapons immediately.

"You don't have any weapons, do you?" Shammo asked Cutto, and the man shook his head.

"We will not hurt you," said the loudspeaker voice. "We are here to protect you."

There was a loud knocking on the door.

Cutto stood up, then froze.

Amina screamed, "No, don't open the door."

Ahlam crumpled in her grandmother's lap, crying.

They stayed still, and the sound of knocking grew more enraged. When the door was about to be broken down, Cutto opened it.

Behind the man banging on the door, a Kia car was in front of the house. Five men in Kandahari outfits stood nearby, carrying rifles.

"All of you, come with us, just for ten minutes," said one man, indicating the direction with his gun. "We'll take you to the sheikh so you can repent, and then we'll bring you back."

"Oh God, what do we repent?" Cutto asked him.

But the man, instead of answering, asked, "Will you become Muslims?" He added, "We will teach you the Muslim prayer."

"We have lived peacefully with Muslims all our lives," said Cutto, "and we know how they pray and how they fast."

"Come with me and, God willing, everything will be good," said the man. "But only men come with me. Women go to that other bus."

—⁓—

They took Amina to the bus for married women, and her daughter Ahlam went with her grandmother Nassima to the other bus.

It didn't occur to Nassima when she uttered it that the number nine was so dangerous. When the gunmen asked about ages, and

Nassima answered that Ahlam was only nine years old, she had thought the opposite. Nassima thought this would mean that Ahlam was still a child. She did not yet know that her truth was different from theirs.

One of the armed men separated grandmother from granddaughter, ordering Ahlam to the unmarried girls' bus. Ahlam pulled Nassima closer to her, refusing to be separated, and Nassima wrapped her arms around Ahlam.

The gunman pulled them apart as Ahlam screamed and cried. For them, a nine-year-old girl was not a child but an adult, and therefore she would not remain with her grandmother. It was too late. Nassima could no longer change Ahlam's age to a lower number so that they'd allow them to stay together. Nassima begged the armed man, "For the love of God, do not take her from me. You took her mother to the other bus that just went away, where to I don't know."

"For the love of God, I'll take her," the gunman said, laughing. He moved away, dragging Ahlam behind him.

Her father and mother did not see her dragged and crying. They were in other vehicles with the blinds lowered. Amina did not know that they later captured her sheep, too. After they emptied the houses of their people, they entered the barns and drove the animals out into trucks. Cats with dogs, sheep with donkeys. In ordinary times, dogs and cats annoy each other and bark or hiss or meow, but the animals were all quiet on the way to the unknown, as if they smelled the danger.

—⁓—

In the Kia, Shammo asked one of the gunmen, "Brother, we are coming with you to the sheikh, but please just tell me, why do you separate the women from the men?"

"Of course, it is not permissible for women to sit with men. Do you not know this?" the man replied.

There was no more talk. About an hour later, the car stopped in front of an ancient castle on a hill. They got out of the car, along with other prisoners getting out of other vehicles lined up in front.

"I know this place," said Cutto. "This is Tal Afar castle," he told his group.

They entered as ordered by the armed men. There was a large clock on the wall, its hands indicating 4:20 A.M. The gunmen then abruptly left, abandoning the gathered men inside the castle fortress, with guards outside.

It was a hot, dusty day with no fans, no water, and no answers to questions like "Why are we here?" and "What are they going to do with us?" and "Where did they take the girls?"

These questions were repeated throughout the day. The sun went down, and nothing happened but the *ticktock* of time. After midnight, they heard shots outside.

The guards came in and informed them someone had tried to escape from the window, and they had killed him. "It is better for you *not* to think about such foolishness," one guard said before leaving with the others.

One of the prisoners was crying, and the other prisoners crowded around him. He told them the man they had killed had been his oldest son.

—⁓—

Two days later, the armed men brought them water and packets of biscuits past their expiry date. On the third day, when the clock's small hand pointed to nine, the gunmen again entered the castle. One of them loudly addressed the prisoners. "This castle is a place of infidelity so, God willing, we will destroy it. The infidels called it Ishtar temple because they did not realize the existence of God and worshiped gods of their making. In a little while, Caliph Abu Nasser will come to tell you about the correct religion. A photographer will come to photograph you as you enter Islam so that others see you and take the right path. Do you agree?"

The prisoners were murmuring while the speaker added, "If you agree, we will bring your families to you and will care for you and protect you from harm."

More murmurs.

"But I cannot agree," said one of the prisoners. "My religion does not allow this."

"Same with me," the young man next to him said. "I don't agree."

"Are you sure?" asked the armed man. "Come with me."

Cutto whispered to Azad, "Those two brave men have no families. Let us stay silent in order to avoid them and return to our families. Love is humiliation, brother."

Azad nodded and said, "We will let them hear what they want to hear since they do not know what is in our hearts."

Shammo said nothing. He was thinking of Helen and Elias, of Ramziya who was likely worried about them being delayed. Yahya and Yassir sat next to him, and he was saddened to see them eat the bad biscuits.

"Ha, what did you say? You agree?" the gunman asked the others.

"Yes, not a problem," said one of the prisoners from the front row. "There is no difference between religions."

"There is indeed a big difference," said the armed man. "Your conversion today to Islam is in your favor because you will enter Paradise through the widest gates."

There were numerous gunshots. Gunmen walked here and there, talking on their phones. Half an hour later, when the gunfire subsided, they distributed bread and triangles of cheese to the prisoners. When the clock's small hand passed ten, they took the prisoners to a natural spring near the castle.

"Take off your clothes," said a gunman with a loudspeaker. "And if you still have anything—telephone, ring, key—you must hand it over. Anything."

Naked, one by one, they washed in the spring's water. When they got out of the spring, the gunmen called on the boys, twenty or younger, to board a bus that was waiting for them.

Shammo wanted to hug Yahya and Yassir before the two boys boarded the bus, but he lowered his head and avoided looking at them because he was naked and embarrassed.

The bus filled up and drove off, out of the prisoners' sight.

An armed man raised the loudspeaker to his mouth and said: "Your sons are ours, and therefore they are the sons of the Islamic State, and we congratulate you because they are now on their way to the Raqqa training camp, which will prepare them to become great fighters."

A man moved through the naked prisoners, distributing cotton shirts and wide trousers.

Wearing the clothes, Shammo whispered to Azad, "What fight? Your nephews are afraid even of snakes."

The loudspeaker continued, "Now, with your clean clothes, get ready to meet the caliph."

They were brought to a grove not far from the water spring, and the armed men seemed on high alert. They seemed to be moving in every direction while directing the prisoners to sit in organized rows.

Finally, the caliph arrived in a black outfit and black turban, carrying a rifle and accompanied by numerous men with large cameras. He took a seat in front of the prisoners. Next to him was a young man in a military uniform, also carrying a rifle.

The caliph spoke to the prisoners: "We came to liberate you and introduce you to the right religion. You are safe once you convert to Islam. Any unbeliever, whether crusader or Jew or Yazidi, has a chance to survive by reciting the two testimonies of faith. We only fight people so we can get them out of blasphemy. And now Sinjar is under the command of the jihadis. We offered them Islam in exchange for peace, but they did reject it, and chose to fight us. But I have good news. There are many families who have accepted our offer and are now happy. They were in the dark and have come into the light. We ask the Yazidis to descend from the mountains and to join us so that they will avoid the fire of Hell in the afterlife. If they remain in the mountains, they will die of hunger and thirst. But we are willing to defend them. We would rather be killed than let anyone harm them. You only need to recite the two testimonies of faith to become brothers for us. You have rights and duties, just like us."

Behind the caliph, in the trees, several birds were singing.

Shammo looked at the trees around him, astonished at how anyone could make life complicated in such a beautiful garden!

His thoughts were interrupted by the loudspeaker proclaiming that the jihadis would talk to the prisoners while the photographers shot videos of them.

A cameraman approached Azad and asked him, "What do you think of what the caliph said?"

"As he said. We are in the light," Azad replied.

As soon as the photographer left, Azad turned his head toward Cutto and whispered to him, "We will be blinded by all this light."

Other gunmen strolled among the prisoners, asking them if they had requests.

When a young man approached him, Shammo asked, "Where are the rest of the prisoners?" The young man did not answer him, so Shammo added, "My son-in-law, whose name is Elias, was taken prisoner, we heard. You know where he is?"

The young man looked to the right and to the left as if waiting for a different question.

Shammo said, "And the girls? Where did they take them?"

The young man looked annoyed. He left him and moved on to another prisoner.

13

THE VILLAGE OF
THE FAITHFUL

The gunmen instructed the prisoners to board a bus which, they said, would take them to the archaeological sites in Tal Afar—just as a tour guide would take a group of tourists to see ancient historical sites. The difference was that the gunmen took these prisoners to those monuments not to visit them and hear the stories about them that had been told for generations for thousands of years, but instead to witness their demolition.

The Khidr Elias dome was the first place they started to destroy. Cutto thanked God because his mother was not with them. She could not have endured this scene. Since he opened his eyes to the world, Cutto knew that the third Thursday of February meant that his mother would take him to that green dome. She would first make the Khidr Elias dessert stuffed with seven kinds of fried, ground nuts, following her faith, which believes in seven angels.

She never missed a spring without a visit to that place with the many other visitors who came from near and far to send candles on small pieces of wood floating down the river as they made wishes in their hearts. When Cutto grew up a little, he asked his mother who Khidr Elias was, and why she made him this dessert every year.

She told him Khidr Elias was a good man, who had lived in the dome a long time ago. He was known to bring good luck. Every dry place that he set foot on turned green and full of plants. In his time, people felt blessed and called him "of green feet." When he died, reverent followers visited his home. He had been a vegetarian, so Eid for him was a time when no blood was shed. Therefore, on his day, his followers would not slaughter an animal or eat any meat.

Members of the Organization had a different idea. They told the prisoners that requesting the fulfillment of wishes from Khidr Elias was now *haraam*—forbidden—because wishes could only be fulfilled by God.

Cutto observed the dome as it exploded, and the gunmen cried, "God is great!" Cutto found himself shouting "Allahu Akbar" like them because he was so agitated seeing the dome leveled with the ground. He remembered the important dream he'd had on the day of Khidr Elias: Amina had brought him water. His mother had interpreted the dream to mean that this girl was meant to be his bride, and so Cutto married her. He was boiling with anger not only because they had torn down a site of his childhood memories, but also because he wanted to know what they had done with Amina, Ahlam, and his mother. Where had the buses taken them?

Surprised at Cutto's hysterical shouting, Shammo murmured to Azad, "Why are they destroying this beautiful place? Shame on them."

A hum of protest went among the prisoners, which the gunmen silenced with shots fired randomly into the air. One of them came and stood in front of the prisoners, shouting through a loudspeaker, "Listen, God created man in the best image, and it is not permissible for human beings to compete with God in his creation. What are these stones that you feel sorry about? Nothing."

The Tal Afar castle was the second monument they witnessed being demolished. This time when the prisoners protested, the gunmen shot three of them. They fell to the ground, stained with blood.

The rest of the prisoners tried to run to the injured men, but a pickup truck drove at them and dispersed the crowd. Two gunmen got out of the vehicle and took the three wounded men into the car. Another shouted through the loudspeaker, "They will go to the hospital for treatment, but we do not want to hear your voices anymore as we carry out our jihad missions. Otherwise, we will fight you. We will now go demolish the rest of the idols because they are *haraam*. Graves, too, should not be higher than an inch above the ground."

It was a long and draining day. At its end, when darkness fell, they took them to Kasr al-Mihrab village. They told them to choose from the village whatever houses they wanted to live in until the rest of their family members arrived.

Shammo wanted to make sure he understood what they were saying. He approached the speaker and asked, "Did you say you would bring the rest of our families here?"

"Yes, tomorrow morning we will bring them, as these homes will be the core of a good society," the man answered. "Each one of you will have a role in building this village which, starting from today, is to be called the Village of the Faithful."

"Call it whatever you want, brother. The important thing is that Helen, Elias, the boys, and the girls, and all the rest of our group are with us," said Shammo.

"What's your job?" asked the man.

Shammo was late in answering, so Azad replied instead, "This is my father, and he does circumcisions."

"I'm glad you told me this. We will need his services here for sure. My name is Ali Economist. I'm a specialist in economics. Whatever you need, I am here." The man extended his hand to Azad, so he shook hands with him.

Azad entered the first house he saw. Shammo came along too, then motioned for Cutto to join them, and he did. They did not notice that the house was missing a door until the next morning. Were there any signs of their relatives coming? Seeing guards posted along the street, Shammo approached one and was motioned to halt. "Do not leave your homes. We will call a meeting with you shortly."

Half an hour later, an announcement was made, giving the instruction to gather at the big square at the end of the street. There, armed men stood in front of the prisoners. Other guards appeared on the street behind them, surrounding them. An Organization member stood in front of the line of prisoners and addressed them: "Listen, my brothers. We want you to help us in building a good society, and in return we will protect you and bring your families to you. We will give you ration cards so that you receive food every month."

"Why? How many months will we stay here?" asked Shammo.

Azad breathed a sigh of relief. It seemed they hadn't heard Shammo's question, as they did not respond. He whispered, "Don't talk to them, Dad."

The armed man continued: "You are 276 men. Seventy-five of you will be working on construction. We want to build a big mosque here so we can all attend and pray together. Twenty-five men will work in the municipality to clean the streets. Twenty-five men will herd sheep as they graze and will also collect hay. Twenty-five men will plant and care for trees. Fifty men can work in the administration and offices of the jihadis. Twenty men will transport goods to offices. Fifteen men will distribute food. Thirty-five men will make explosive devices. One will do circumcisions. The five remaining are for emergency work. Abu Mu'taz will now give you jobs and will write down the names of your family members so that we can bring them to you."

When he said this, he was staring at Azad and Shammo. He motioned for Azad to approach.

"Listen, brother. Tell your father to stop his questions, as it is safer for him. I swear by God if he was not specialized in circumcisions, we would have gotten rid of him immediately. Understood?"

Azad lowered his head and returned to his place. His father looked at him, wondering, but Azad remained silent.

The day passed, and their families did not come. In the evening, the men ran outside at the sound of car horns, but this was only an invitation for them to come out and face the gunmen.

Standing in front of the houses, the man with the loudspeaker said, "The women were delayed, but news came to us that they will be arriving soon, God willing. So do not worry about that. Married women will reach their families. As for the unmarried women, they are owned by the fighters as a mission of jihad."

"No, I do not accept this," shouted one of the prisoners. "I want my entire family."

"Yes, we all want our entire families," Cutto shouted.

Azad poked his father to stop his questions, which had started with "Why is that so?" and "How come you do everything your way?" He continued despite Azad's warnings. "Let's understand, son, what is going on here. This is not right."

Other prisoners joined the shouting. They left their places and gathered in the middle of the street, raising their hands in the gunmen's faces.

They started shooting randomly. Some prisoners fell to the ground, and others retreated behind the fences of the houses. Blood streamed from the prisoners who fell while other prisoners ran to embrace them. They all shouted in the faces of the armed men. They were too angry to care anymore about the bullets that confronted them.

Shammo moved in front of Azad to protect him, but Azad pulled him hard, trying instead to shield his father, and they both tumbled to the ground. The gunmen stopped shooting.

One of them called to the prisoners. "Go inside, and we will deal with you tomorrow."

The prisoners did not move until an armed man shouted from his pickup truck, "Move away from here. Let us take the wounded to the hospital."

After another car approached, armed men threw the dead and wounded into the two cars.

Cutto lay on the ground near the fence of their house. He checked himself out and found no wounds on his body. He spotted Shammo and Azad and said to them, "Come inside. Let's make a plan."

Once indoors, Cutto told them, "Once it's dark, I'm getting out of here. Do you want to go with me? We can jump from the house's roof in the back. There are no guards behind the houses."

Shammo and Azad exchanged looks, then Shammo said, "But what if our families come and don't find us waiting for them?"

"You believe that?" asked Cutto. "Do they have any honor to keep a promise? They are lying and will not bring our families."

Shammo looked to his son, awaiting his opinion.

Azad said, "If we wait a day or two, and if it turns out that they are actually lying, we'll run away."

"I can't bear to stay here any longer," Cutto said. "Let me try first. If I succeed, you can follow my lead later."

After one hour's sleep that night, Shammo woke to the sound of gunshots outside. Azad was awake as well. With the first rays of the sun, they, like the rest of the prisoners, took to the street after being summoned by the car horns.

A gunman with very thick eyebrows and a long beard but no mustache, raised the loudspeaker to his mouth and said, "Today we redistribute the tasks among you because your number has decreased to 213. Last night, some of you tried to escape, but they failed."

He raised his voice. "We have told you: be brothers to us, and we protect you. But some of you chose to violate the will of God, so we could do nothing but fight. This is the fate of traitors. They end up in a hole. As you saw, we treated your wounded in hospitals because we wanted to give them a second chance so that they might be well guided. You said you became Muslim, but it seems that some of you were lying to us. We promised you to bring your families to you, and indeed they are now on the way here. Abu Qutaiba will now write your names again and redistribute your tasks."

Azad was assigned work in the management offices. He was standing with the rest of the people given this task when he spotted his father wiping away tears. It was the first time Azad had ever seen his father cry. Not even at funerals of relatives.

Some of the prisoners went to work in groups and some as individuals, depending on the orders of the armed men. Ali Economist motioned Azad into the car with him, saying, "I will take you to a warehouse to help me move some stuff to the management center."

"All ready," said Azad.

After a period of silence in the car, Ali said, "Listen, you are a good person, and I want you to talk to your group to urge them not to flee. Last night we had to kill a large number of your group. They ended up in a big hole. We don't want you all to end up there."

"Can you take me to the hole?" Azad asked.

"Why?"

"I want to see if my friend is among them."

"When we're done, we'll pass by there, and I'll let you take a look," Ali said. Just then, his phone rang. "Next week," he said to the person on the line and hung up.

"That was my daughter," Ali said to Azad. "She asked me when I am going to be back home."

Azad was surprised to hear this, as if he did not expect the man next to him to be a human being who also had children.

"Are you married?" Ali asked him.

Azad hesitated to answer and then said, "No." He was afraid they would take his wife from him if he uttered the truth. She must have been worried about him being this late, but at least she was safe with the baby, and he would try to survive for them. He would be patient in order to return to them safely.

"Whenever you become a true jihadi," Ali said, "you can marry whoever you want, and even if you are martyred, you will meet a nymph in heaven. Your jihad will not go in vain."

"God willing," Azad replied. But in his heart, he said, *God willing, you will be martyred so you are disappointed, finding no nymph waiting for you.*

"I have three wives," Ali said. "The last one is a real jihadi. She left her husband and joined us."

"She divorced her husband?" Azad asked.

"He was beating her every day," said Ali. "Despite that, she could not get rid of him until she joined the Islamic State."

———

In the evening, Azad returned to his father, exhausted—not only because of all the boxes that he'd carried but because of the corpses he'd seen piled up in that hole. When his father looked at him, inquiring, Azad said, "Cutto was not among the dead. I saw them with my own eyes. Some were lying facedown, so I couldn't recognize them, but it did not seem to me that Cutto was there. Among the dead, I did not see a hand as big as his."

———

Tasks varied, and everyone started doing a bit of everything. Azad gained new experiences in building, repairing, cultivating, and even reciting the call to prayer in the mosque, which he helped to build, also bringing microphones to its large hall.

The sun shone more than 120 times on the Village of the Faithful and its prisoners, who were forced to work without pay except for the food that kept them alive. The prisoners had a special kind of hope that was not unlike despair. When hope is repeated every day, despair becomes as familiar as hope itself. Over time, they become so similar that it is difficult to tell them apart.

The guards no longer stood in the streets. They moved to the outskirts of the village to control who went in and out. Yet it was not easy for the prisoners to flee, as they had no means of transportation other than their feet. They needed to walk at least seven hours to get out of the danger zone, crossing areas where they themselves had planted landmines under the gunmen's supervision. If someone tried to escape, they killed him—hanging him on a tree in front of the other prisoners. When the sun went down, the prisoners would take down his body from the tree and bury him.

—⁂—

On a day of hope—that twin of despair—in mid-December 2014, came the sound of the morning horns: the bus they had been waiting for! Women and children ran from the bus, searching for family members among the prisoners. When located, they hugged so hard and long, they cried. Some found their other halves and relatives, and others did not.

They cried together. Everyone cried. Shammo wiped his tears at the scene of the embracing families, but Helen was not there for him to embrace.

"Is there another bus on the way?" Shammo asked one of the guards, but the latter pretended to be busy on the phone.

An old woman rushed toward Shammo. She was holding the hand of a nine-year-old girl. When she got closer and greeted him, he recognized her as Cutto's mother. The girl's hair had been cut in a very haphazard way, and it was dirty with dust. The edges of her clothes were oddly cut or ripped. She appeared neglected or disturbed.

"Where is Cutto?" Nassima asked him.

Before Shammo could answer, Azad stepped forward, looking around, and whispered in her ear: "Cutto fled."

"What about Amina and Helen?" she asked.

"We had hoped you might have news of them," Azad said. "Weren't you together?"

"I have not seen them since that day," Nassima replied.

The gunmen were bothered by all the questions they were getting, and one of them declared through the loudspeaker: "This is the first group of your families. Stop asking questions, or else whoever comes here will not find you. There are empty houses in the area. All yours. Be patient, for God loves those who are patient."

"There are two rooms in this house that we are in," Shammo said. "Azad and I in one room, and you and Ahlam in the other. Or do you want a house on your own?"

"No, of course we do not want to be on our own," Nassima replied.

Soon after the four of them entered the house with no door, Nassima asked, "Are there scissors here?"

"Not sure," Azad said, "but there are abandoned houses, and I can look for stuff in them. Or I can ask the neighbors. We help each other and share everything. We even found arak liquor. We drank it in secret, as alcohol is prohibited. I would assume scissors are not forbidden."

"What would you do with scissors, Umm Cutto?" Shammo asked her.

"I rescued Ahlam with scissors," Nassima said, "but they took my pair away before they brought us here."

"Is it true? How is that?" Shammo asked, motioning her to sit down. "Azad, make some tea and bring bread. Excuse us for not being hospitable enough," he added, "but this is not our home, as you know. There we would offer you more appropriate food."

"Of course, I know," Nassima said.

"Where did they take you, Umm Cutto?" he asked.

"They separated us from each other at the beginning," she replied. "Oh, they destroyed us. They killed the men before our eyes. They threw them in pits and shot them. They burned the hearts of their mothers."

Nassima could barely breathe as she cried. Azad brought her a bowl of water, and she thanked him. She continued: "A prince bought me as his servant. One day I begged him to bring me Ahlam. He did bring her for two hours and then took her back to the girls' hall. She was allowed to come and visit me once every month. When she arrived the third time, the prince had just died in the fighting. So the guard said someone would come and collect us. I had an idea. I cut Ahlam's hair and messed it up and cut the edges of her clothes. I instructed Ahlam to act crazy when they arrived. She played her role very well, so the person who came to purchase us actually believed she was crazy. He refused to buy us. Another one came, and he refused as well. They said, 'You are useless,' and then brought us here. So I need the scissors in case they change her clothes, so I can cut them again and pretend she's doing it."

They heard a car horn. Azad spotted Ali's car in front of the house, so he went out. He returned a few minutes later and said: "Dad, they want you to come and circumcise some boys."

Shammo stood up and told Nassima, "If we can't find regular scissors, you may use circumcision tools."

The following day, Azad's task was to carry food boxes from the warehouse to the distribution office two streets away from the house. In the end, they gave him his share of food, and Ali said he could leave. On the walk back, Azad entered an abandoned house, hoping to find scissors. While searching, he found a phone charger. He picked it up and left, imagining that if he should find a phone too, he could call random numbers. Perhaps hear a voice from outside these prison walls.

Once back at the house, Azad emptied his bag of tea, bulgur, potatoes, onions, and tomato paste.

"No flour this time?" Shammo asked him.

"Do you know who I met today, Dad?"

"Who?"

"The son of Helen's neighbor. His name is Hameed, and he is a friend of Yahya. He was at the food distribution office."

"Is he a prisoner too?" Shammo asked.

"No, he is Daesh," Azad replied. "He was with them and carrying arms like them."

"Did you ask him about Helen?"

"He left with his group before I could, but he knew me and where I live. He looked embarrassed." From his pocket, he pulled the charger. "I found this, and now I need to find a phone, though I'm not sure if there's service here."

"What does this mean?" Shammo asked.

"Without it, no connection would happen," Azad replied.

"Glory be to God," Shammo said. "Even devices do not function without connection."

14

THE WHISTLE

Helen had always loved the forest in Mosul and the beauty of its giant trees. But seeing them now, a sense of disgust overcame her, as if they were a group of rapists who would take turns with her. The driver had told her only that he was taking her to the "guests' place" because Ayash had died. In the back seat of the car, not knowing where they were going, she covered her eyes with her hands.

She lowered her hands to her lap and looked again out the car window. The moon was full in the sky as it followed her. It kept following her until the driver stopped the car by a building with a sign reading GALAXY WEDDING HALL.

So they had not brought her to the school they took her from, as expected.

The driver placed his pistol in his belt and ordered Helen to enter the hall. Inside, more than 150 women sat on the floor, but the driver told Helen to follow him to a side room. There he handed her over to a young man seated behind a desk. The driver said, "This is Ayash's widow," and left.

The young man wrote something on the paper in front of him and, without looking up, said, "Wait there in the hall until your turn comes."

Shocked to see this young man in front of her, Helen said: "Hameed?"

As she was wearing the niqab, Hameed did not recognize her at first, but he knew her voice.

"Aunt Helen?"

"What are you doing here, Hameed?"

He was silent for a moment before answering, "Just work."

"Take me to your house so that I can see my daughter."

Once again, he kept silent, looking down, and then said, "This is very difficult for me."

Helen looked at him with tears in her eyes.

"I will try my best to help you," he whispered, "but for now you should go to the hall."

Helen did as he said, feeling as if she were in a strange dream. Children she had loved and looked after grew older and grew long beards, and now they gave her orders. She sat on the floor with the other women and looked around, hoping to see Amina. Some of the women were wearing the niqab, and it was difficult to distinguish them, but she spotted a sleeping Layla in the corner of the hall.

Helen crawled to her through the small gaps between the women and whispered her name. Layla opened her eyes. Helen smiled at her and said, "I am Helen. Do you remember me?"

Layla nodded and then said, "I saw you in my dream two days ago."

"Really?"

"You were with Mayada, and she was playing with a little ball."

"Who is Mayada?" asked Helen.

"Your daughter."

"Her name is Mayada?"

"That was her name in the dream."

A woman entered the hall and announced that they had to get in line to take a bath and change their clothes. A merchant had bought them in bulk and would sell them individually in Raqqa.

After encountering Hameed, Helen was disappointed to leave. She had been hoping he might still help her, despite his terrible job. Seeing him there had been a shock. But after three hours, her hope was gone: the women were ordered onto a bus that would take them to Raqqa. But the bus was not large enough to fit all the women, so some of them had to ride in small cars.

Helen was sitting on the bus next to Layla when a young man boarded and said: "Which of you is Helen? Come down."

When she got off the bus, he told her to follow him. In the distance, she saw two young men with Daesh headbands around their heads, so she thought they would rape her. She stood in her place and said to the young man who was walking two steps in front of her, "May God protect you, let me go with the rest of the girls. I'm sick."

"Move quickly. Don't stop," he said.

When she reached the men in headbands, she saw that Hameed was one of them. Standing next to a car with an open trunk, he said, "Get in quickly."

Helen got in, and before Hameed closed the door on her, she lifted her eyes to him and said, "A girl named Layla is with me. She's on the bus. Let her come with me, please."

"That's a risk, and we want to move quickly. We'll see," Hameed said. He closed the trunk, and she was in the dark.

Minutes later, they opened the trunk again, and Layla joined Helen. They curled up to make the space enough for them both.

The car went back to the caravan, waiting for the signal to head toward Syria.

"I'm about to die of fear," said the young man sitting next to Hameed. "What if they find out? That's Abu Tawfiq coming toward us. I swear he's going to slaughter us."

Hameed lowered the car window and said to Abu Tawfiq, "Are we leaving now?"

"The order hasn't come yet," Abu Tawfiq replied.

"Our car is old, and sometimes it breaks down. What if we go ahead of you so that we won't be late?" asked Hameed.

Abu Tawfiq signaled to them to go ahead, and they pulled away with a sigh of relief.

Hameed turned his head a little bit toward Helen and said loudly so she could hear him back in the trunk, "In one of these houses is your brother. I don't know which one exactly, but once we stop, you're both to get out quickly, and of course don't let anybody know about this. The people in these houses are all captives, and they may tell you where your brother's house is. We cannot do more than this because we must get back right away to join the caravan."

Once the car stopped and Hameed opened the trunk, they got out and quickly walked away. Helen grabbed Layla's hand, and they fled to the nearest house, which was deserted. But the kitchen tap worked, and they drank from it.

"Is Azad really here?" Helen muttered. "I'm afraid they will catch us if we walk on the street."

Overcome with exhaustion, Helen and Layla found themselves sleeping on the floor. The next day, Helen kept watch at the window.

She glimpsed long-bearded Azad as he walked quickly in front of the house. She hesitated a little because she was not sure whether this person was Daesh and looked like Azad or was Azad and looked like Daesh. She released a whistle that meant in mountain language, "I'm here."

Azad froze in his place when he heard Helen's whistle. He looked back and turned around. And when he was in front of the house, Helen let half of her body out of the door, and Azad hurried to her, looking stunned. She hugged her brother for a long time, wetting his long beard with tears.

"I thought you were Daesh," she said, pulling away and wiping her tears.

"I am not allowed to shave my beard, just my mustache," he said.

He went out to the street and looked right and left, then came back and said, "Hurry. We're going to the third house from here."

Helen held Layla's hand, and they all walked quickly, entering the doorless house.

Shammo exited the bathroom and found himself face-to-face with Helen. He embraced her as she wept on his shoulder. They all cried.

"What brought you here?" Helen asked.

"We were looking for you," Azad replied.

"Was Amina with you?" Nassima asked Helen.

"I only saw her for one minute, and then they separated us," Helen said.

"We scattered like sumac seeds," Shammo said, looking at Helen's young companion.

"This is Layla," Helen said. "Since she is ten years old, they separated her from her family."

"Like Ahlam," Nassima said, standing aside and pointing to Amina's daughter, Ahlam. "Also, they think she's crazy," she added.

"Perhaps it is normal to be crazy here," said Helen.

Shammo bent down and smiled at the shy girl. "What is your full name, Layla?" he asked.

"Layla Hassan Khan."

Shammo thought a little and then said: "Do you have a brother named Zedo?"

"Yes, he is younger than me."

"I circumcised your brother. You are from Tal Qasab, right?"

"Yes."

"Zedo?" asked Helen. "Wait a minute, what is your mother's name, Layla? Is her name Ghazal?"

"Yes, that is her," Layla answered.

Helen opened her mouth in surprise and added: "I met your mother! And with her was Zedo and your little sister."

"Where were they? Was my dad there too?"

Helen was silent. Right now was not the time to tell Layla that her mother Ghazal had seen her father being killed and that she had lost her voice.

"I did not see your father," Helen replied as she remembered how Ghazal had motioned to Helen, urging escape.

The happy group was startled by the horn of Ali's car.

"Go to the bedroom. Sometimes Daesh enter without warning," Azad said and quickly departed.

—␣—

His mission on that last day of 2014 was to clean up Ali's office, and he took great care of it. When he'd finished, Azad said to Ali, "I want to ask you a favor, please."

Ali regarded him silently, waiting to hear.

"Yahya and Yassir, my nephews, are at the Raqqa training camp, and I miss them. Could they come to visit me?"

After a pause, Ali said, "I know that fighters have two days off each month. I will ask and let you know."

"Thank you so much," Azad said, filling a box with Organization pamphlets. He was about to say "Happy New Year," but he refrained, fearing this was *haraam*. Azad put the box on top of another when he heard Ali stuttering on the phone, trying hard to say something he couldn't, as if his tongue was heavy. The phone fell from his hand. He tried to pick it up and couldn't. He fell on the floor. It looked as if he had lost control of himself.

Azad rushed to his side and tried to rouse him, but Ali had lost consciousness.

Azad ran out to the street and stopped the first car he saw. He asked the driver to take Ali to the hospital. The man helped Azad get Ali into the car.

Azad accompanied Ali to the hospital and stayed with him in the emergency room until late that night. The driver, who was a member of the Organization, informed the hospital administration that Azad was a prisoner, so they needed to monitor him. In the end, they moved Ali to another room and instructed Azad to leave, arranging for a driver to take him back to his house.

———

In the kitchen, he recounted the events with Ali over tea with Helen, and she said, "I wish you had let him die. The fewer of them, the better. Anyway, when are we running away from here?"

"I have been thinking about this since the first day we arrived, but I have not done anything about it because it would be so hard for Dad. Escape would require walking long hours, and that would be difficult for him. Also, another reason prevents us," Azad replied.

"What's that?" asked Helen.

"Yahya and Yassir are at the training camp in Raqqa, Syria."

"What?" Helen looked stunned, as if she could not believe the words.

"Calm down, thank God they are alive."

"I cannot leave without them."

"I know," Azad said.

———

A week later, Ali had recovered enough to return to his job. Azad was also back to clean up Ali's office.

Ali was incredibly grateful. "They told me I would have died had it not been for your swift reaction. I am indebted to you, brother. And I have news for you," Ali added. "There is a man named Khalid Omar. Do you know him?"

"He's my friend and like a brother to me," Azad replied.

"He saw you on the YouTube video of Yazidis entering Islam, and he praised you a lot."

"I am his son's godfather because my father circumcised him in my lap."

"Khalid Omar met Caliph Abu Waleed, and he asked to visit you," Ali said. "It seems he's a relative of the caliph. And because you are in my squad, the caliph called me and asked about you."

"I will be very happy to see Khalid again," Azad said.

———

Azad had just returned to the house from evening prayer when Khalid surprised him with the visit. They exchanged kisses on the cheeks, and Khalid kissed Shammo's hand. He brought with him a box of baklava, cheese pastries, and a bag of salted almonds.

When they were sitting down, Khalid stared at Azad. "Your beard is so long! You look like Daesh."

"No. But when I heard you wanted to see me, I thought that you had joined Daesh," Azad said.

"I am Muslim and not Daesh," Khalid said.

"I know you very well, Khalid."

"Tell me, Azad. Do you need anything from me?"

"I need something important if you can get it."

"I'd be glad to do it."

"I have a charger and need a phone."

"Don't worry, I'll bring you one," Khalid said.

"Phones are not allowed here, so be careful when you bring it."

"They inspected me when I arrived, but rest assured I will hide it well."

On his second visit, January 13, 2015, Khalid was accompanied by a guard and brought them a large bag of bulgur. He said: "I am in a hurry. I only came to deliver this bulgur for almsgiving. But the bag got a little wet, so it needs to be emptied into another bag."

Azad assumed the presence of the guard had prevented Khalid from bringing the phone. After Khalid left, Azad put the bag on the table.

Shammo brought a plastic bowl and said: "I heard him say the bag is wet."

As Shammo emptied the bag in the bowl, a phone fell out with the bulgur seeds. Azad picked it up and said: "Oh, that's why he wanted us to empty the bag."

Another surprise came the following morning when the prisoners went out after being summoned by the car horns. An armed man declared, "We made a deal with the local government to hand over to them the elderly and the disabled in exchange for providing our area with electricity. Buses will arrive shortly to transport the eligible among you to Kirkuk, and from there, it is up to you where you go, so be ready to leave."

Ali approached Azad and said to him, "Your father is not that old."

"He is almost eighty," Azad said.

"He can leave then, unless he wants to stay with us."

"I will ask him," Azad said, wondering if there was anyone who wanted to stay with Ali.

—⁓—

Shammo was bewildered and reluctant when the announcement came through the loudspeaker that the buses were ready.

"How can I leave you here?"

"It is better for all of us that you go," Azad said.

"So you get rid of me?"

"No, so that you can help save us. Listen, Dad, memorize this number, and when you arrive in Kurdistan, give it to someone so that they can communicate with me. I have a phone now, but I don't know any numbers."

The horn blew again, so Shammo had to hurry now to catch the bus.

"How can I memorize the number this quickly?" Shammo said. "Write it for me, my son, on a little sheet of paper that I can hide in my clothes."

Azad picked up a pen but could find no paper. Nassima ran in with a pair of scissors and cut a small piece of Ahlam's dress, giving it to him.

"How smart," Shammo said. "You can solve any problem with scissors."

Many of the men and women in the line for the bus walked with canes. When it was Nassima's turn to board, the person at the door looked at Ahlam and asked, "Is she with you?"

"She is mentally disabled," Nassima whispered, and he allowed them to get on.

The day after their departure, eight prisoners fled successfully, and this angered Daesh, so they imposed a curfew in the area for three weeks. Silence prevailed in the village, interrupted only by the crowing of a rooster in the early morning and the noise of generators at night.

The prisoners heard that Daesh had destroyed more archaeological sites and burned the central library of Mosul, turning its priceless books and historical manuscripts to ash. Those books, in Daesh's opinion, brought atheism and thus were something demonic.

"It reminds me of Hulagu, who invaded Baghdad and threw its books in the Tigris," Helen said to Azad over breakfast. She had visited the central library once with Elias, and she remembered well the building's four floors, its old architectural style and longitudinal windows. Helen wiped her tears as she recalled studying the library's rare antiques with her husband. He had been fascinated by a sand timer used to measure the passage of time by the flow of fine sand from its upper bulb. *How much sand will flow before I see you, Elias?* Helen wondered.

After the curfew ended, members of the Organization announced their decision to transfer the prisoners to Tal Afar. They would move them in two rounds. When they summoned the houses in the first round, Azad's was among them.

Helen hid the phone under her clothes because Daesh usually inspected men, while they didn't approach the veiled women. This would be the first time Helen and Layla had gone outside the house. They had to be careful, lest the Organization discover they'd been smuggled from the wedding hall. It was the niqab, their shield, that protected them. They quickly headed to the first group gathering by the buses, mixing in with other families.

Once in Tal Afar, the armed men again ordered the prisoners and their families to enter and occupy any of the abandoned houses there. This time, however, there were also Daesh families living in the area. The prisoners helped each other, carrying furniture and blankets, whispering that their lives would become harder with Daesh families next to them.

Two days passed, and the second round of prisoners did not come. The first group started asking Organization members about their relatives and friends. On the third day, when Azad went with Ali to help him move a refrigerator to his office, he asked, "Where are the rest of our group?"

"Don't ask about them," Ali said.

<hr />

Finally, the group of prisoners received an answer that made them weep and wring their hands. Daesh had killed the men from the second group and sold their women and children. That news was leaked to them by a female neighbor whose husband was a member of Daesh. But why did they do this to the second group and not the first? None of the remaining captives knew if there was a reason or if the decision had been made randomly.

———

It was a cool April day in 2015 when Helen, in the living room, felt the phone vibrating under her clothes. When she took it out and looked at its screen, she saw a message and Abdullah's name.

But just then, Azad heard a car horn and said, "Hide the phone quickly. Ali has arrived."

After Helen watched the car drive away with Azad heading to work, she sent a text: *Hello, my dear cousin. This is Helen.*

An answer came immediately: *Where are you?*

Tal Afar.

Can you escape?

Not now, I will let you know after Yahya and Yassir come. We will all leave together.

Okay. Be well.

———

On that day, Azad's work duties were different. He'd been tasked by Ali to pack a large car with improvised explosive devices. Naturally, he did this with great caution, lest one blow up in his face. He also had a strong headache and was very tired.

"What's wrong?" Ali asked him.

"My head is about to explode," Azad replied.

Ali stopped at a pharmacy and bought him several paracetamol pills.

"Thanks," Azad said.

"I wanted to tell you that I did not forget your request to see your nephews. I met them yesterday. Masha'llah, very intelligent boys."

When Azad did not respond, Ali added, "They will come to visit you on the last Friday of this month. I will bring them with me to the mosque, and we will meet you there after the noon prayer."

———

Azad went to the mosque at six A.M. to clean the hall and fill its tank with water before the noon prayer. He joined the praying men, and when he turned his face to the right, he glimpsed the boys with Ali. A second look confirmed they were Yahya and Yassir.

He waited for the prayer to finish, then hurried over to them.

"Tomorrow morning, Abu Sufyan will stop by and pick them up on his way to the camp," Ali said and left.

Azad hugged them and tried to talk to them, but he got little response. He didn't know what to say. He wanted to tell them that their mother would be thrilled to see them, but for some reason he refrained from talking. Yahya was now seventeen and Yassir twelve. They were in their Afghan outfits, knee-length shirts and baggy trousers.

They left the mosque and walked silently down the street together, Azad casting stealthy looks at them every minute or so. Moving without any expression, they looked like robots.

The uneasy feeling deepened when they entered the house and did not show very much emotion at being reunited with their mother, though Helen almost passed out with elation. Even when she removed her niqab and revealed her face, their reaction was muted.

Helen brought out lunch, which was bread, eggs, and tomato. When they had finished eating, Azad served tea.

"I want to tell you that you have a little sister," Helen said. "She'll turn one on July 10th."

"Where is she?" Yassir asked.

"With Hameed's mother," Helen replied, wiping away a few stray tears.

Azad went closer to the boys and spoke in lower tones. "Listen well. We have an opportunity to escape from here, but we waited for you so we could all go together. Friday is the best day to flee. At prayer time, the roads are clear of passersby."

Yahya and Yassir exchanged looks.

"We didn't want to escape without you," Helen said.

"We won't come with you," Yahya said. "Before us is a big task, greater than the family. Our family is the entire Islamic State, and we strive to make the State win. The rest of the world's nations only pursue money. They conspire to weaken and eliminate Muslims. Western countries interfere in the Islamic world and sow disputes and wars. Colonialism tries to divide and rule, but our State rules with justice. And in the end, the whole world will become fair under the banner of the Islamic State."

"All religions call for justice," Azad said.

"But Islam is the final religion," Yahya said. "If it was not an integrated religion, God would send another prophet to complete it."

"And you, Yassir, what do you think?" Azad asked.

Yassir shrugged his shoulders. But Helen was looking intently at him, as if awaiting his answer. Finally, he said, "It is not right to disappoint our group. They trust us and tell us we are among the best Muslims because we converted with satisfaction and faith."

Helen jumped to her feet and shouted, "Your *group* raped your mother, and even this child Layla was raped. Her father is missing, and your father is missing too."

"Calm down, Helen," said Azad. "Remember, we didn't even believe the Organization would bring the two boys for us to see. Let's not spoil this meeting."

Helen's sleep that night was interrupted several times. In the morning, the two boys were ready to go.

"I heard you have leave every month," Azad said as they gathered their bedrolls.

"We'll be waiting for you next month, okay?" Helen asked.

Yassir looked at Yahya, and he nodded.

Helen made cheese sandwiches and tea, and before the end of breakfast, Abu Sufyan's car arrived. Azad went outside to greet him, asking him to give them a minute.

Helen hugged the boys, kissed them, and sent them off with tea and a sandwich for Abu Sufyan. From the window, she watched them drive away, then turned toward Azad, whispering, "How did the Organization manage to brainwash our boys like that?"

15

GOOFBALL

ike the rest of Sinjar's people, the life of Abdullah the honey merchant changed forever on August 3, 2014, when his family left home. They joined an exodus of thousands forced to flee from their homes, carrying their children on their backs while behind them the dust was rising. Among the desperate were hospital patients who had left their beds and women about to give birth. They struggled to walk seven hours through the mountain's green woods and over its rustic brown rocks to reach the cave where they would shelter, a natural refuge like their grandmothers' laps.

Along the way, some footsteps slowed and could not continue. They stayed behind. Some Sinjaris, in the middle of the journey, turned back and returned to their homes. They had heard that members of the Organization were announcing through loud-speakers that the reason they had come to Sinjar was to change the government, not to harm people or interfere in their affairs.

Other Sinjaris hesitated too long before leaving their homes. Now, appearing in front of their thresholds were menacing Daesh cars with black flags.

Abdullah took with him only his cell phone and bread and honey. His mother had just left the hospital after heart surgery. Yet instead of taking rest for recovery, she joined the convoy, walking with Abdullah and his wife and their two sons and two daughters.

His older daughter had asked him whether they would return to their home or if she should take her belongings with her.

He had answered that they would return.

On the way, Abdullah called his brother-in-law and found him still at home. Urging him to leave as soon as possible, Abdullah said, "No, I don't think they'll leave us alone. I don't trust those extremists. They call us infidels and consider our food and water dirty. How can I trust them?"

The first week in the cave passed. The hundreds of gathered Sinjaris were struggling to decide whether to stay or attempt to return to their homes. Food and water were already running low, even as people shared what they could like one large family.

The painful sight of babies crying for milk pushed Abdullah and a few other men to milk a stray goat wandering in search of water. Abdullah said, "It is not fair to take her milk and not give her water."

Their water was not enough. Abdullah held out one bowl of water and was suddenly surrounded by a herd of goats. He journeyed two hundred meters down the valley with the bowl in hand and the goats behind him. He knew where there was a big water basin, and it was worth the risk. Once there, he opened the tap for the goats to drink while he hid behind an adjacent barrel, as Daesh were nearby, perhaps just another two hundred meters away.

After a few minutes, he turned off the tap and returned up the mountain with the herd behind him. Their original shepherd must have left them to join the convoy. The animals probably thought Abdullah was his replacement.

On the walk back, Abdullah saw people gathered on the path around the fallen corpse of an old woman. Next to her was an empty water bottle. He understood from them that she had stopped walking at that spot after asking her family to continue going up and return later, that she only needed to rest a little. She had refused to take water from her grandchildren and had persuaded them that the bottle in her hand was enough. "She died of thirst," said her son, crying. The water bottle he had brought back to her was too late. But he was able to save an old man who lay near the dead's body. He was about to die of thirst too.

The next evening, the goats came back, running toward the people stationed on the mountain, as if wanting to exchange milk for water again. Children drank the goats' milk and shared it with their grandparents. The herd appeared in this way for several consecutive days, until finally the Sinjaris dared to venture up to the nearby fruit and vegetable farms to pick and eat from them. But soon after they arrived, they lost their appetite.

This was the moment they learned that the rest of their relatives who were late or had stayed behind in their homes had fallen into captivity. The Sinjaris sat on the ground and cried, tired and in pain. A clergyman, trying to calm them down, said, "Our God, who sent us that herd to save our children from hunger and thirst, knows how to save us from this crisis."

After a week of life on the mountain and enduring hunger and thirst and the cold of the night without blankets, they began to spread over the villages of the mountain and in other rugged areas too difficult for non-mountain folks to reach.

Abdullah brought more than a hundred people with him to his uncle's house in the village of Halliqi. No one was home but Ramziya. He asked her, "Where's Shammo?"

"I don't know. They all went to Helen's house and never returned," she replied. "Did you hear anything? And is it true that a gang came to our area to steal girls?"

When she did not receive an answer, Ramziya started to howl. "O, owelli, owelli, neither my night is night, nor my day is day. It is the end of the world." She sat on the ground, crying and singing funeral tunes. Around her, a crowd gathered, also singing and crying. She took a handkerchief from her pocket, wiped her nose, and said, "Thank you all for coming here. Sadness wants company. If Shammo was here, he would invite you to pick figs from the garden. Please go ahead and do that as much as you like. I am going to bake."

Ramziya took out all of her stored bags of flour and started to knead.

By that evening, more people arrived in Halliqi until there was no room for any additional feet. They slept in the orchards, using stones for pillows, grass for beds, and large pieces of nylon as their covers. A newcomer who arrived a few days later said he had heard that a Daeshi caliphate had announced a prize for those of his men who could climb the mountain and raise the Daesh flag above it. The prize was to be female captives.

"What do you say?" an old man asked. "Did they go up?"

"No, a helicopter bombed them," the man replied. "I don't know where it came from, but it landed and took some of our people from the mountain. Others waited for the helicopter to return and take them as well, but it did not come back."

"We should not stay here any longer," another guest said. "We must leave because people here in Halliqi, may God protect them, must be tired of kneading and baking for us."

Another new guest, who'd just arrived at Halliqi, told Abdullah that a group of Kurds in the Syrian Hasaka region were setting up tents to receive the displaced.

When Ramziya's guests grew to more than ten dozen, they gathered to sit on the ground, discussing what to do next. In the end, they stood up like one person, having decided to go to the Hasaka camp. They began to go down to the village of Adika at the foot of the mountain. From there, they could reach the Syrian camp within half an hour by car or six hours by foot.

After two hours of walking, Abdullah's mother was too tired to continue. She sat on the sidewalk, so Abdullah, his wife, and four children also sat down beside her. Abdullah remembered the grandmother who had died from thirst on the rocks of the mountain.

His five-year-old daughter asked him, "Will Daesh come after us, Dad?"

"No, we will not let them," Abdullah said.

She released a sigh of relief, then asked, "Where are we going?"

"To our friends in Syria."

"Will they allow us to watch cartoons?"

At that moment, a car stopped in front of them, and the driver waved to Abdullah.

Abdullah rose and hurried over. It was his friend Saleh, the fig merchant. When Saleh heard of their intended destination, he volunteered to take them. His car was hardly big enough for them all, so Abdullah and his eldest son squeezed into the space at the very back of the vehicle.

The road was incredibly crowded with caravans of people and chickens, cats, dogs, donkeys, camels, and sheep. Abdullah lowered his head, ashamed when he saw some of his relatives walking and could not help them. Their families were large, and this was not his car.

Two hours passed as they sat in traffic, and they still had miles to go.

—*m*—

Getting out of the car, Saleh took Abdullah aside and said that he just received a call from his wife, telling him that all of their neighbors had left their homes and that she and the children were going to die of fear because they had heard that Daesh was on the way to their area.

"Go to them, Saleh, and all of you get out of there immediately," Abdullah said.

"I am sorry to leave you here," Saleh said as he looked toward Abdullah's mother.

"We are now very close to our destination," Abdullah said. "A thousand thanks to you."

—*m*—

On the Syrian border, Syrian Kurds awaited them with large trucks and transported them to the Roche camp. There had been a dust storm, so when it rained, they were covered with mud. They had to choose between staying in the camp or being transferred by car to Iraq—east of the Tigris, because west of the Tigris had fallen under the rule of Daesh. Most of them chose to go back to Iraq, including Abdullah and his family, who were brought to Dohuk. They lived in the skeleton of a large three-story building which had been donated by someone from the area to the displaced.

Abdullah and his family, as well as about eighty other displaced people, were living there when Cutto appeared in the second week of September 2014, having escaped from captivity. The building's inhabitants often gathered on the roof to get fresh air and exchange news. Now they surrounded Cutto, eager to hear any possible news about others who were missing and who else had escaped with him. But he, too, was searching.

A month later, people once again congregated on that roof, this time around Abdullah. On his phone, he had seen a picture of a captive woman put up for sale online.

The blood froze in Cutto's veins when he saw that it was Amina. Beneath her picture was her owner's phone number in Raqqa. Cutto hit his head with his hands and began screaming incomprehensible words.

"I have a friend in Raqqa," Abdullah said. "Let me ask him for help."

Abdullah phoned his Syrian friend, asking him if he could buy a captive woman from Daesh and return her to her people in Iraq.

"You mean to smuggle her?" His friend's voice signaled his apprehension.

"Yes."

His friend fell silent for a short time and then said, "I know one of the cigarette smugglers in the areas under Daesh control.

They are used to danger. Maybe they can help you." Abdullah was given his number.

He called it immediately. "Hello, my name is Abdullah Shrem. I got your number from Sabir Abu Hussein."

"You got it."

"I need your help in smuggling."

"How many packets of cigarettes do you need?"

"First, tell me: Are you sure you can cross the border patrols safely?"

"I know my job. Don't worry about it."

"What I need from you is very important—more important than cigarettes."

"What is it?"

"Can you smuggle a woman?"

There was silence on the line, but the man had not said no.

"You will receive a double reward: from me and from God."

"Where is she?"

"In Raqqa. I have her owner's phone number."

"Raqqa is in a danger zone, but I will not say no to a friend sent by Abu Hussein."

"Thank you. Wait a minute, I don't know your name."

"They call me Goofball."

———

Abdullah gathered his people around him and said, "We need to raise money to pay smugglers and bring back our girls. Contact all your acquaintances, and we'll create a fund to rescue the kidnapped women."

Abdullah's requests for help reached the Yazidi emirs, so they came to the rescue. They donated from their pockets at first, and when the costs increased, they contacted the local government in their area to take over the task for them.

This was the reason the Office of the Abductees Affairs was opened. By the end of November 2014, they had appointed employees to take survivors' statements and worked to coordinate and compensate the rescue costs needed to recover captive women.

Abdullah put on his coat and went up to the roof, as he felt the need for some fresh air, although it was cold that first night of 2015. He stood by the fence, contemplating the reddish sunset. A few minutes later, Cutto came and stood by him. He said nothing, but his broken look made Abdullah guess that he badly needed to hear something new about Amina.

Abdullah called Goofball and asked, "Is there news of the captive woman?"

"My partner is disguised as Daesh and is now monitoring the situation to find the best way to get her out."

"Listen, Goofball," Abdullah said, "Daesh stole thousands of women from us, including my relatives, and I want to give you a big mission. Are you ready for it?"

"It is a shame to have doubts about a prison graduate like me."

"Why were you in prison? You committed a crime?" Abdullah asked.

"Yes. I killed the hunger."

"You mean you stole money?"

"No. I got arrested on purpose."

"Why?"

"In prison, you get food. I was hungry."

"How long were you there?"

"They kicked me out a few days later, so I had to think of a new way to get arrested. But then I fell in love, and after that did not want to go to prison. But Daesh and their control over our lives is not normal. I couldn't control myself and said what I thought of them. I was in trouble again. My sweetheart helped me through her relative, who was a lawyer. By the way, he works in the Daesh court and knows their laws well, though he hates them. He could be useful."

"Great," Abdullah said. "How about we make a network for rescuing the kidnapped women?"

"Let me think about it. It's dangerous work."

"Much more dangerous than smuggling cigarettes?"

"I know. Cigarettes are risky too."

"So is it possible to switch from cigarettes to women?"

"I'll ask others in my group whom I trust and let you know. For example, one of my men is a garbage collector whose monthly salary is $100, but he receives $200 when he smuggles cigarettes. His wife hides them in her clothes because they don't inspect Muslim women. Also, I currently rent a house for hiding cigarettes which I could possibly use to hide captives."

"Excellent, and we would pay them more for our kind of smuggling. Would your group agree to take part?" Abdullah asked.

"I guess so," Goofball said, "but we will have other expenses. Daesh allows women to receive visits, so I imagine that one of our female smugglers might be able to find a way to contact and visit your captive. Then one of our drivers could get her from there to a safe place. Another person takes her to the border. Each one of these people would need to be paid a fee."

"Of course, of course," Abdullah said. "I'll pay any expenses, and when the captives arrive, the Office of the Abductees Affairs will compensate me. They don't give a penny before a kidnapped woman is safely returned, so if one of our rescue operations fails, her family will bear the cost. We should avoid this as much as possible."

"This work is not without risk," Goofball said, "but this is life."

16

SON OF DAESH

Goofball arranged with a female smuggler to distribute free bread to the houses on the street where Amina was kept. The smuggler would present the bread as a charitable gift, and if she managed to get a chance to be alone with Amina, she would offer to help her escape by taking her to a waiting car and driver.

This plan was successfully completed, and the driver gave Amina his phone so that she could speak with Abdullah. He explained the rest of the plan to her. Abdullah recommended that she be especially careful about Daesh spies, so if she spotted them, she should flee and pretend that she was lost.

However, the day of the escape, Amina instead slipped away from Goofball's smugglers and returned to Daesh. Fortunately, her owner had not yet returned home when she arrived back home that night, so he did not even know that she'd gone out.

The last thing Abdullah could imagine was that Amina would escape from the smugglers, but that was what she did. After all the dangers she had gone through, and the smugglers themselves had gone through, to deliver her to the safe house, she had returned to Daesh.

"I can't believe she did this, Goofball," Abdullah said when he got the call.

"I swear," said Goofball. "She went back."

"How do you know?"

"We left her at the safe house last night, with a plan to take her to the border today. It seems that she ran away as soon as we left her. First, we thought that Daesh police found her, but one of the women who work for me called to inform me that she saw Amina returning. When she went and gave her the bread again, Amina avoided looking at her."

"I wish she'd asked Amina why she did that," Abdullah said. "She is free to stay there if she wants, but I want to know why."

After the torture of waiting and feeling humiliated as all kinds of men raped his wife every day, and after the opportunity to rescue her from them, Cutto almost went crazy when he heard what had happened. But then he learned that Amina had with her a newborn baby.

———

On that same mid-January day in 2015, Cutto was reunited with his mother, Nassima, and daughter, Ahlam, who returned from captivity on a bus filled with the disabled and elderly. The Daeshi bus driver had brought them to the Mosul-Kirkuk border—the dividing spot between Daesh and the government of Kurdistan.

After getting off the bus, the freed captives had continued on foot. Once they reached the safe side of the border, they sat on the ground, too exhausted to get back up. Members of the Kurdish Authority were waiting for them there, with a bus parked near the checkpoint to take them to a shelter in Dohuk.

Extremely tired, the people on the ground struggled to rise. Seeing this, nearby street vendors used their small carts to help transfer them to the bus door. The boy who transported Nassima with his two-wheel cart had shoved aside open bags of raisins to make room for her. He lowered the front of the cart to the ground, and she got in. He pushed her to the bus, and before she got off the cart, Nassima took a handful of raisins and put them in her pocket.

Later, sitting on the shelter's floor, Nassima took the raisins from her pocket and gave them to Ahlam. Then journalists came and photographed those returned from captivity. They'd publish and broadcast their arrival so their relatives could locate them and come for them.

A journalist approached an old woman and asked her why she was crying.

She told him that at the checkpoint, they took her blanket and threw it in the garbage, and she had used that blanket during all the days of her captivity, and now she could not sleep without a blanket.

"Don't worry, auntie, I'll get you a new blanket," the journalist promised her.

When the news of the arrivals reached the people in Dohuk, Abdullah accompanied Cutto to the hall. Cutto saw his mother and daughter. Hurrying to their side, he sat with them on the floor, crying.

Shammo stood, leaning against the wall, and when he saw Abdullah coming toward him, he opened his arms widely, just as he used to do in the village. Abdullah asked him about the rest of the family, and Shammo took from under his shirt the piece of cloth with the phone number written on it and said, "This is their number in the Daesh house."

At that moment, a man sitting on the floor grabbed Abdullah's leg, saying, "Oh, my son, you are finally back? I cannot believe my eyes."

Abdullah lowered his gaze to the man and did not recognize him, yet he bent and kissed the man's outstretched trembling hand.

The man smiled at Abdullah and said, "Take me home, Eido. I thought they had killed you. This is the happiest day of my life because you are alive."

Abdullah looked around, unsure what to do. In the end, he had to leave the man, with a heavy heart.

Abdullah wanted to take Shammo to his house in Halliqi, but the road to the mountain was not safe, as there were areas by the mountain under Daesh control. But Shammo told him that he was already going home by helicopter.

"A security man registered my name and asked me if I wanted to go to the camp in Dohuk or go to Zakho by car and from there to Halliqi by helicopter," said Shammo.

"This will be your first time in an aircraft, right?" Abdullah asked.

"I am afraid to get on the helicopter, but I will," Shammo said. "I have been a long time away from home, and Ramziya must be worried."

Cutto and his mother and daughter left the hall for the camp where the three of them would live. But Cutto spent most of his days in the building where Abdullah lived, returning to the tent only at night. This way, he kept up-to-date on Amina. He heard that the female smuggler had found an opportunity to be with Amina alone, saying that someone wanted to talk to her on the phone.

It was Abdullah on the line.

"I want to know why you went back," he said.

"Didn't you tell me if I saw Daesh, to escape from them?" asked Amina.

"Yes."

"The driver took me to a house full of Daesh with their long beards and clothes, and even on the wall of their house there was the Daesh flag and their slogans," Amina said.

"They are not Daesh. They are disguised as Daesh, so they could save you."

"I didn't know that."

"So we have to smuggle you again."

"Yes, please."

"This time do not run away, no matter how long their beards are."

"But I want to wait a little here until I find Ahlam. I heard the Organization killed Cutto and his mother and sold Ahlam."

"No, all of them are here in Dohuk," Abdullah said, "and they are waiting for you."

"You swear to God? You're telling the truth?"

"Believe me."

"Oh my God. This is the best news I've ever heard. When will the bread woman come again?" she asked.

"This Friday," Abdullah replied.

———

For four days, Amina hid in that same smugglers' safe house while the Daesh police searched for her. After that, she walked to the border accompanied by Goofball. The roads had been planted with mines, so she needed his guidance to avoid them. Amina walked slowly while carrying her newborn, and Goofball trod carefully as well.

But when they heard gunshots behind them, Goofball took the baby from Amina and ran, motioning for her to follow, paying no attention to the mines. When the gunfire calmed down, they were at the end of the dangerous road.

Goofball stopped and handed her son back to Amina. "It was only by luck that we made it."

He left a voicemail for Abdullah, informing him of the latest. "When I heard the sound of bullets behind us, I forgot the mines in front of us," Goofball said.

—⁓—

As soon as Amina crossed the Iraqi border, she spotted a large crowd of people on the hill waiting for her.

Her daughter, Ahlam, was the first to hug her. She said, "Who is this baby, Mom?"

"Your brother. His name is Adam," Amina answered, still crying.

Cutto stood behind Ahlam, and said, "Is this son of Daesh?"

Amina did not answer.

"This boy will not enter my house," Cutto said.

Nassima hugged her and turned toward Cutto, saying, "My son, let your wife rest, and leave the rest for tomorrow. Poor one, her face is yellow like turmeric."

—⁓—

With baby Adam in her lap, Amina was transported by people from a humanitarian organization to the survivors' camp in Dohuk. They gave her a tent, some cans, and milk powder for newborns.

Just before sunset, Ahlam came out of the tent and found Cutto standing outside. When she told her mother, Amina put her baby in Ahlam's lap and went out to Cutto.

She looked at him with tearful eyes while he was frozen in place. She hugged him, and he cried.

"Everything that happened to me in captivity was not of my choice," Amina said, "and this boy knows nothing of this world."

"I know, Amina," Cutto said. "He has no guilt, but how can I live with a creature who reminds me every moment of the man—the men who raped you and did all of this to us?"

"This is difficult for me too. The memory of his father disgusts me. But what should I do with an innocent child?"

"It is not only me," Cutto said. "Our whole community will not accept him here."

Amina kept silent.

"We will never forget what they did to us," Cutto added. "As for raising their children, this is too much."

Amina cried and did not say anything.

"As you know, Adam will never become Yazidi," Cutto said. "The clergymen will not change the laws for him."

"The clergymen are not mothers, and they will not understand my feelings," Amina said through tears.

"Come with me tomorrow to the court of civil affairs," said Cutto. "Ask them about the boy's registration, and let's see what they say."

"You promise to come with me and ask them to register Adam?"

"I am not Cutto son of Nassima if I don't keep my promise."

The next morning, carrying Adam, Amina stood beside Cutto in front of the judge and requested that he be officially registered as Cutto's son.

"Adam should follow his father and therefore can only be registered as a Muslim and not a Yazidi, son of Cutto. The Yazidi are only so by birth," the judge said.

"Let's register him in my name then," Amina said.

The judge did not answer.

"Adam Amina," she said.

"This is not permissible," the judge said.

"This is my husband. His official name is Cutto Nassima, and Nassima is his mother. Why is Cutto Nassima permissible and not Adam Amina?"

"His name registration must have happened by mistake," the judge said.

"What should we do now?" Cutto asked the judge.

"The boy must be taken to the Orphans Center, and you can visit him whenever you like," said the judge.

As they were leaving the building, Amina asked Cutto, "What if we don't follow the judge's order?"

"Let's take him there even if only temporarily, and then I will see if among my Muslim acquaintances, someone can take him and return him to you," Cutto said.

"Will they do that?" she asked.

"Our Muslim acquaintances buy female captives from Daesh and return them to us, so why can't they do that for Adam?"

"If so, then let's take him to the center," Amina said.

All the way back to the camp, Amina could not stop crying.

"Will you come with me tomorrow to see him?" she asked her husband.

"Yes, I'll go with you," Cutto replied.

"I love you," she said.

He embraced her as she continued to cry on his shoulder.

"I'm so lucky they didn't kill you," Amina said. "They killed so many of our men."

"I ran away. They shot at us and killed some of those who were with me," Cutto told her, lifting the edge of his pants to show her a scar on his leg.

"Ah, the scars they left on us will never go away. What have we done to them to harm us like this?" Amina asked.

"Even people of their religion are astonished by their deeds," Cutto said. "But I'll also never forget the family that helped me while I was between life and death. I had been running with my wounded leg and lost a lot of blood. I kept falling down until I knocked on the door of a house. When I asked for water, they gave me water, food, and shelter, and they took me to a doctor who was their relative. I stayed three weeks in their home. On top of that, they apologized and said, 'Daesh damages our reputation as Muslims.'"

―⁓―

The next day, Nassima fell sick with a stomachache that intensified, and she began vomiting. Cutto took her to a clinic. Cutto's promised visit to the Orphans Center was postponed by two days. When he and Amina did go to see Adam, Ahlam asked to come along.

But at the center, Amina received a shock. Adam had been adopted by a Syrian family, and they had just left with him.

"How did this happen in just two days?" Amina screamed.

"Boys are more desirable than girls, so they take them quickly," the woman said.

"Who took him? How do I know they will really take care of him?" Amina asked.

"They are a husband and wife without children, living in Deir Al-Zour. This is the address," said the woman. She picked up a pen to write the address for Amina.

"I am going there," Amina announced.

"I'll go with you," Cutto said.

"Me too," Ahlam added.

"No, I'm going by myself," said Amina. "I will wear the niqab, so they don't recognize me. You, Cutto, can't wear the niqab."

"But I can," Ahlam said.

"No, my love, you are staying here with Dad until I return," Amina replied.

Cutto was bothered by Amina's decision, but he knew that she was stubborn and that no attempt to convince her would work.

"Here's my new phone number," Cutto said.

Back in the camp, when Nassima learned that Amina had gone to Deir Al-Zour in Syria, holding Ahlam's hand, she asked Cutto, "How could you let her go like that?"

Cutto did not answer.

Two days passed, and there was no news from Amina. "My heart is uneasy," Nassima added.

"My phone rang a few times and was cut off," said Cutto, standing in front of their tent. "I called the number that appeared on the screen and did not get an answer."

His phone rang again.

"Here it is again," Cutto added, putting the phone on his ear.

"Are you related to Amina?" asked the person on the other end.

"I am her husband."

"She is in intensive care, and we found your phone number with her."

"Why? What is the matter with her?"

"Deir Al-Zour was bombed. Her driver was killed, and she's wounded."

"Which hospital?"

"Deir Al-Zour Hospital."

"Mama is sick?" Ahlam asked.

"Yes," Cutto replied, trying to control himself.

He avoided his mother's questioning look and went away from them to cry.

After, he phoned a relative of his who was a driver, asking if he could take him to Deir Al-Zour.

"Give me half an hour, and I'll let you know," said Cutto's cousin.

—⁓—

Cutto was waiting on the street across from the survivors' camp. It was raining heavily when his phone rang on that third day of February 2015. He assumed his cousin the driver was calling him back.

But it was a nurse on the line, who told Cutto that Amina had died of her wounds. The words hit Cutto like a bolt of lightning. He did not say a word, and his tears could not be distinguished from the raindrops on his face.

17

WHEN SHE CLOSES HER EYES

Layla noticed that Helen closed her eyes for long periods of time without being asleep. She did this several times during the day while sitting. Layla wondered if she was praying. She did not want to interrupt her.

But if she had asked her, Helen would have answered that she did it because she saw her missing people whenever her eyes were closed. She went to them in her mind because they didn't come to her. She took time each day to be alone with them. She kept her eyes closed as tightly as possible because she wanted to see them for as long as possible. Sometimes they talked to her. Other times they looked at her without talking. Elias told her, "I love you." She asked him "When are you coming?" He gave her that deep look and disappeared, as tears flowed from her closed eyes.

Her daughter did not leave her eyes as quickly as Elias did, but Mayada acted as if she did not know her mother. Helen opened her arms to her, but the little girl didn't respond. She paused a moment, then carelessly stepped toward the table's edge, stumbling like someone who had just learned to walk. Under her two little feet were tiles with square motifs intertwined around drawings of wildflowers.

"Amina? Where are you?" Helen asked as soon as she saw her in her eyes.

Amina, instead of answering, asked, "Why are you still there?"

Helen explained that Yahya and Yassir had changed a lot and did not want to go home with her, and that she, despite this, had not lost hope that she would get them back. Amina, as usual, listened attentively to Helen and waited for her to tell her everything. But first Helen wanted to know where Amina was. When Amina did not answer, Helen changed the question a bit and said, "Are you coming back with us?" Amina shook her head and turned away from Helen's eyes. Helen called for her, but Amina did not come, and Helen grew upset with her.

The pulse of the phone hidden inside her clothes made her open her eyes to read the message:

> *Hello, this is Abdullah. Who is with me?*
> *Hello, my dear cousin. This is Helen.*
> *Your parents ask when you can return.*
> *We were waiting for Yahya and Yassir, but they refused to come with me.*
> *Try to win them over in any way.*
> *With us here is a girl. Her name is Layla, and her family is captive in Mosul. Can you help rescue her family as well?*

Where in Mosul?

In a two-story house—at the end of the street, there's a store that sells tahini and date syrup. It's close by the Galaxy Wedding Hall.

Any other detail that would help us?

The woman is mute, her name is Ghazal, with a boy and a girl. Their jailer is called the desert emir, and he was originally a tailor.

———

Abdullah entered the site of the Islamic State Mall, which sold everything from needles to women, but he did not find Ghazal there. The smugglers network could not find her nor any trace of the desert emir in Mosul.

"Maybe this desert emir sold Ghazal to someone else?" Abdullah asked Goofball.

"Be patient with me. My friend Fawaz can help," Goofball replied.

———

Fawaz had a sewing shop in Mosul, and after he took on the task of searching for the desert emir, he started asking everyone who passed through his shop the same question: "Do you know the desert emir who was a tailor as well? He paid me for textiles, and because of the bombing in the area, he did not come to pick them up, and I want to give him back his money because I work at the door of God and do not take *haraam* money."

After numerous negative answers, in the third week someone said, "Yes, I know him."

"For the sake of God, give me his address so that I can send him back his money," Fawaz asked.

"His house is in Raqqa in front of Al-Rasheed Park, near the National Hospital," replied the man.

———

The smugglers monitored the area until they saw the desert emir. They watched him as he entered his house. Abdullah wrote to Helen, *Ghazal is now in Raqqa and we will try to save her from the desert emir. What's up with you?*

Helen replied: *We are preparing to escape on the last Friday of this month.*

How many people are you?

Three. Azad, Layla, and me.

———

The last Friday of June was the date they set for their escape, the day following one of Yahya and Yassir's visits. They would see the boys for the last time after Helen's failed attempts to persuade them to leave with them.

Four days before that Friday, Azad heard a horn from Ali's car at dawn. He went outside, still in the dishdasha in which he had slept, grumbling at this early morning arrival.

"I will change my clothes and be right back out," Azad told Ali, rubbing his eyes.

"You have only two minutes to do it. It's urgent," Ali said.

But then Ali left Azad in his office and departed without giving him a specific mission. Azad was confused. Hours passed, and Ali did not return nor send any instructions. The evening came, and

Azad thought that Ali might have forgotten him in the office. He was about to go back to the house when Ali finally returned.

"I thought you must have forgotten about me," Azad said.

"I did not forget you, Azad. Because I did not forget you, I brought you here to save your life. You are a good person, and I love you," Ali said.

Azad waited for Ali to explain to him what he meant.

"We got an order today to kill all the captive men and keep women only," said Ali. "I need to hide you somewhere away from this place. If anyone knows you are here, they will kill you and me."

Shocked, Azad didn't know what to say. He was surprised to see Ali risk his life in order to save him from death, but he also felt his blood boiling with anger because the Organization intended to kill his people one by one. How could he leave with Ali and abandon Helen and Layla?

"You must hide here until I manage to get you out of the area," Ali added.

"But I can't cross the checkpoints without a State badge, right?" Azad said.

"You didn't bring your badge?"

"No."

Azad pretended he didn't have the badge as a pretext to return to the house and inform Helen of these developments.

"It's dangerous for you to go home, but let me explore the possibilities," Ali said, and he started making calls.

A few minutes later, he told Azad, "You'll have to hide here until morning because I have an order to go tomorrow to Mosul. I'll take you with me to a spot close to Kirkuk. From there, you can manage on your own. But you have to bring your badge first. Tonight, I'll drive you home so you can quickly get it."

Azad felt a severe headache coming on as he tried to make the decision whether or not to tell Ali about Helen. In the end, he said, "Ali, you have helped me in many situations, and I know the risk you are taking for me now, but there is something I must tell you. My sister is now in the house for the sake of meeting her two boys when they come from the camp during their monthly leave. Can they still come to visit her even if I leave with you?"

"I'll tell Abu Sufyan to bring them and take them back, as usual," Ali replied.

It was after one A.M. when Azad got out of Ali's car and quickly entered the house.

"Oh my God. Where were you?" Helen asked.

Azad briefly informed her of the situation.

"Ah, go quickly," Helen said.

"You're going to run away with Layla in accordance with Abdullah's plan this Friday, right?"

"Yes," Helen replied.

"Don't delay this time, because there is a possibility they will soon move the women to another area," Azad said and left.

Near the last checkpoint before Kirkuk, Ali stopped his car and said to Azad, "If at the crossing, they ask you why you are going to Kirkuk, say you need to buy insulin."

Both got out of the car, and Ali stopped a taxi. He paid the driver to get Azad to the Kirkuk border, five kilometers away. The two men hugged, and Ali put money in Azad's pocket and said, "You might need this."

———

The taxi driver stopped at the Kurdish border and said, "Here is my limit. I can't go any further."

Azad crossed the border on foot. On the other side, he heard a driver calling, "Dohuk, Dohuk."

Azad went to him and asked, "How much is the fare to Dohuk?"

"One hundred fifty thousand dinars," the driver answered.

Azad counted the money Ali had put in his pocket and told the driver: "I only have one hundred thousand dinars."

"Okay, get in," the driver said.

At the Kurdish control, the inspector ordered Azad into a back room to be interrogated.

"Why is your beard so long?" they asked.

"I was a prisoner of Daesh," Azad replied.

"Do you have an identity card?"

Azad took out the Islamic State badge and said: "They took my original ID and gave me this."

The inspector made calls to inquire about Azad's identity to make sure he was actually a prisoner. He asked Azad to tell him his story in detail, and after that, they released him.

When he got out, he couldn't find the driver. Azad sat on a bench at the side of the road, confused and disoriented. Ali the Daeshi had given him money, while this driver from his own people had stolen from him and run away. Or had he waited a long time and then given up because he thought Azad was a criminal and they had arrested him? But shouldn't he have returned the money to him before leaving, since he was not going to take him to the agreed place?

In the midst of his questions, Azad spotted a taxi in front of him. He thought for a moment that the driver had come back, but this was a different driver.

"Taxi?"

As Azad got in, the driver asked, "Where to?"

"To the house of the Yazidi emir in Sheikhan."

"From my eyes."

"May your eyes be well."

"Where are you from?"

"From Halliqi. I just got back from Daesh."

"You swear to God? Is that why your beard is long?"

"I spent almost a year in captivity," Azad said.

The driver stopped at a barber salon and told Azad, "Shave your beard at my expense, and I will return for you shortly."

The driver soon returned and paid the barber his fee.

"Big difference! You look a hundred years younger now," he said to Azad, who was smiling widely.

"Thanks, ah, I feel good. It was itching me," Azad said.

The driver gave him a falafel sandwich and said, "I ate one while you were at the barber's; this one is for you."

Azad was starving, and he found the sandwich especially delicious.

"How much money do I owe you? I'll pay it all when I arrive," Azad said.

"I will take nothing from you," the driver said.

"Why is that?" Azad asked him.

"I had a health problem that prevented me from working for about a month, so I vowed to work three days for free if I recovered.

Since yesterday I have been transporting people for free, so if you want, I can take you to your destination tomorrow as well, but after tomorrow I'll start charging."

"May God protect you," Azad said.

"Thanks, and may He protect your family. Do you have kids?" asked the driver.

"I have a child that I haven't seen yet. I was captured before he was born."

"Oh God," the driver said, shaking his head before introducing himself. "My name's Hoshyar. My seventh grandfather was Yazidi. Well, all of us Kurds, we were Yazidis in the past, and we became Muslims after various invasions. But the language and the customs that we share with you remain, you know. Only the Yazidis who had hidden in the mountains remained Yazidis. And what's your name?"

"Azad. I did hear from my relatives that the mountain has always been our refuge."

"You are now truly 'azad'—free, as your name means."

The car stopped in front of a white building with a front garden. Azad told Hoshyar, "You may come with me into the diwan if you would like to have some rest."

"No, thanks. Are you a relative of the prince?"

"No, but this is the Yazidi public house. I had no money when I got into your car, so I thought of coming here because they would pay you on my behalf. But thank you for everything."

"Welcome back home."

———

In the diwan of the Yazidi emir, they gathered around Azad, listening to his account of all the things that had happened to him.

In a big white hall, he was brought food and tea. Everything in the room was white: walls, curtains, sofas, and furniture.

After one of the emir's assistants made several calls, he told Azad that Shammo had been taken to Halliqi by helicopter.

"So I need a helicopter now to go to Halliqi?" Azad asked.

"No, the areas around the mountain have now been liberated. We can take you by car to the mountain and you can walk from there."

"Thanks. May I use your phone for a minute?"

Azad texted Helen: *I arrived. Tell me you are safe.*

Helen replied: *Praise be to God. My appointment with the smuggler is the day after tomorrow.*

On the night before Yahya and Yassir's next visit, Helen could not sleep as she tried in vain to imagine a life without them. She wanted to be able to postpone their escape plans again if she could not change their minds this time. Finally, the morning came.

Helen tried to take in their presence as much as she could with her eyes. She was silent and did not talk to them about the escape and did not try to persuade them of anything. But she could not stop crying.

"Why are you crying?" Yassir asked her as they were sitting in the living room in the early afternoon.

Helen did not answer.

"Where's Uncle Azad?"

"He went back home, and I'll do the same tomorrow. I am not sure if I'll see you again in this life," Helen said, but she looked at them searchingly.

Yahya and Yassir looked tired, as if they had not slept for days. Their faces were paler than before. Even their voices sounded fractured and faint. It was true that during previous visits, they had behaved in a manner unusual for their young age, as if they had aged several decades, but there was something different about them today.

"We have decided to go back with you," Yahya said.

Helen could not believe her ears. "Is this true, my son?"

"We had decided even before we got here," Yahya said.

Helen stood up and kissed them on their heads, then asked, "But what changed?"

Yahya and Yassir exchanged another sad look. Yassir bowed his head, avoiding her gaze.

"What happened?" Helen asked again.

Yahya hesitated again before saying: "During our training, we saw something terrible." Yahya paused for a moment to collect his breath, then continued. "On screens, they showed us the beheading operations. They said we should learn this and carry it out against our enemies."

"You used to shiver whenever you saw a sheep slaughtered in the village, Yahya," Helen said, "and I was wondering why both of you were so pale."

Yassir put his hands over his eyes as if trying to avoid seeing something in his mind.

Helen went to the bedroom and took out the phone from under her clothes. She wrote to Abdullah that Yahya and Yassir had agreed to return with her. They were known among Daesh members so there was a danger of them being recognized at the checkpoint.

The original plan had been for a driver to pick them up during Friday prayers when the street was empty of passersby, but that plan had changed at dawn, when explosions had intensified in Tal Afar. The nearby airport had been bombed, and the bombing had also reached Tal Afar residents, including Daesh families.

Abdullah and his smugglers used the bombardment in their plan to hide the two boys. They sent a car with two coffins for Yahya and Yassir to sleep inside, along with sleeping pills for them to take so that they might more easily bear their temporary death. They wrapped the coffins with Daesh flags. A smuggler sat next to the car's driver, and he was also disguised as Daesh with a beard and Afghani outfit.

In the back, Helen and Layla hid as usual inside their niqabs. It was assumed that the martyrs of the Islamic State were not to be stopped at the checkpoints, but the security guard stopped them anyway and said: "Who are the martyrs?"

The smuggler replied: "My nephews, killed by the bombing, praise be to God for their martyrdom in the path to Allah. Here in the back are their mother and sister."

"Wait, I will come with you and help you bury them," said the guard.

"Thanks," the smuggler said, "but we don't want you to go to the effort for us."

"This is less than duty, brother, just tell me which cemetery."

"Badush Cemetery," the smuggler replied.

"Why Badush? There are closer cemeteries."

"We have dead relatives there, and you know the traditions," the smuggler answered.

"Then I'll follow you in my car," the man said.

From time to time, the driver slowed the car down as he tracked the security man's car behind. Those in the car exchanged extremely anxious looks.

Helen wanted to beg the driver to change lanes and directions and escape from the other car, but she found herself unable to speak. She saw Yahya and Yassir in her mind as they were buried alive. Would they go so far as to bring them down to a gravesite and spread dust over them? She would be pushed away a distance from the grave, because the traditions of the place do not allow women to see the burial process. She saw herself running to the coffins, indifferent to tradition this time. She would prevent them from killing her boys. She would beg them to leave them alone.

Another smuggler was waiting at Badush Cemetery, pretending to be the gravedigger, and he almost lost patience because he was digging and digging, and no one had arrived yet. He called Abdullah and told him, "The soil has become soft from overturning, and they have not arrived yet."

They were late because the driver took the longest route possible. The phone was vibrating under Helen's clothes, and she knew it was Abdullah, but she couldn't answer for fear that the security guard behind would take notice. Her hand was trembling, even though it was not cold.

She jumped suddenly when a powerful bombardment reverberated behind them. She pulled Layla, who was also shivering, closer. The sounds of successive explosions increased, and they were yards away from the cemetery.

Helen said: "Tell the guard that I fainted, so you cannot perform the burial now. Actually, I feel as if I really might pass out."

They saw in the car mirror the guard getting out of his car and heading toward them. He stood by the smuggler's open window and said: "The airplanes are bombing hard, and the flag on the coffin may attract the attention of the infidels. Take off the banner quickly and bury your dead. I just heard that many of our people have been injured, and I have to rush to the rescue sites. Excuse me, brother, for not completing the duty with you. May God be with you and bless your dead."

"May God bless your dead as well," said the smuggler.

———

As soon as the man's car disappeared from view, they opened the two coffins and unloaded the two boys, who seemed drunk, neither awake nor asleep. They handed the empty coffins over to the fake gravedigger and quickly returned to the car.

The smugglers drove down an unpaved road to a remote area. The driver left, and the smuggler stayed with them. They hid in a tent made of goat hair, with ten strings inserted into the soil with pegs, leaving a space between the tent and the ground. The tent was furnished with rugs, on which lay packets of biscuits and bottles of water. The smuggler told them this was one of the "bats" tents. He explained that the smugglers call themselves "bats" because their journeys require sleeping in the morning and walking at night.

Thus, when the sun was completely gone, they walked six hours north until they reached the village of Tal Al-Reem, and there they slept among the ears of yellow corn, which the sunshine brightened. When the sun went down again, they walked a few more hours to reach the river separating Daesh from their people. Under normal circumstances, the distance could be covered in an hour, but in order to avoid the Daesh side and landmine routes, they had to take double the number of steps.

They were used to walking between trees and valleys for long distances, but it was different in darkness, with the fear that those trees would turn into an enemy that blocked their path or a landmine that exploded beneath their feet.

The end of that road seemed to be the end of the world, but at the far end after a long dark night, the beginning of their freedom emerged with the first glimmer of the sun. At the shore of the Tigris River, another smuggler awaited them.

He motioned for them to lie down in the boat and not show their heads until they reached the other bank. He loosened the rope so two others could pull the boat from the other bank with great caution. They wanted the boat to look as if it was floating in the river with no people on it.

Shortly before the boat arrived, Yassir raised his head slightly and shouted, "We arrived."

Helen took off her black niqab, revealing colorful clothes beneath.

Yahya said, "One more minute."

Once the boat reached the safe side, Helen threw the niqab into the river and said, "May the water return it to them." Layla did the same with her niqab.

Security officers from the region were waiting for them. Abdullah had informed them in advance of the time and place of their party's arrival. They were quickly moved by car to security headquarters away from the river, at a distance safe from gunfire. After they had their case documented, Abdullah met them outside the headquarters, saying, "Thanks to God for your safety."

Helen hugged him warmly, crying.

"Masha'llah, the children grew up," said Abdullah, embracing Yahya and Yassir.

Helen held Layla's hand and introduced her to Abdullah: "Layla is the daughter of Ghazal, whom I told you about."

"I have good news," Abdullah said. "We found Ghazal's place."

Layla stepped forward to hear more. She smiled, her first smile in a very long time.

Abdullah asked her to speak and direct her words to her mother while he took a video of her on his phone.

———

In his pickup, Abdullah took them to a nearby restaurant and ordered enough food for five.

Helen took a sip of water and asked Abdullah, "When was the last time you went to Halliqi?"

"Last week. They do not yet know that you have arrived."

"I don't want any of them to come here and get tired out," said Helen, "I'll go to them."

"If you like, we can go together," Abdullah said.

"Yes, please, I'm longing for Halliqi," Helen said.

"But first we have to go to Lalish," Abdullah said. "Baba Sheikh recommended that returnees from captivity should renew their baptism for spiritual purification, wiping the Daesh chapter from their lives and starting a clean new page."

"We will need two pieces of white cloth for Yahya and Yassir because this will be their first visit to the temple," Helen said.

"No problem," Abdullah said. Then he drank some water and added, "Helen, there is a camp for survivors here in Dohuk. How about if you all stay overnight in the camp and we go to Halliqi tomorrow morning?"

"Okay," Helen said. "Anyway, I would not stay in Halliqi for more than a few days, as it is difficult to catch up with the news of the missing from there. I need to look for my husband and daughter."

Yahya and Yassir exchanged a look, then looked back at Helen.

"You are right, it's easier to follow up in the camp," Abdullah said. "And I'll keep you updated as much as possible."

"Thank you," said Helen. "You really are a savior."

Abdullah smiled, picked up his phone from the table, and said, "Let me announce your arrival on Facebook so that people get ready for you in the camp."

"Are there other survivors I know in the camp?" asked Helen.

"I'm not sure," Abdullah answered.

"Any news of my friend Amina?"

Abdullah kept silent. He could not find the words to inform her of the sad news. The waiter had just put the food on the table, and Abdullah thought that revealing the truth might spoil Helen's first meal after her captivity. Helen was looking at him, waiting for an answer, so he said "No," stood up, and went to the bathroom.

After lunch, Abdullah bought new clothes for each of them and two white handkerchiefs for Yahya and Yassir to wrap around their heads. When they did, Helen remembered the black Daesh headbands.

"Is this why people call us 'of white head'?" Yahya asked.

"White is our symbol of transparency," said Abdullah. "It's easier to see dirt in white than in other colors."

Driving east toward the Sheikhan district meant an hour of winding roads through a mountainous valley. Finally, the three domes of Lalish appeared in front of them.

Leaving their shoes in the car, the five of them entered the temple barefoot like all other visitors, as there should be no barrier between their feet and the ground of the temple.

On the right side of the temple gate, an image of a black snake attracted Yassir's attention. He asked his mother, "Why is there a snake here?"

"After it hit a rock and got a hole in its hull, Noah's Ark sprung a leak. It almost sank, but a black snake plugged the hole, saving mankind. Therefore, we hold the snake in high regard." Helen crossed over the threshold, saying to the boys, "Be careful. Do not set your feet on the threshold. It's sacred."

In the temple's inner courtyard, seven columns were draped with colorful cloth. Abdullah untied a green one and then retied it. Helen did the same with a red cloth. Layla came closer to the column, and Helen encouraged her with a smile. Layla picked a pink one.

Yahya and Yassir watched all this with interest.

Abdullah told them, "Each of these knots represents a wish made by the visitor who tied it. The ones we untie are the wishes to be granted. We hope that the next visitors will untie ours as well."

They walked on ancient smooth rocks into the entrance to the sacred spring. Here was the water of baptism. The temple servant was called Faqrai—a dedicated woman who must stay single. She stood by the white spring with a metal bowl of water in hand. After they entered the room enclosing the spring, she poured water from her bowl over their five heads, one by one, reciting the prayers of blessing and salvation. She pronounced the words with a distinctive musicality and extension of the long vowels.

Afterward, Helen bent over the spring and washed her face and hands, and the rest of them did the same. When they came out of the spring, Faqrai said, "Congratulations."

In the outdoor courtyard, they saw wicks lit on stones beside the caves' doorways, and trees along the valley beyond.

Helen felt an inner comfort, and at the same time she wanted to cry. Everyone here felt emotional at being reunited. Others embraced the hopeful survivors who emerged from the healing waters. On the rocky fence, young men sat, silently looking at the horizon, like a flock of birds.

It was evening when they arrived at Qadia camp. The management officer in the camp accompanied them to their assigned tent. Helen was astonished to see over a hundred people gathered by her tent, welcoming her.

A group of women sprinkled candies over her with ululations.

Deeply moved, Helen sat on the ground crying, and others sat around and cried with her.

When the crowd dispersed and went to their tents, Abdullah told Helen, "They do this every time a new female survivor arrives at the camp." Then he added, "So tomorrow morning, we will go to Halliqi."

"Where do you live now?" Helen asked.

"In Dohuk," Abdullah said. "A crowded building with two families per room. The other family with us is nice, and my family gets along with them."

"How are Sari and the children?" Helen asked.

"Sari lost her brother. Daesh killed him in captivity."

"Ah, I'm so sorry to hear that."

"She told me to say hello to you."

"My heart is with her."

"See you tomorrow."

As the group approached Halliqi in the late afternoon, Abdullah rushed ahead with great purpose. He found Shammo in his living room, filling a big can with dried figs.

Panting from the effort, Abdullah said to him, "I have guests today. Would you accept them in your house?"

"Hello, Abdullah," said Shammo. "You and your guests are always welcome."

Abdullah looked behind him, and minutes later, Helen, Yahya, Yassir, and Layla arrived.

After tearful hugs, Shammo released several whistles.

Ramziya entered the house, not believing her eyes. "Oh, how I have missed you," she said to Helen, weeping as they embraced.

Then Azad, his wife, and their son came in. They all hugged and cried.

Ramziya could not stand any longer after hugging them for so long. She sat on the floor and began her sad song.

"When she gets too emotional, she sings those songs," said a joyous Shammo, his arm around his daughter.

After her long cry, Ramziya went to the kitchen, returning with a large watermelon. She broke it for them to eat.

After Abdullah had eaten a slice, he said, "I must go now."

Ramziya protested. "You barely took a rest from the road, Abdullah. How can you go without dinner?"

"There is a captive on the way. I must follow up with her step by step, and I am afraid that I will miss important calls, as my phone will not ring here. But I will come again as soon as possible," Abdullah said before parting.

When Ramziya noticed that Layla had not taken her share of watermelon, she said to her, "Come on, my dear Ahlam, eat some."

"This is Layla, Mama," Helen said. "She's almost the same age as Ahlam."

"I thought she was the daughter of the late Amina," said Ramziya.

Helen took a minute to process the words. "The *late*? Amina is dead?"

"Oh, you didn't know?" Ramziya said.

Helen did not answer. She stood up and left the house.

Ramziya followed. "I am sorry, my daughter. Come back, darling. Where are you going?"

Helen turned back to her mother. "I just need to walk a little by myself."

Helen went toward the valley. After her first tear fell, the rest poured in abundance. On the road she used to traverse with her friend, Helen imagined herself and Amina. They were fourteen years old, walking together on Eid in April among red anemones and yellow-white chamomiles. The mountain was covered in those three colors, like every spring. She remembered how Amina gathered a bouquet of anemones, braided them flower by flower into a red necklace. She did it as fast as she usually braided her own hair. Amina had put the flower necklace around Helen's neck. Helen collected chamomile flowers in her straw basket as her mother had asked her to do. Ramziya would later give them to Umm Khairy, as many villagers did, and Umm Khairy would make pain-relieving herbs with them.

Helen stopped walking, touching her neck, trying to trace Amina's necklace.

All of the April chamomile herbs would not be enough to relieve her pain.

18

THE VOICE

Abdullah descended the mountain and soon reached a low meadow where he could use his phone. He called Hadla, the woman who had taken over the task of saving Ghazal. Hadla was only one of the women who worked for the network Abdullah and Goofball had set up. There were now fifteen members taking part in the rescuing of kidnapped women.

Hadla was the most active of them, by virtue of her work as a nurse in the Raqqa women's hospital. Among the patients in that hospital were captives who were being treated for fractures and wounds after men beat them with cables, perhaps because they resisted rape or were too tired to do their housework. Other times, the harm was caused by explosions and bombardments in the area.

When Hadla heard from Abdullah that Ghazal could hear but not speak, she had answered him that she had a sister who was the same way, as a result of which she knew sign language. Hadla donned her white nursing clothes for a trip to the home of the desert emir.

With a hospital card in hand, she told Ghazal that she needed to come to the hospital to have a vaccination. Hadla assured Ghazal that after the shot, she would personally accompany her home so that she would not get lost.

In a small nursing room at the hospital, there was another nurse with them as Hadla busied herself preparing the vaccination. When the other nurse finally left, Hadla closed the door.

She opened her cell phone in front of Ghazal and urged her to watch the short video: "How are you, Mama? How are my brother and sister? Is Dad with you? I am back home and waiting for you."

Ghazal's eyes opened wide when she saw Layla. She almost spoke, but the words did not form as they should. A sound more expressive than any words came out of her.

Ghazal took Hadla's hand and placed it on her chest and then on her mouth.

The other nurse entered the room and saw Ghazal kissing Hadla's hand, so she assumed that Ghazal was very grateful for the vaccine.

Hadla left with Ghazal to accompany her back to the desert emir's house. The walk took a quarter of an hour on foot, during which Hadla told her about the escape plan. She explained to Ghazal that she should come to the hospital the next day at ten in the morning with her daughter, on the premise that her daughter needed to be vaccinated as well. It was not permissible for a boy to enter the women's hospital. Therefore, her son should be disguised as a girl. He would wear female clothes while waiting in the garden behind the hospital.

Ghazal indicated by putting her hand to her shoulder how tall her son Zedo was. Tomorrow, Hadla would bring a niqab that

Zedo could wear. Ghazal and her daughter would leave the hospital's back door and keep walking to the park, where Zedo would join them. The smugglers' car would be stationed in front of the park, its trunk open as a sign that this was the right car.

Hadla gave her phone number to Ghazal because she wanted to be informed when they arrived safely at their destination.

Ghazal nodded, promising to send her good news, if there was any.

The next day, all went well. The smuggler closed the trunk after the three of them got in the car's back seat. He drove them to a rural area on the outskirts of Raqqa, stopping at a house where a grandfather, grandmother, father, mother, and five children lived. Along with them, in a large room, their animals also lived: sheep, cows, and donkeys.

The father was a relative of Goofball's. For a fee, he periodically let Goofball use a room in his house as a shelter for a day or two, sometimes for five days.

Ghazal felt a sweet warmth as the family surrounded them in this peaceful atmosphere, one which they had not known for a long time. Every hour, the mother insisted that they eat something.

On their second day there, the host family gathered around Zedo, and the boy told them what had brought them to their home.

After he told their story, the grandmother said, "You are the fourth family we have hosted. Throughout our life we have never known anything like this and have never heard such strange tales, not even in the stories of a thousand and one nights. We don't know where these people came from or why they are doing this to you."

On the third night, it was time to leave. The mother made egg sandwiches and put them in a nylon bag. She said to Ghazal, "This is for the road."

Ghazal hugged her and stood waiting for Zedo. The other children stared at Zedo as he put on the niqab. The grandfather, knowing that Zedo was embarrassed, said to him, "You are not the first one we've seen in disguise. The boys who were hiding here before you did the same."

Outside the house, two motorcycles waited for them. Ghazal got on one behind her daughter and the driver. Zedo hopped on behind the second driver. After a two-hour ride, they arrived at a remote dirt road.

From there, the three of them had to walk three hours to reach the Kobani border. The motorcycle driver gave Ghazal a white plastic bag to lift when she saw the border from a hundred meters away. That was the agreed upon sign by the receiving party on the other side. They had to remember *not* to cross those last meters by themselves. They were full of mines.

Ghazal walked, anxiously thinking: What if they made a mistake and did not know where the boundaries of that last distance were? Whenever Zedo sped up, Ghazal motioned for him to slow down, lest they forget themselves and walk right into danger.

The clouds were scattered in the sky, and at the break of dawn, the features of a new day appeared, and also the figures of several women standing at the border, waving their hands.

When Ghazal lifted up her white bag, a woman hurried toward them. She told them to follow carefully in her steps. Ghazal was surprised by the trilling cries of joy greeting them and the candies they spread over them. Those gathered started singing Kurdish songs that were familiar to Ghazal.

She found herself singing along with them. Zedo was shocked to hear his mother singing. He shouted, "Mama, you got your voice back!"

Ghazal stopped singing because she too was astonished. She tried to say something to Zedo, but only a rattle came out.

The crowd fell silent as Zedo addressed them. "My mother lost her voice in captivity, and she is now singing. Did her voice come back?"

One of the women said: "Sing, sing," and she motioned for the others in the group to resume singing.

Ghazal also sang, and her words were fully comprehensible, causing them to dance and sing louder. They raised their hands, rejoicing, and some wiped away their tears. At the end of the song, they looked at Ghazal, waiting for her to say something.

She tried to speak again, but at first she stumbled over the words. Then, when she repeated them, they came out right. For a year, her mouth had been like a solitary confinement room in which the words had been trapped. Now, Ghazal said, "Thank you for liberating me and releasing my voice."

———

Abdullah went up again to Halliqi at the beginning of July 2015. The summer sun made his gray hair shine. It had been black just a year earlier, but recently it had turned half white. Once in his uncle's home, Abdullah asked Helen, "Where's Layla?"

"She went with Yahya and Yassir to the fig orchard," Helen answered.

"I wanted to tell her that her mother has reached a safe place and will reach the Iraqi border tomorrow," said Abdullah.

"Oh, this is wonderful news," said Helen. "Let's go tell her."

Layla was picking a fig from the tree, and Yahya said, "Let me show you a better way." He shook the tree, and ripe figs fell down. Yahya and Yassir started collecting the figs from the ground.

Layla turned when she noticed Helen and Abdullah at the orchard's entrance.

Hearing the good news from Abdullah, Layla's face brightened with a cheerful smile, a fig still in her hand.

Helen, Abdullah, and Layla would travel to receive Ghazal at the border. Yahya and Yassir wanted to go too. At dawn the next day, Ramziya also woke early and decided to accompany them.

After the group descended the mountain, they walked to Abdullah's pickup truck, which he had parked in front of a house in the meadow. It was midday when at last they reached the no-man's-land between the Iraqi and Syrian borders. They waited five hours for Ghazal, during which time Abdullah lost phone contact with the smuggler, due to a lack of cellular coverage. It wasn't until that evening that he was informed that the road to the border was not safe enough, and the meetup would be postponed until the next day.

They returned to the mountain, and the following morning arrived back at the same waiting area on the border. They sat again until late afternoon without Ghazal.

"You look pale today. I am embarrassed by the trouble we have put you through," Ramziya said to Abdullah.

"In fact, I am the embarrassed one because you have waited two days here in the open air, and the weather is hot," Abdullah said.

"This is nothing in return for the arrival of a survivor. As if she rose from death," Ramziya said, "but tell me, Abdullah, how's Siham doing?"

"My niece's health has improved, thank God," Abdullah replied.

"I was so sad to hear that she had returned from captivity with broken ribs," said Ramziya.

"When did Siham return?" Helen asked.

"Two months ago," Abdullah said.

"Tell me more, cousin," Helen said.

As the group sat on the ground around him, Abdullah began telling the story of how Siham was rescued.

—⁓—

Siham had been thirteen years old when she was bought by Bilal, the director of Daesh security. One day in his office, she saw a picture of Abdullah. She did not know that her uncle had become a wanted person by Daesh, so she asked Bilal, "Where do you know my uncle from?"

Bilal used her innocent question to concoct a scheme. He said to her, "If this is your uncle, I can sell you to him. What do you think?"

Of course, Siham jumped with joy. Bilal called Abdullah and sent him Siham's photo, offering him a deal: Siham would be freed in exchange for help smuggling Bilal's family to Turkey. This was hardly the first time that such an agreement had taken place. Abdullah had recently made a similar deal, so he was not surprised by the offer.

He made an agreement with Bilal that Siham would wait at the Jarrah roundabout in al-Mayadeen and that someone would pick her up from there. That was the first ambush, for as soon as the smuggler arrived near Siham, Daesh members surrounded them. They returned Siham to Bilal's house and killed the smuggler.

They forced Siham to speak with Abdullah on the phone to tell him she had waited, and the expected person did not come.

Abdullah did not know that they had beaten her to get her to say this, so he replied that he would send another of his operatives.

The second time, the appointment was in a park in front of Al Mayadeen Hospital. The smuggler had looked around in the park and found nothing hinting at danger. He spotted no suspicious men, and near Siham there were only women wearing the niqab.

But when he approached Siham, he found her crying and refusing to go with him. She told him to leave so he would not be arrested.

Just then, the women in niqabs surrounded him. They were undercover, disguised as women in order to catch him. Later, they tortured him and also Siham because they had heard her telling him that he was about to be arrested.

That had been a terrible day for Abdullah and Goofball. They had discovered too late that Bilal had used Siham to trap the smugglers. Amid the sadness and frustration that Abdullah felt, Goofball decided to take charge of Siham's rescue himself, saying, "Let me take revenge on this Bilal."

"I don't want to lose you too," Abdullah said, "and it is dangerous because they will lie in wait for anyone who goes near her."

"All you have to do is make an appointment with Bilal again, as if nothing had happened, and I'll take care of it," Goofball said. "But try to arrange with him for the smuggling to be from Manbij, because that's my area, and I know it like the back of my hand."

About a month passed, and Bilal had not called. When he finally did, he told Abdullah that he had not called because he had been wounded in battle and lost a leg. But he was still ready to complete their deal.

Abdullah said to Bilal, "I have a friend who is available to pick up Siham, but he is in Manbij. If you give us an appointment in Manbij, I can let him know."

"Manbij is far from here, six hours by car," Bilal said. "Why don't you come, Abdullah, and collect Siham from me yourself? Isn't that better?"

Abdullah replied that he would do it if his friend couldn't.

"Well, I'm going to send her with someone on my behalf. I'll give you his phone number, and you two can make arrangements," Bilal said.

After three days, Siham waited as scheduled at Markaba roundabout in Manbij. The person who brought her was sitting at the internet cafe across from the roundabout. He was looking at Siham and at the same time writing to Abdullah that Siham was standing in the roundabout and had a diaper bag in her hand as a sign for his friend to recognize her when he came to pick her up. An hour later, he wrote to Abdullah, *Your friend has not yet come.*

Abdullah wrote to Goofball to check on him.

Hahaha, Goofball texted back.

What is so funny? Abdullah asked.

I am sitting in the cafe next to him as he writes to you. I greeted him, and he replied to me with a better greeting, and I am now chatting with him about the gas crisis, Goofball replied.

———

Goofball had quickly noticed a person closely monitoring Siham through the cafe window, and he also spotted two other men loitering outside near Siham, who appeared to be tired of waiting. After an hour and a half of observation in that hot afternoon, the two men entered a nearby refreshment store.

Goofball wrote to Abdullah, *Tell the hajji that I will arrive in half an hour.*

Goofball watched the Daesh read Abdullah's message and then phone the two observers. Goofball saw one of them answering the call, which made Goofball sure that they were the ones charged with arresting him. He wrote to Abdullah, *Send the hajji many questions to distract him. His group are drinking Pepsi, and the poor woman is standing in the sun. They did not even give her a sip of water.*

Goofball stood up and once again greeted the person next to him, telling him: "May God bless you, pray for me today so I get some gas."

"May God grant you success," the man replied.

Goofball got on his motorcycle and rode around the area. When he saw the monitors entering the store again, he approached Siham and said to her: "Get on quickly. I am from your uncle."

She threw the diaper bag from her hand and climbed up behind him. He flew with her into the first alley. The Daesh monitors were on their tail, racing behind them in their car down the alley, which was barely wide enough for the vehicle. On either side were old buildings that looked like they were about to tumble down on any passersby.

Goofball turned his motorcycle down an even narrower alley, where no cars could enter, and from there to other narrow alleys and ultimately to a safe house.

The next day, Goofball called Abdullah to tell him that he and Siham had reached the town of Tal Tamr in the Hasaka governorate. He told him that Siham could barely walk and needed to see a doctor.

Abdullah decided to go by himself to fetch her in his car and also to finally meet Goofball in person. The trip to the restaurant meeting place took four hours by car, and their meeting did not last more than ten minutes. Although excited, they could meet only briefly to ensure their safety. The three of them were in a situation that could easily lead to interrogation by the authorities, if not worse. Siham had no identity card, Goofball was a frequent traveler to Daesh areas, and Abdullah was now in constant danger if he happened to be caught in the wrong place at the wrong time. The three of them were innocent, but their innocence did not ensure their safety.

Abdullah had imagined that he would meet a huge, muscular man. He was surprised when he found Goofball to be a slight person. "I thought I was going to see a giant man in front of me," Abdullah told Goofball.

"I am like gold, small and valuable," Goofball said.

"Your deeds are more valuable than gold, Goofball, and I brought you a gift," Abdullah replied, handing him a jar of honey wrapped in black duct tape.

"This is royal food," he added, "and since you are saving our queens, this is their gift for you."

Goofball hugged him and left. Abdullah was unable to hug Siham for fear of hurting her. Her fractures had not yet healed. He gave her his daughter's identity card for crossing the border and said, "Your cousin is waiting impatiently for you."

Waiting for Ghazal at the border, time went by faster as they listened to Abdullah recount Siham's story. But in the end, they stood up to return to Halliqi, for Ghazal's return had been postponed again.

Making a call, Abdullah wiped his forehead, asking his contact, "Will Ghazal come tomorrow?"

"God willing," the smuggler answered. "Be optimistic."

On the third day, after waiting two hours, Helen spotted Ghazal, Zedo, and Joan crossing the border. They stood to receive them.

Helen cried as Layla ran to her mother's side. But when she asked, "Where is my dad? Why did he not come with you?" Ghazal fell to her knees crying.

Helen, Ramziya, Yahya, and Yassir surrounded her, and she said, "Daesh killed them all. Since that day I have wanted to scream, and my scream was not coming out as it should."

Ramziya sat, as usual, singing a sad song.

As she hugged Ghazal, Helen asked her, "Remember me?"

Ghazal nodded and kissed Helen again.

Helen glimpsed Abdullah as he stood alone to one side, watching them. Helen said to Ghazal, "Come, let me introduce you to my cousin. He's the man who arranged your return home."

Ghazal had not forgotten her promise to Hadla. As soon as she hugged Abdullah and thanked him, she asked him to call Hadla to let her know she had arrived safely. Abdullah did not respond. She waited a little and then repeated her request.

Abdullah lowered his head, looking weary.

"Are you okay? Do you need water?" Ghazal asked.

"I am not thirsty. I am sad, more than you can imagine," he replied.

"What happened?"

"I did not want you to grieve like me, but Hadla . . . They caught and killed her."

Ghazal put her hand on her mouth and asked, "Because of me?"

"No, Hadla rescued another woman after you, and Daesh found out. They killed her in the public square in front of a crowd. They announced by loudspeaker that she had been a spy working with the infidels. Her husband had also worked for our network. But when they interrogated her, she told them that her husband had no hand in this and that he did not know anything about the smuggling of women. She took full responsibility. They offered to release her if she gave them information about the network. Hadla did not utter a word. She died alone in silence."

Hadla had been forty years old when she'd started this dangerous job, her goal at the beginning to collect the amount of money she needed for her child's transplant. She thought that she would stop after raising the required amount, but she changed her mind after she saw the change she was making in the world by rescuing women.

Two hours after her execution, her picture was hung on the wall in the square and, under it, the word *HERO*.

Daesh ripped down the picture. The next morning, they found two more pictures of her hanging on the city walls, inscribed with the same word. After they tore down those pictures, dozens of others appeared. Daesh were assigned to monitor the walls of the square, with the intention of arresting those who were hanging the pictures.

A symbolic battle broke out between the Hadla supporters and the Daesh group. At night, rebel hands were putting up Hadla's pictures, and during the day, Daesh hands tore them apart. In the end, the pictures disappeared, but a phrase written in thick marker remained on many walls. It read: "Hadla's shoe is worth more than your heads."

19

THREE PASSWORDS

Helen was standing by her tent in the camp when she heard Bahar, the woman in the neighboring tent, yelling at some children, "Shit, damn it!"

Their soccer ball had just landed in her large pot of boiling water. Bahar waved her hand to Helen and said, "It's my lucky day. The ball fell before I added the tomato paste."

The children of the survivors' camp played soccer from morning until evening in the dirt space in front of the tents. Nearby adults did their cooking and washing, also drinking tea and exchanging news of who had returned from captivity and those who had not yet come back. Whenever their hearts could no longer withstand the space, the camp residents emerged from their tents, especially in hot and dusty times. They were the lucky ones, who had survived, but their survival was not absolute, for they all had memories of loved ones who were missing or dead.

Linda was a Yazidi resident of Germany and worked for a humanitarian organization affiliated with the United Nations. That day, she entered Helen's tent to discuss her needs, as she did with other survivors.

"What I need most is to have my husband and daughter back," Helen said. "Their absence is the reason I can't sleep."

"Where are they?" Linda asked.

"My husband is a captive of Daesh, and my daughter is in my neighbor's house in Mosul," said Helen. "She does not even know me."

"You should take care of yourself *for* them," Linda said. "Remember the safety rule on planes, when a passenger is in need of oxygen, she should place the oxygen mask over her mouth and nose *before* assisting others."

Helen did not comment on this, but she thought this law was difficult for mothers.

"Do you have nightmares?" Linda asked her.

"In my dreams, I am always hiding," Helen replied, "and once, in a strange dream, I was a husband even though I was a woman, and they raped my wife in front of me. I screamed at them, but they did not see or hear me."

Linda was taking notes when she noticed a large hole in the roof of Helen's tent. She offered to bring a piece of cloth to patch the hole and prevent leaks when rain came.

Helen refused, saying the rain didn't bother her.

She preferred to leave it. Through that hole she saw the stars at night, which gave her a sense of hope in that darkness surrounding the tent. Sleep did not come to her quickly, so—while Layla slept beside her, and the two boys were sleeping in the corner—Helen contemplated a future life while looking at that glittering spot in the sky.

Like the rest of the camp's residents, Helen followed the daily group chat on a special website they had created for themselves called "People of the Kidnapped." It had nearly nine hundred active members who published pictures and information for mobilization, awareness, and fundraising—all with the goal of rescuing more kidnapped women. They had been motivated by the "Islamic State Mall" website created by Daesh, which displayed kidnapped women for sale.

Only Mall members had access to the Daesh site, but they could invite friends, and that was how Abdullah managed to penetrate the site with a fake account. A disguised member added him. Abdullah passed on Mall advertisements to his network, as well as to the "People of the Kidnapped" website.

When he spotted an ad by someone offering a woman and an explosive belt for sale, Abdullah wrote to the seller: "I would like to buy the belt from you."

The man replied, "Come here, sheikh, so we can agree on a price."

Abdullah took the address from him and gave it to the smugglers to watch his house, awaiting an opportunity to rescue the imprisoned woman. Meanwhile, Abdullah continued to procrastinate with the man on the pretext that a bombing had caused him to delay his visit. In the end, he said to him, "May Allah reward you. We bought a belt from another jihadi and used it for the sake of God."

"May God bless you," the man replied.

After two weeks of monitoring the house of that man, Abdullah's network was able to rescue the captive woman whom the man had offered for sale.

Whenever Helen heard the special ringtone of the group chat, she immediately looked at the thread. This time she found a message from Abdullah: "Open the site quickly. There is a woman who entered the chat and said a one-year-old girl is with her. The woman gave your name and Elias's as the girl's missing parents."

Helen felt her heart pounding as she located Shaima's online statement and phone number. She called her right away.

Shaima's eager voice came to her. "For real? Helen? Where have you been all this time?"

"I just returned from Daesh," Helen replied.

"Oh my God."

"Can I talk with Mayada?"

"Mayada?"

"My daughter who is with you."

"I didn't know her name was Mayada," Shaima said.

"Are you at home?" Helen asked.

"No, we fled to Turkey. Our house is not our home anymore," Shaima said in her Mosul accent, the accent that reminded her so strongly of Elias.

Helen kept silent, so Shaima added: "Be reassured: your daughter is okay."

"Oh, my dear. I have no words to thank you."

"I became attached to her, and so did Mustafa. She became his sister as I breastfed them both, even though your religion prohibits kinship to Muslims."

"You are my sister, Shaima, even without breastfeeding."

"Of course."

"Tell me, Shaima, is Hameed with you in Turkey?"

"No, Hameed is in Tal Afar because he found a job there."

"I know. He works with Daesh," Helen said.

"What do you say?"

"I saw him there with them. He helped me escape."

"Such good and bad news! His father will destroy him if he hears this. Oh God, where did all this misfortune come from?"

"My boys also cooperated with Daesh, but they returned to themselves. I hope Hameed returns as well."

Helen took Shaima's address. She gave it to Abdullah to arrange smuggling Mayada from Turkey back to Iraq.

The person assigned to transport Mayada had originally been a truck driver between Syria and Turkey, and he knew how to smuggle prohibited goods. He had joined the "bats" network, which Abdullah called "the beehive."

Goofball had joked with Abdullah, saying, "The bats have become bees. This is an upgrade."

When Abdullah's contact arrived at Shaima's house, she was confused: How could a stranger take a child away from the woman she thought was her mother? But he had come prepared for his mission and gave Mayada a sleeping drug. When she closed her eyes, he put her in the back of his truck inside a carton with small holes. He put that inside a bigger carton, one meter long and half a meter wide, used to store eggs. On top of the small carton and around it, he placed cartons of eggs.

Shaima watched all this in amazement, and he told her that during his trips, he noticed that at the border they didn't open the egg cartons one by one, perhaps because they were similar and they got bored, while they inspected various other items with greater attention.

The driver's intuition was right. The Turkish border inspector opened three layers of eggs and returned them to their place, and then went on to inspect the rest of the truck.

Finding nothing, he gave the sign to the driver to go. He crossed the bridge overlooking the Tigris River. The Kurdish border control on the other side had been anticipating Mayada's arrival.

The inspectors at the Ibrahim Khalil border crossing in Zakho, surrounded the driver and thanked him after he handed over the carton to them. Abdullah received the carton from them and transported it in his car to the camp in Dohuk, thinking it was as if Mayada was sleeping in a nest.

"This is your daughter, and eggs on top of her too," Abdullah said as he placed the carton in front of Helen's tent.

Many of the camp's residents gathered by Helen to congratulate her on the arrival of her daughter, and among them were journalists taking pictures of the little girl as she opened her eyes in the arms of a woman she didn't know.

She did not cry at first, but minutes after entering the tent, she wept.

Helen took her in her lap and kissed her repeatedly on her head. When the girl calmed down a little, Helen picked up a sketchbook and a box of colors that Linda had given her after she learned that Helen liked drawing. Helen drew a qabaj bird and placed the paper in front of Mayada on the floor with the coloring box. Helen began to color in the bird's wing. She did it slowly, leaving enough space for Mayada to add color too.

Mayada picked up a green pen and started scribbling. The stroke of color filled Helen with euphoria, as if something dry had just turned green. The bird became real and full of life and flew before her in that moment. Mayada was fully engaged in coloring, tears still in her eyes.

Yassir cut a sheet from the sketchbook and made a paper missile and threw it over Mayada. She lifted her head for a moment and went back to coloring. He lay beside her to see what she was doing.

Linda had asked Helen if she needed a table to draw on. Helen had answered her that she, like the rest of her people, was used to doing everything on the ground. They wept on the ground. They sang and played music on the ground. They ate on the ground. They hung out and drank tea on the ground. They made love on the ground. They waited on the ground. They were happy on the ground. They were sad on the ground.

———

The following day at noon, Yahya and Yassir went to the empty space behind the tent to play soccer. Dirt bounced between the players' feet, and the grass was stiff from the summer heat. Yahya was overseeing the game as a referee. He had learned from Helen how to put his fingers to his mouth and whistle whenever he wanted to catch a player's attention or call an end to a match.

Yassir left the match and returned to the tent. After warning him twice, Yahya had expelled him for breaking the rules. Linda was in the tent with Helen, and Yassir heard her talking to his mother about an opportunity provided by the United Nations for a survivor like Helen and her family to travel and live in one of the countries that granted refugee status. Helen said that she had never thought of leaving Iraq and that her stay in this camp was for the purpose of following up with news of the missing, as she hoped to return in the future to Halliqi or to Mosul when the city was fully liberated from Daesh. After Linda left the tent, Helen tried to fix a zipper that they used as a virtual door.

Yassir asked, "Mama, why can't we travel? We don't want to stay here in the camp."

"We can go to Halliqi," Helen said.

"But there is no phone and no TV there," Yassir said. "I like the village for short visits only."

"When your father comes back, we will return to Mosul," Helen said.

"Dad will never return," Yassir said.

"Why do you say this?"

"Because the dead never return, Mama."

Helen gave up on the zipper and stared at Yassir. She saw disappointment and fear in his eyes.

"I saw them kill my father with a sword," he told her.

"Where?"

"In a video I watched with Yahya."

Yassir told her how he and Yahya had seen Elias in a YouTube video. Onscreen, they had seen members of the Organization beheading Elias, the blood flowing from his neck. The coldblooded trainer who had shown them this said, "These men are traitors and infidels and should be fought like this with swords." When he saw the boys' tears, he scolded them. "The State will not be strong with the weak, and you are men, so it's shameful for you to cry."

"What if this beheaded man was my father?" Yahya had asked the trainer.

"If your father was a disbeliever, then you must be the first to fight him," the trainer replied. "Your brother, who is here next to you, is not your brother if he is on the wrong path. The State is your family, and to the State should be your loyalty and sacrifice, first and foremost."

Hearing this, a disconnect with the Organization formed in the minds of the two boys, as final as a period at the end of a sentence. They became extremely fatigued, unable to resume that day's training.

Yassir suddenly bent over, trying to vomit, but nothing came out. The trainer thought that he had been infected with a virus.

That video would fester in their minds, but at the same time it functioned as an antidote, the pain leading the two boys to wake up from death, even though the hurt would not go away.

Yassir, reliving the memory and weeping himself, sat down in the corner of the tent. Helen let the thread fall from her hand. She sat on the floor and started beating her hands on the rug and on her feet. Her tears poured as if a large glacier had melted at once, and its water cascaded down a mountain.

Her sobbing awoke Mayada from her nap, and when she saw her mother like this, she also cried. Yassir grabbed his sister's hand and took her out of the tent.

Helen remained in the tent until the next day. Exhausted, she sat in the corner, her hands on her forehead. She closed her eyes. She kept them closed until she saw Elias. In the beginning the view was blurry, but little by little his features became clearer. He wore the gym clothes she had bought for him just before his disappearance. He smiled at her, so the two dimples appeared on his cheeks. Waiting for him to tell her something, she saw a shadow coming from behind. She panicked, as she glimpsed a sword in the shadow's hand, rising up to kill him. She shouted at him. She shouted louder, "No, no!"

Linda heard her screaming. She sat with her in the tent for half an hour, but Helen's mind had gone far away. She had no desire to answer Linda's questions that day. She had no desire to speak or do anything.

Helen's hope of reuniting with her children and Elias had been what had kept her going through her torture and torment in captivity. The memory of her loved ones kept her together when she was sliced in pieces, each piece barely aware of what was going on with the other piece. After all that panting to escape and help rescue her children and others, there was one last strand of hope she was clinging to: Elias. Now she had lost it. She lost it now, when she was barely hanging on from the death of Amina. This turned her into a statue with no center to hold her from falling apart. Unable to get up, only her soul was wandering around in search of that part of herself that she was still longing for. She was still frozen in her spot when women entered her tent. They kissed her on her cheeks and sat down, murmuring words of condolence. Wailing and chanting the names of their dead who did not survive with them, the women were wiping their tears.

"We could not even bury our dead," one of the women said, and several other women repeated her words.

Helen's tears fell hot on her cheeks. She could not bury Elias. In her village, they would wash the dead and dress him in a white robe of round neck. His coffin would be carried on shoulders, accompanied by sad flute music. His closest relatives would be dancing the pain dance of the wounded bird.

Helen's eyes were closed when the women left. Only Linda stayed.

Linda called for her. "Helen, Helen." But she did not respond. She was in another world. Linda patted Helen's shoulder, and Helen looked at her as if she had just woken up from a nightmare.

"I have a story for you," Linda said, taking Helen's hand in hers. "I'll tell it and go. There are three villages that you must cross in order for your wound to heal. Each of the three villages has an entrance with a key. The key is the password to get in. I'll give you the three passwords. The first village is not difficult to cross. Its password is 'Realize.' In order for you to pass through the first village safely, you must realize what happened and believe that it really happened. You must understand that the injustice and violence you endured is *one* part of your life and not your *entire* life. The second village is further and requires more effort. Its password is 'Remember.' Maybe you will say that remembering is painful. I know, but it is less painful than forgetting. Remembering and mourning those missing is part of recovery. Remembering and talking about what happened to you helps you cross that second village. You might say that talking about the disaster will reopen the wound and make things worse, but on the contrary, talking about it in the past tense prepares you to cross into the future. As for the third village, it is difficult to reach. It is on the top of a mountain, and you will be gasping for breath before you arrive. But we rest in the end, even survive. Its password is 'Reconnect.' You must reconnect with people, especially the ones you trust. You cannot cross the third village without reconnecting to normal life. What happened to you and your family cannot be erased or undone, but something meaningful in the coming days can be found. The time you spend in each of these healing villages depends on you. I would be lying if I told you this can all be accomplished quickly, but it is possible. Believe me, everything is possible."

—

Helen went up and down the mountain to Halliqi more than ten times in the three months that followed the terrible news. But neither walking in the meadows, nor sleeping or awakening, nothing could distract her from the pain of missing her husband. Even the sound of birds caused her sorrow. She felt the presence of Elias all around her. Like threads stitched on an embroidered canvas, her life was seamed with the color of his absence.

A year after her arrival in the camp, Helen was receiving new survivors and bidding farewell to others who left the camp and returned to their liberated villages. Some left the country. Bahar was granted refugee status in Germany, along with her son and sister. Daesh had killed her husband, her father, and three of her brothers. On the day in October 2016 when she was leaving the camp, Helen went to visit her for the last time.

"Have you filled out your refugee form?" Bahar asked Helen.

"No, not yet," said Helen.

"This is an opportunity that may not always exist, Helen. Who knows what will happen tomorrow? Did we ever imagine this could happen to us? How will we guarantee it will not happen again?"

"Yahya and Yassir are both nagging me to submit the application," Helen said.

"Well, their future and your daughter's are better abroad," Bahar said.

"So you think I should fill out the form?" Helen asked.

"Yes, of course," Bahar said. "What do you have to lose? You can withdraw it later if you change your mind."

———

During Linda's next visit, Helen asked for her help in submitting the refugee application. After ten months, on August 7, 2017, Linda arrived at her tent and informed Helen that her request had been accepted by the United Nations: she and her family had been granted refugee status in Canada. All they needed to do was get medical examinations in the next six months.

After delivering this great news, Linda noticed that Mayada was carrying a plate with a colorful fish drawn on it and a spoon. Yassir had in his hand a tray and a ladle.

"Tonight is the lunar eclipse," Helen said to Linda. "Would you like to join us?"

"Where?" Linda asked.

"There are no roofs here in the camp, so we will gather in that open space." Helen pointed to the area behind the tent.

"What will you do there?" asked Linda.

"We knock on trays and plates, and we say, 'Hey whale, leave our moon alone. It's our moon, our precious moon.'"

"Then what?"

"Nothing. We just hope we send evil away from our country."

"Sounds good, but I have a meeting with my colleagues, and I'm afraid I'll be late," Linda said. "I am happy for you, Helen, that you and the children will start a new life," Linda added before departing.

"Thank you for your help, Linda," Helen said with a last embrace.

—⁂—

It was not sunset yet, and the moon was still on its way, but some of the camp's residents had already gathered in the open air. Mayada stood with the crowd, carrying her plate which she struck with her small spoon, imitating the others.

The faint sound she caused might not scare the whale, but Mayada loved the idea of this ritual—so much so that as soon as she opened her eyes the next morning, she ran to that spoon and knocked on the same plate inside the tent.

"Okay, my love, the whale became afraid and fled," Helen told her, and then tried to coax her back to sleep.

20

DANCE OF PAIN

The city streets were lit by cars rushing by, their windshield wipers moving furiously right and left. Helen walked fast to avoid getting wet. The woman behind her walked even faster, catching up with her and raising her large umbrella over them both.

She included Helen in her safe little world under the umbrella, and Helen felt a sense of gratitude to this kind-hearted stranger. They exchanged a smile that would remain in Helen's memory—not only because she was touched by this small kindness but because the woman looked so much like someone she knew, and Helen could not just then remember who. She stayed in her mind throughout that day as she worked at the cafeteria. As she made nearly twenty hamburgers, Helen kept searching her memory for this woman, every face from Halliqi and her time in Mosul, but nothing materialized.

Their faces gave her a mixed feeling of joy, sorrow, and nostalgia. She followed their news from Azad, who called her on a regular basis. He had opened a radio shop in Halliqi. Sometimes when he went to import the radios from Dohuk, Shammo and Ramziya accompanied him so they could get the net to speak with Helen.

She learned that Abdullah went back to Sinjar. The town was all in ruins. Abdullah's home was destroyed, but he decided to rebuild it. Cutto and his daughter, Ahlam, moved to Australia as refugees. Cutto's mother did not join them. She had died of a heart attack. Every now and then, Helen called Ahlam to check on her and also to find a trace of Amina in her voice. Helen had not tried to keep in touch with Shaima, although every time she saw Mayada, she thought of her and was grateful to the woman who literally nursed the baby as if she was her own.

It had been almost a year since Helen had arrived in her new country, and she was beginning to learn places and even the dates of holidays. In winter, she wore a thick coat and special shoes to keep her from slipping in the snow. That was what the Canadians who had welcomed her and her two sons and daughter at the airport had recommended. She had been amazed to hear their warnings about the cold and snow. She wanted to tell them that snow was fragile and peaceful for someone like her who had experienced the hardships of life at its extreme.

Yassir loved heavy snowfall because then the schools were closed. Mayada enjoyed making snowmen in front of their home, laughing when she added a carrot for a nose. For Yahya, snow meant money: he had bought a snow plow, which he used to remove snow from neighborhood driveways for pocket money.

But the absence of Elias was felt among them all. His memory was not snow that would melt away. He was painfully present when Mayada turned to her mother one day and asked, "Where is my father?" She had asked because she was watching *Finding Nemo*, and the fish had inquired about her father.

The second time Mayada pained her mother's heart was when she returned from school saddened because her fellow students had drawn pictures of their fathers on craft paper with hearts and balloons for Father's Day. Mayada did not know how to draw her father. She could only draw hearts and balloons. Helen tried to hide her emotion in front of Mayada and did not let her see how her heart was breaking. She quietly drew a picture of Elias and gave it to Mayada saying, "This is Dad. You look like him."

Mayada grabbed the paper with both of her hands as she scrutinized her father's features. She said: "Is he still in heaven?"

"Yes, my love, but his soul is also here with us," Helen said.

"How do you know?" Mayada asked.

"I see him in my dreams," Helen said.

"Does he talk to you? What does he say?"

"He said he's happy because you are so smart and doing so well in school."

"But I want to show him myself how I did my homework," Mayada said.

"When he comes to visit you in your dream, he'll see what you've done," Helen said.

"Mommy, you are not going to heaven, are you?"

"No, not now," Helen said and took Mayada in her lap.

———

Every morning, when Mayada went to school, Helen headed to the Institute of English as a Second Language. She liked the class she was attending with other refugees. They had all left their homelands with empty hands but packed memories.

Mario almost always sat at the desk next to her. Their friendship had been growing since the day their teacher paired them off to read sentences to each other and guess their meanings.

That day, Helen had forgotten to bring her book, so Mario put his book between them for her to read.

When they had to write a sentence using the words "I have," he seemed fascinated by her sentence; he looked at her with admiration, and she smiled. She had written: "I have a star in the sky," and Helen had drawn a star instead of the word because she did not know the word in English.

Mario didn't know the word either, but he searched his phone, showing Helen so she could write it down.

At first, she knew no more about him than his name and that he was from Guatemala. But one day during a class break, Mario told Helen that he used to run a ceramic shop at Lake Atitlan, a beautiful area surrounded by mountains and wildflowers in Guatemala's western highlands. From his village he would cross the lake by boat and then walk or ride the little *tuk tuk* to his shop. Despite its small size, the shop was making money. It was popular because its ceramics looked different: they had traces of cracks.

One day a man entered the store and was looking suspiciously around. When the customers left, the man approached Mario and said, "You should start paying money for protection." When Mario refused, the man proceeded to threaten him, saying, "You're gonna have a problem," and left.

Two days after that threat, Mario's wife Ivanna was killed in a hit-and-run, her corpse left on the road. Shocked, Mario stayed home for three weeks with his two-year-old son, Luis. He couldn't face going to work and was too angry to figure out what to do. He couldn't get the man's words out of his mind. Overwhelmed with guilt, Mario regretted that he didn't pay the money the man had demanded.

After that terrible day, Mario was fearful for his son. He could not go on with his life as before. He quickly sold his shop and paid the money to a smuggler who helped transport him and his son to America. But his fear of the gang did not qualify him for asylum. So he crossed overland from America to Canada with the help of a humanitarian organization.

———

In their first lesson, the teacher asked them to introduce themselves. When it was Helen's turn, the teacher said, "Your name is Western. Where are you from?"

Helen replied: "I am from Iraq. The second *E* is pronounced long, and my name in Kurdish means 'bird's nest.'"

"So you speak Kurdish?" asked the teacher.

"And Arabic," Helen replied.

"Wonderful," said the teacher.

Helen did not add that she spoke in whistles too.

———

Whenever the teacher instructed students to work in groups, Helen and Mario formed a team. Together they learned new words and more about each other. They recounted funny situations they'd faced as immigrants, such as how, in the cafeteria where Helen worked, on the first day she had been surprised to hear about a "hot dog." She had thought that Canadians ate dogs!

Mario laughed when he heard this and said he had faced a similar dilemma when two words that sounded similar got mixed up in his mind. When he had wanted to eat something light, he had asked his employer for a "snake" instead of a "snack."

———

Every day, Helen learned to put new words together to form useful sentences. But there were things in her heart that words could not express. She spent a long time in Linda's second village and was not sure that she would make it to the third. It was as if Helen stood at the border between the two villages, and a checkpoint prevented her from crossing.

She wanted to meet Linda again and ask, "Is everything really possible?" When Linda had recommended that Helen "reconnect," she had meant to reconnect with the living and not the dead, and that this would make life in the third village bearable.

But being unable to reconnect with Elias was too much for Helen. And she would also not reconnect with Amina. How could she endure missing her loved ones when her emotions were stable and deep like the roots of trees? What would she do with her sorrow, which was not a tree branch to be cut? What did it mean to be captivated by her memories after being freed and no longer the captive of anyone?

<hr/>

July 8, 2019, was the first time Helen missed her English class. She had woken up late after being unable to sleep until four in the morning. She stayed at home rather than going to the lesson late. She did not leave their apartment until the evening when it was time to go to work.

There, as she was filling up the box of plastic spoons in the cafeteria, she glimpsed Mario. He was sitting at a table near the window. She assumed he was there by chance, but when she went to greet him, he said that he had come to see her workplace.

She said, "I'll be done in twenty-five minutes."

"I will be here waiting for you," Mario said.

She completed her work and headed toward his table. She said, "Do you want to drink something?"

"How about we go somewhere else?" he suggested.

She agreed, so they walked to another cafeteria.

"Why didn't you come to class today?" he asked.

They spoke like old friends who had met again for the first time in years. Sometimes they communicated using signs because so much of what they wanted to express they didn't yet know how to say in English. She understood that when he was five years old, he had lost his mother in a massacre. Mario had been unable at the time to understand that she could disappear like that, so he had kept crying and asking his father for her. His father told him that his mother would return to him if he could mend a broken vase. His father was working in a place that repaired broken ceramics, and so from that day on, he took Mario with him to the place to help him fix the broken vessels. Mario worked passionately, waiting for his mother's return.

Mario drew vessels with cracks on the paper tablecloth in front of Helen, then he drew kites over a coffin.

Helen tried to understand. "Were you flying kites when your mother died?" He shook his head. She thought that perhaps he meant that many children had also died in the massacre. But through his words and signs, she finally understood that in Guatemala, they fly kites as a ritual during funerals, celebrating the souls of the dead.

Helen drew a heart with a crack. She wanted to say that she was sorry for the loss of his mother, and that she, too, had lost loved ones who had no graves to visit. She drew a flute next to the heart.

He said, "You play the flute?"

She replied only "Yes." But she wanted to say that her people did not bury their dead and did not pray for their souls until the sad music, which would start from the moment the coffin was raised until the burial, was completed.

"This is a good drawing. Are you an artist?" Mario asked.

"I have loved to draw since I was a girl," she replied.

"Have you thought about displaying your drawings?" he asked.

"No."

"Why not? Think about it, and I will help you frame the paintings."

"Thank you. But what about your ceramics? Why don't you display them?"

"We could do a joint show," he said excitedly. "Paintings and ceramics with cracks. What do you think?"

"Lovely idea."

"Let's do it!"

Mario walked her home, as it was near her work.

"I like that we don't need to think about what to do when we meet. I enjoy talking and walking with you," Mario said.

"The day after tomorrow will be my daughter's birthday party, and you and Luis are invited," Helen said.

"Sure, we will be there."

"This is the first time we are throwing her a birthday party."

"How old is she?"

"Five."

Helen agreed for Mario to come early to her apartment, an hour before the birthday party, so they could work together on their homework. The teacher had instructed the students to write a paragraph describing their cities using shapes, colors, and geographical characteristics.

Yahya and Yassir took Mayada to McDonald's to play in the restaurant's playroom before the celebration at home. Yahya's friend Ashley joined them there.

Yahya had met her while attending a soccer game at Yassir's secondary school. Yassir was playing for the school's team, and Yahya had gone to watch. Like him, Ashley had been sitting in the stadium bleachers. Her enthusiasm for the game had attracted his attention. It was the first time he had seen a girl excited by a soccer match. At a subsequent game, he found himself searching for the girl who wore comfortable sportswear and pulled her hair back with a white ribbon. He took a seat in an empty space next to her. He summoned his courage and spoke to her with his foreign accent. He did not know if his words made sense, but he was strangely confused and happy. After watching several games together, Ashley agreed to go out with him. Yahya shaved his hair and started wearing cologne. He asked Helen for her opinion about his appearance before he went on his date. Helen smiled as she said to herself, "I can't believe that once he wanted to fight with Daesh."

When Mario arrived, holding his son's hand, he praised Helen's apartment while looking at the large balloon tied to a chair with the words *Happy Birthday*.

Little Luis was holding a gift, which he gave to Helen.

She smiled at him and said, "Oh, thank you. Mayada will be happy with this. You look the same age as her. Are you in kindergarten?"

"Yes," said Luis, who seemed an adorable boy with a round face and a missing front tooth.

Helen asked them what they would like to drink. Mario chose coffee, and Luis shook his head, wanting nothing. When Helen returned from the kitchen with two coffee cups, she found Mario writing with Luis on his iPad. She peeked at their work and said, "It looks like you are about to finish the homework."

"Without Google dictionary, I wouldn't be able to write anything," Mario said. "I make so many mistakes and forget that adjectives come before nouns in English, unlike in Spanish."

"In the Arabic and Kurdish languages, the adjective also comes after the noun, but most of my mistakes are with verbs. I don't use the tenses correctly," Helen said, also starting her homework.

When she finished and put her pen down, Mario took another sip of coffee and said, "May I read to you what I wrote?"

Helen nodded, so Mario began reading aloud: "In Guatemala, schools are not closed because of snow but because of volcanoes. It is a city of volcanoes, mountains, temples, and outdoor markets. It's been said that the name Guatemala comes from the ancient Mayan word meaning 'the mountain that vomits water.' On the mountain, there is a beautiful bird. Its name is quetzal, and its feathers are green, white, and red. This bird became a symbol of freedom because they found that he would die of sadness when put in a cage."

Helen smiled. "That reminds me of my village, Mario," she said. "Guatemala must be beautiful."

"Yes, even its ruins are beautiful," Mario said, "but of course I'm not mentioning its negative aspects."

"Like what?"

"Drugs and poverty. Anyway, tell me about your country."

"My country is also beautiful when there's not a war on," she replied.

"Read me your paragraph."

Helen began. "In a village that is not on the map, I had a family who loved me. Homes were open day and night, and in them people with hearts pure like spring water, and in their hearts people from everywhere. Their world is the color of their birds and the shape of fig trees. All that remains of it is an empty place here in my heart, and it hurts me. You can refer to that place as if it is on a map, although like love it cannot be seen."

"This is very impressive," Mario said.

"Words of a broken person," Helen said.

"You are not broken. You just have a scar," Mario said. "Listen," he added, "there is something I learned from my work mending broken ceramics. The vessel with a crack has its own beauty, because true beauty is imperfect. Perfect beauty is false. One thing that I like about you is the trace of sadness."

Helen smiled at him. He touched her left hand, looked at it for a little longer, and said: "Even your tattoo is different."

She looked at her tattoo and closed her eyes. She saw a patch of light, and it quickly grew into a familiar face. It gradually receded until it turned back into mere light. She waited for the face to come back, but it did not. Yet that patch of light in the darkness gave her a special feeling that only the image of a loved one would give.

When she opened her eyes, Mario said to her, "Close your eyes again."

"When I close my eyes, I see the past," Helen said.

"Can you see the present when you close your eyes?" he asked.

She wanted to say that with her eyes closed, she saw her life as photos printed on her eyelids. And that her pain did not know the difference between the past, present, and future; it was only pain.

Mario noticed tears in her eyes.

"Don't worry, everything will be okay," he told her.

Something inside her was moved by Mario. His presence alongside her gave her deep comfort, but she didn't want him to initiate any physical intimacy with her, no matter how small. Helen was still afraid and angry at all those men who had raped her. A man's touch, no matter how innocent, brought to mind that nausea she had felt during her ongoing ordeal. Mario was a gentle man, but there were rapists standing between them.

The doorbell rang, and Helen rushed to open it. Mayada ran inside, behind her Yassir, Yahya, and Ashley.

Helen introduced them to Mario and Luis, then went to light the candles. They gathered around Mayada, singing "Happy Birthday" while Mayada blew them out. Mario stood before them, taking a photo.

After eating some cake, Yahya said, "We have to hurry up and get to the stadium. The match will start soon."

Helen played a song on her phone. She took Mayada's hands in hers and started to spin with her in the middle of the room. After a few random movements, their motion became a coordinated dance.

When the song was done, Mario applauded and said, "Beautiful."

"Sad," Helen said.

"Sad?" Mario looked confused.

"Sad, no, happy, no, dance, no, its name is the dance of pain," Helen said, bewildered as to how she might explain to him without a dictionary that people in her old village imitated the dance of wounded birds. Their bodies swayed to the sad tones of the flute. It looked like a beautiful dance because there was beauty when trying to express something within. Even pain became beautiful when expressed this way. Just like the crack on a ceramic pot.

EPILOGUE

The joint exhibition of Helen and Mario, *Imperfect Beauty: Paintings and Ceramics*, was opened in the autumn of 2019. Helen was nervous as she caught sight of visitors who were contemplating her art for the first time. Mario was handing them copies of the exhibition flyer.

The painting that attracted the most attention was the canvas of women sitting on the ground, their bodies shaped as circles: faces, hands, feet, eyes, and tears all circles. Some of the paintings were unfinished. Helen did this on purpose, perhaps to give the impression of the beings in their unfinished state. The largest in size was a painting titled *Good and Evil*. In one part of the canvas Helen drew Ayash's face as she knew him, and in the other part she drew Ayash's face as a child as she imagined him. It was inspired by a story Helen had heard from Amina's grandmother during one of those storytelling evenings in the village: There was an artist who wanted to embody good and evil in a painting. He saw an innocent child and asked him to sit down in front of him to draw his face. The artist was happy with the result and paid the child some money. But thirty years passed, and no evil face was found, so the painting remained incomplete. The day came when the artist heard about a man who committed awful crimes in the area and was arrested. Through his acquaintances, the artist managed to get a permit to enter the prison cell and meet that evil man. He asked him to sit down for the artist to draw him, and at the end he gave him some money. At that moment, the man said to him: "You drew me thirty years ago, and you gave me money as well."

—⁓—

In front of that particular painting, a woman stood contemplating the two faces of Ayash. She was about Helen's age, short hair and wearing eyeglasses. She was staring at Ayash's adult face as if she knew him. After a few minutes, she approached Helen and said: "I love this painting of good and evil very much. The angel child became evil when he grew up, right?"

"Yes, they are one person," answered Helen.

"Beautiful exhibition. I loved the ceramic vases too," said the woman.

She looked so familiar to Helen, as if they had met before. Ah, wasn't she the woman who once raised an umbrella to protect Helen from the rain? And then, it all flashed before her. She was the woman Helen saw in the photo album in Ayash's house. She had the same features and smile. Could it really be her? Had she also taken refuge here after she and her family were displaced?

"Thank you," Helen said.

"You are Iraqi, aren't you?" asked the woman.

"Yes, from Sinjar. Your accent is of Mosul," said Helen.

"Yes, I'm from Mosul," the woman said.

It took Helen a moment of hesitation before she said, "I want to ask you something."

The woman looked at Helen, waiting for her question.

"In your home in Mosul, was there an Arabic calligraphy that reads: "Half of a person's beauty comes from the tongue?"

"Yes, how did you know?" the woman asked, raising her eyebrows.

After a moment of silence, Helen answered, "I was a captive at your home."